Why does Dulce have so profound an impact on the artistic lives around her?

A lesbian has ended her conventional marriage and is free—or is she?

In the most traditional of romantic settings, on board a ship that travels the Inland Passage, two women discover new possibility . . .

These and many other soul-deep, gentle tales explore the conventional and unconventional relationships in all our lives—relationships among lovers and friends and wives and husbands and children and family . . . and the power we all have to sometimes damage, sometimes ennoble those around us.

The broad range and depth of these stories, their insight and humanity, reflect the fully matured talent of Jane Rule.

# INLAND PASSAGE

# INLAND PASSAGE

# JANE RULE

THE NAIAD PRESS INC.
1985

ACKNOWLEDGMENTS

"A Chair for George" under the title "A Delicate Balance" was first published by *Chatelaine,* as were "Seaweed and Song," "A Migrant Christmas," and "Joy." CBC's *Anthology* has broadcast "You Cannot Judge a Pumpkin by the Smile upon its Face," "Blessed Are the Dead," and "The Pruning of the Apple Trees." "Slogans" appeared in the Women and Words anthology. "The End of Summer" appeared in the English magazine, *Aquarius.* All the other stories in this volume appear for the first time.

Printed in the United States of America
First Edition

Cover design by Susannah L. Kelly
Typesetting by Sandi Stancil

Library of Congress Cataloging in Publication Data

Rule, Jane.
    Inland passage and other stories.

    1. Lesbianism—Fiction.  I. Title.
PR9199.3.R7815  1985      813'.54      84-20770
ISBN 0-930044-56-8
ISBN 0-930044-58-4

*FOR HELEN*

# WORKS BY JANE RULE

*Available from The Naiad Press.

# CONTENTS

# DULCE

I was not perfectly born, as Samuel Butler prescribed, wrapped in bank notes, but I was orphaned at twenty-one without other relatives to turn to and with no material need of them. I was, in a way everyone else envied, free of emotional and financial obligations. I did not have to do anything, not even choose a place to live since I had the small and lovely house in Vancouver where I had grown up to shelter me from as much as developing my own taste in furniture. I did not, of course, feel fortunate. Ingratitude is the besetting sin of the young.

If I had been rich rather than simply comfortable, I might have learned to give money away intelligently. What I tried to do instead was to give myself away, having no use of my own for it. It was not so reprehensible an aim for a young woman in the 50s as it is today. I was, again with a good fortune I was far from recognizing, unsuccessful.

My first and greatest insight as a child was being aware that I was innocent of my own motives. I did not know why I so often contrived to interrupt my father at his practicing. Now I understand that he, otherwise a quiet and pensive man, frightened me when he played his violin. Or the instrument itself frightened me, seeming to contain an electrical charge which flung my father's body around

1

helplessly the moment he laid hands on it. Though he died in a plane crash on tour for the troops in the Second World War when I was fifteen, I never quite believed it wasn't his violin that had killed him.

Wilson C. Wilson, a boy several years older than I, lived down the block with his aunt and uncle who gave him dutiful but reluctant room among their own children because he had been orphaned as a baby. That fact, accompanied by his dark good looks, had made him a romantic figure for me, but I had never expected him to climb up into our steep north slope of a garden where I made a habit of brooding on a favorite rock and often spying on him through the fringe of laurel, dogwood, mountain ash, and alder which grew, and still does grow, down at the street. No handsome boy of my own age had ever paid the slightest attention to me.

If he had not come with such quick agility, I would have hidden from him and let him pay his respects to my grieving mother to whom I suspect he might have been more romantically drawn than he was to me. I was too terrified of him even to be self-conscious. I sat very still, hardly at first hearing what he had to say, waiting for him to leave, but he was so gentle with me and at the same time so eager that gradually I began to listen to him.

"Some day," he said, "you'll be glad you were old enough to remember his face."

He offered his own grief as a way of sharing mine, but I had not had time to let my raw loss mellow into something speakable. He did not expect me to be adequate then or, I suppose, ever.

After that, once or twice a week he would come to find me. Sometimes he talked about his week-end job as an apprentice to a printer, but more often he talked about the books he was reading. He did not expect me to be older or more intelligent than I was, but he did begin to bring me books to read. When I asked him a question that pleased him, he would say, "Dulce, you have an old soul," but he was normally content to have a good listener.

Sometimes he suggested a walk on the beach just several blocks below the house, even in winter weather. We both liked the mists that obscured the far views across Burrard Inlet to the north mountains and focused our attention on the salty debris at our feet. We liked finding puzzling objects and making up histories for them as we walked among gulls and crows, past ghostly trees emerging only a few feet from us.

Neither of us liked wearing a hat or hood, and we would come back as wet-headed as swimmers to a hearth fire and tea, to the personal questions my mother asked which always began, "If you don't have to go . . ." or "If you're not called up . . ." or "If the war's over . . ." I never asked Wilson questions like that though I could see my mother's concern for his peaceful future gave him more confidence in it. He wanted to go back to Toronto where he had been born. He wanted to study literature and philosophy.

"And after that?" Mother asked.

"I'll be a philosopher . . . and a printer to feed myself."

I watched him, his strong, dark hair glistening rather than flattened, as I knew mine was, by the damp, his dark eyes glistening, too, and wished he were my brother or at least in some way related to me.

Wilson was called up two weeks before the war was over. Then his orders were canceled, and he packed to go to Toronto. Before he left, he asked for my picture in exchange for his, taken for his high school graduation, on which he had written, "For a good listener, Wilson C. Wilson."

"I so dislike my name," he once told me, "that I'll simply have to make it famous."

"How?"

He shrugged, but I wasn't really surprised when he sent me the first of his poems to be published in an eastern magazine. Some few of the images in them were ones we had found together, which made it easier for me to comment on them. Now that we were exchanging letters, I discovered that being a good listener by mail was learning to ask interesting rather than personal questions.

When Wilson came back the following summer to take up work with the printer, his aunt and uncle asked him to pay room and board. I was shocked by their lack of generosity, particularly since it would mean Wilson could not afford to go east again.

"My uncle points out that my cousins are perfectly satisfied to go to UBC."

"He doesn't charge them room and board, does he?"

"They're his own children," Wilson explained reasonably.

"You could pitch a tent in our garden," I suggested, "and you could pay Mother just the bit it costs to feed you."

"Don't make offers for your mother," he said.

"Are you in love with Wilson?" my mother asked me.

"I don't think so," I answered, both surprised and embarrassed by the question. "I just want us to help him."

"Is he in love with you?"

That I knew was preposterous. "I'm just a good listener," I answered.

The tent did go up on the flat square of lawn by the roses on the understanding that I would not visit Wilson in it. I would not have dreamed of invading his privacy.

More like a grown man, he assigned himself chores about the place without being asked. Mother and I had been used to a man who protected his hands and anyway had no eye or ear for the complaints of a house. By the end of the summer, nothing squeaked or dripped, and I had decided to go away to college myself and major in English.

I liked the idea of a women's college, for boys, except for Wilson, began to alarm me, taking on sudden height all around me, their noses and fingers thickening, their chins growing mossy, their voices cracking to new depths. I walked as defensively among them as I would through thickets of gorse or blackberry.

I chose Mills College in California partly because it was

in the Bay Area, and I liked San Francisco, the city of my mother's girlhood. Though my mother had been sent to the Conservatory of Music and attended concerts with her handsome and handsomely dressed parents, they hadn't approved of her marriage to a fellow student who wanted to sit on the stage instead of in the prosperous audience.

"They said, 'he'll never buy you diamonds,' " my mother told me.

"Did you mind?"

"About the diamonds?"

"About their not approving."

"Yes, but it gave me the courage to do it."

I found it hard to associate courage with love.

Wilson did not come back to Vancouver the summer I graduated from high school. He had found a printing job in Toronto, a less expensive solution than living in a tent in our garden. I sent him my high school graduation picture without signing it because I didn't know what to say. I signed my letters "As ever." He signed his "Yours" which I understood to be a formality.

Two of the poems he had published that year were love poems, dark and constrained, which made me unhappy for him and a little bewildered, too, for I could not imagine anyone incapable of returning his love. Since he wasn't in the habit of confiding in me about his personal affairs, I could hardly answer or question a poem. He wrote to me that his first collection of poems was about to be published, sent me a picture to be used on the cover, and asked permission to dedicate the book to me.

"Does it mean anything, Mother? I mean, anything in particular?"

"It's not a proposal, if that's what you mean," Mother said. "But it certainly does mean you are important to him. It's all right to accept if he's important to you."

I accepted, feeling a new self-conscious place in his life which I did not really understand. Surely, if he'd been in love with me, I would know. I studied the picture and saw simply his familiar intent and handsome face. Experimentally I kissed it, a kiss as chaste as any I gave my mother. Then quite crossly I thought, "If I'm so important to him, he could at least have come to my graduation and taken me to the dance."

Yet who of my school friends could boast of having a book dedicated to her? Wilson would never have taken me to a dance. Nor would I have asked him to. He did not belong to my silly social world. Even I had outgrown it and longed to begin my own serious education in a part of the world nearly as beautiful and far more sophisticated than my own.

To the relief of some of my disgruntled, liberal professors, I shunned the child development and dietary courses newly introduced to make servantless wives out of my post-war generation and to redomesticate those few female veterans who had returned. Instead I chose traditional art history, religious history, and philosophy courses as electives around my requirements in literature. If there had been a history of science, I would have chosen that over biology, the least mathematical of the sciences available. In that lab, cutting up flat worms, crayfish and cats, I came as close to domestic experience as I would get in college. I sent my laundry out every week to a war widow, left not as well off as my mother.

Thanks to Wilson, I was better read than many of the other incoming freshmen, and, though I rarely offered an opinion in class, I asked very good questions. My written assignments were not immediately successful, but again Wilson had trained me to listen and comprehend not only the material but the mood and bias of the instructor before me. Once I got the hang of being a logical positivist in philosophy, a new critic in contemporary literature, a propounder of history of ideas in Milton, my grades bounded upwards.

There were students at the college who actually engaged in the arts, notably in music, but I avoided the rich offering of concerts. In fact, any performing art was difficult for me to deal with; for, like my father, the performers all seemed in the grip of an energy which made spastic victims of them, leaping inexplicably around the stage, shouting in unrecognizable voices, faces either entirely expressionless or distorted in unimaginable pain. Poetry was for me a superior art. I had never had to watch Wilson write a poem. It was a relief to me to study Shakespeare on the page, a prejudice I shared with my professor who considered any available production a defiler of the poetry of the bard.

At a performance of *MacBeth*, put on by St. Mary's, a men's college in the neighborhood, the wife of a faculty member played Lady MacBeth in the same red housecoat even after she'd become queen; the wind for the witches' scene was her vacuum cleaner. MacBeth himself was a speech major with a lisp, who murdered more than sleep. His severed head was presented at the end of the play in a paper bag which looked like someone's forgotten lunch and perhaps was.

Granting the limitations of amateurs, I could not imagine even great actors tastefully gouging out eyes on stage on the way to a climax of corpses. The blood and gore were a convention of a barbarous time, which the poetry transcended.

In my letters to Wilson, both of whose pictures sat framed on my desk, I sometimes confided academic puzzlement. Though styles of poetry changed through the ages, particular poems were recognizably great in each period. Prose, on the other hand, seemed to improve, become more economical, lucid and beautiful. "Are you going to make an idol out of Hemingway," Wilson demanded, "at the expense of Donne and Milton?" I'd had F. Scott Fitzgerald in mind. I went back to Donne's sermons, and, when I imagined them, as instructed by Wilson, recited by the Dean of St. Paul's with tears streaming down his face, their excesses seemed more appropriate; yet I also had to admit that a man in tears would embarrass more than move me.

I found few fellow students with whom I could raise such questions. Only a small band of rather aggressive scholarship students discussed their studies. The more acceptable topics of conversation were menstrual cramps, other people's sexual habits, the foibles of parents and professors, and God. Nor were academic subjects acceptable topics on dates. Any conversation was impossible over the noise at fraternity parties, football games, and bars. The only virtue of the gross abuse of alcohol at such gatherings was that, more often than not, my young man of the evening was incapable of a sexual ending in the back seat of a dangerously driven car.

At first I was uneasy at the status my pictures of Wilson gave me. When I confessed that he had also dedicated a book of poems to me, it was simply assumed that I was unofficially engaged to the handsome young man with the unhandsome name. He wrote me letters, which was more than could be said for some who had even presented diamond rings.

"Are you going to see Wilson at Christmas?"

"Oh, he probably can't afford the trip. He's putting himself through . . ."

Explanations true enough, but I did not think of myself as the object of Wilson's romantic interest. There were more love poems, flickering with unredeeming fire which certainly had nothing to do with me, but they gave rise to shocked and admiring speculations among my friends who read them.

Gradually I used Wilson as the protection I wanted from a social life too barbarous to bear, even if it meant remaining among the humiliated on Saturday nights. If I was not writing love letters to Wilson, I was writing loving ones, for he was the one human being, aside from my mother, with whom I could really talk.

To Wilson's great disappointment, the only fellowship open to him for graduate studies was at UBC. He frankly confessed that it would be all right with him if he never laid eyes on Vancouver again. The university was inferior, the city really not a city at all, for it was without cultural reality, and he had been personally unhappy there. He did kindly add, "Except for that summer in your garden." But he was competing with too many men older than himself, more mature in their judgments, with Americans and Englishmen as well as his own countrymen, and he had to take what he could get.

Wilson met me at the airport when I came home to bury my mother. It was the first time we had seen each other in four years, and we embraced in the way we signed our letters because we had to do something. Wilson seemed to me more substantial and attentive in those few days, but my need was also extraordinary. It was Wilson who would not hear of my simply staying there, moving into the house to begin a grief-dazed life. He put me back on the plane to finish my education.

In the next year and a half, Wilson became my unoffical guardian. He rented the house for me, effectively preventing me from coming home in the summer, which he said I should spend in Europe where he had not yet been himself.

He outlined a trip he would like to have taken, but I was far too timid to travel alone, and, since he didn't offer to come with me, I elected instead to take the Shakespeare summer session at Stratford.

Younger than most of the other international students and not as well prepared for the work, I was at first intimidated, but my listening, question-asking habits soon provided me with a couple of unofficial tutors, also willing to indulge my uncertain sensibilities at the theatre.

"Why, it's meant to be vulgar!" I exclaimed after a performance of *Measure for Measure*. "All that bawdy fooling around."

If it hadn't been for Wilson, I might have fallen in love with either of the two young men, one English, one American, who also took me punting on the Avon, day tripping to Oxford, to Wales, pub crawling, and simply walking country lanes in the late summer light. While both of them talked nearly as well as Wilson about matters literary and historical, they were also flirtatious and entertaining. Instead I fell in love with England and wrote to tell Wilson that we had both been born on the wrong continent. We were not after all freaks, simply freaks in the new world.

"This bloke of yours back in Canada, are you going to marry him them?" the Englishman asked.

"Oh, eventually," I answered, and I found that I believed what I said.

I spent my final year at college in a postponing aura of serene industry, my essays enlivened by new insights that were my own, for I had been in that green and pleasant land and knew that birds do sing.

But at last I did have to go home to discover that my mother really was dead, that I was alone. If the house had been on an ordinary street in an ordinary city, I might have been persuaded to sell it and live the more vagabond life of my contemporaries, brash and brave among the new ruins of Europe, before returning to mow lawns and pay taxes. But it was built sturdily on a high piece of ground overlooking the inlet, the mountains and the growing city of Vancouver, and it contained my childhood which was prematurely precious to me as my parents were.

Wilson had not met my plane, nor did he come to see me until I'd had several days of blank passivity. I did not think it odd at the time. When he did arrive, I greeted him less shyly than before and felt him pull back. His Dulce was still not a woman but a docile, intelligent child in need of his guidance.

I could not ask him, as I very much wanted to, "What are we going to do with the rest of our lives?" He considered his to be publicly disposed, as a poet and teacher. He would give up printing, though he might one day use that practical knowledge if he founded a literary press.

"Vancouver is changing," Wilson admitted as we looked together at the view, the skyline altered by the first of so many high rises which would eventually make it look more like New York than itself.

Then he asked, as if an uninvolved spectator, "What are you going to do now?"

"I don't know."

"You haven't thought about it?"

"I wondered if I'd get a dog . . . no, I haven't."

"Why?"

"Do I have to do anything?"

"Well, eventually," Wilson said. "You haven't got enough capital to live on, not the way you'd like to live."

I was furious with him for speaking as if I might never marry him or anyone else; yet I knew he would think it beneath me to leave my life to such an eventuality. I must be held accountable for my future.

All the girls I had known at school were either locked in combat with their parents or already married. Only two had jobs, chosen for their proximity to marriable men, which, of course, Wilson was not and would not be for some time until he could translate his years of learning into a modest academic salary. If I had to mark time until then, I might as well do it with him. I could get a teaching assistantship and take my M.A.

At first, witness to all the fawning young women who surrounded Wilson, I was both daunted and repelled, but, as I watched him treat them like bodies on a crowded bus, I was reassured. He was a little aloof from me, too, at first, as if he did not want any display of our friendship, but gradually we formed the habit of having lunch together several times a week. For his birthday, I gave him season tickets next to my own for the theatre and the foreign film series. We became in public rather than in private a pair.

Wilson had rooms in a widow's house on the second floor with only a hotplate to cook on and a glimpse of view through a small, stained glass window in his bathroom which I saw only in the lines of one of his poems. He never invited me there, in deference to the widow's sensibilities perhaps but in keeping with his appetite for privacy.

He visited me comfortably enough, and he did the same

things for me that he had done for Mother as well as advising me about my ownerly responsibilities. But we almost always went out after the simple meals I was learning to prepare under his direction and with his help.

To my relief, Wilson did not want to go to poetry readings. He said he had nothing in common with the other students who claimed to be poets and brought out a magazine called *Tish*. "It's not really necessary to spell it backwards," Wilson said. To focus on the human breath and the heartbeat for a theory of aesthetics was simply an excuse to ignore the great traditions of poetry. For Wilson the roots of poetry were in knowledge, discipline, and concentration. He admired Auden, Eliot, the best of Dylan Thomas, a good reason for avoiding the drunken bellowings of that undersized bull on the stage. About giving readings of his own, Wilson was non-commital. "I'm not ready."

We went instead to the Art Gallery for every visiting show. Wilson was fascincated by the question of great subjects. I was more interested in paint and stone and metal; therefore I didn't have the trouble with modern art which often daunted Wilson, fearful of being tricked by fads and imposters. How could he judge technique without subject matter, he wanted to know. "Think of it as more like music," I suggested.

When he went with me to openings of local galleries, Wilson stood back from the conversations I got into, I suppose because he was more comfortable with answers than with questions, but he did listen, and occasionally he would go with me to parties held after the shows for the artist and his friends.

Wilson would have preferred me to invest in something like first editions, about which he was relatively well informed, but the only first editions I've ever bought are new books. I have no taste for books as objects. What I wanted were paintings. For me they were as pure as poems.

In asserting that aesthetic independence, I did not feel so much Wilson's equal as a better, more independent companion, one he would some day come to see as a woman rather than a fifteen-year-old with an old soul. He dedicated his second book of poems to me with the words, "For Dulce, my muse."

Just the other day I came upon a metaphorical distinction between the romantic and classical poets in Northop Fry: "Warm mammalians who tenderly suckle their living creations and the cold reptilian intellectuals who lay abstract eggs." There were no love poems at all in this second collection. Like the canvases Wilson was drawn to, they were about great subjects. The title came from the longest and most difficult poem in the book, *Exercises in War.* Trained as I had been, it didn't occur to me to wonder whether or not I liked Wilson's poetry. I admired it as intellectually requiring and courageously cruel about the nature of man.

Three months before Wilson received his PhD, he accepted a graduate fellowship in England.

"You'll never come back," I said.

"I hope not."

"Wilson, what about me?"

The eyes turned to me were brilliant with unshed tears. "I'm sorry, Dulce."

Now that Wilson C. Wilson has made his name attractive with international honors, occasionally a graduate student comes to me to ask what Wilson was like as a young man. I can only say what he tried to be like as a young man in order to become what he now actually is, a very good poet whose poems I can't bear to read.

If Wilson was a coward, he wasn't coward enough to marry me. I was coward enough to have married him to seal myself away forever from learning either to live alone or truly with another. Instead, he left me when I was twenty-four in the cocoon of my independence which exposed rather than hid my humiliation, for very soon after Wilson left, Oscar Kaufman, a sculptor at whose studio we had often been, said to me, "I thought at least he'd marry you for the view you've got here."

Perhaps because Oscar was as unlike Wilson as it is possible for a man to be, I was not so much attracted to him
as resigned to him for the medicine I needed as a kill or
cure remedy for the past ten years of my life.

He was, as most of our friends were in those days, older.
Wilson felt safer among people settled in marriage and the
raising of children than among other teaching assistants
like ourselves who were marrying in nervous numbers and
moving into the ugly and cramped married quarters on
campus. Perhaps Wilson thought I might be as put off as
he obviously was by family life if I could witness first hand
the emotional and physical squalor of it.

Oscar and Anita had three children under five years
old. "Catching up after the war," Oscar explained. He was
both efficient and tender with them, and he gave Anita a
day off every Saturday in exchange for a Saturday night
for himself, no questions asked.

When he first stopped by, he had the children with
him, and I discovered very quickly how inappropriate my
house was for any child neither tied up nor caged. The
baby was putting an ant trap in his mouth before anyone
had taken a coat off, and Mother's favorite lamp was smashed
on the hearth in the next five minutes. After that, Oscar
got ahead of them, kid-proofing the room while I got out
cookies.

While the children climbed all over him, covering him
with enough crumbs to feed every bird in the garden, he
said to me, "You know, Dulce, what you've needed for a
long time is a real man."

"What's unreal about Wilson?"

"He's a faggot." When I looked blank, Oscar explained,
"A queer, a homosexual."

"How do you know such a thing?"

"Don't get mad at *me*," Oscar said. "Do you have any
better explanation? Did he ever take you to bed?"

If it hadn't been for the presence of the children, I

would have ordered Oscar out of the house. Instead, we both used them as a distraction, and Oscar didn't speak of Wilson again then or ever.

When he had gone, I took down Wilson's first volume of poems and turned to the love poems which had always bewildered me. What I thought had been about unrequited love was instead forbidden, I could quite clearly see, but nothing prevented the reader from supposing the object to be a female, married or otherwise lost to him. It was not, however, a better explanation. Had they been, in a perverse way, poems also for me, the only way Wilson knew how to tell me that he was incapable of loving me?

I had ignored his absolute lack of expressions of physical affection, rationalizing it as part of his extreme sensitivity or a peculiarity of his being raised without tenderness or his sense of honor or some lack in myself because I had loathed those aggressive and drunken young men when I was in college. And I had been relieved that I didn't have to compete with other women for his attention, but there had been no man in his life, of that I was sure. Was Oscar suggesting that Wilson was the kind of man who sought sex in parks and public washrooms? Such an accusation made Oscar rather than Wilson disgusting. If Oscar thought Wilson was queer, why did he also suppose Wilson might have married me?

I try to explain what happened in terms not only of my own ignorance but of the ignorant intolerance of that time. Oh, I had heard rumors of homosexuality in some of Shakespeare's sonnets, but I had dismissed them as I did suggestions that Bacon had really written the plays. I had heard a couple of very masculine girls at college referred to as lesbian, but I associated that with the inappropriateness of their style and manner, rather than with their sexual tastes. The only homosexual male I had ever been aware of was a very effeminate brother of a high-school friend of mine who cried because someone had called him a fairy.

Wilson was entirely masculine. Even in his good looks there was nothing pretty about him. His body was hard and competent, his voice deep. If there was an error in his manner it was an occasional hint of arrogance. There was nothing of the passive or sycophantic about him. He wasn't exactly a man's man either, without interest in either sports or dirty jokes. He was a loner, learning to command respect rather than affection. Yet who could call a man of such intense feelings cold?

I had never pretended to understand Wilson, but he was realer to me than anyone else, both gentler and stronger. My first wish about him, that he could have been my brother, probably most accurately described what we had been for each other and might have gone on being if I had not tried to break the taboo with one question which created the irrevocable separation and silence between us.

Compared to Wilson, Oscar was transparent, his work hugely, joyously sexual, his needs blatant, his morality patriarchal. He worshipped his wife as the mother of his children; he loved his children, and as a man and an artist he deserved me, but I was also his good deed, part of a sexual altruism he had worked out for himself which drew him to unhappy women. Often in his life he has been bewildered to leave them even unhappier. For some years I let him come to me to be comforted when he was suffering their unreasonable demands and accusations. I can explain that only by my horror at ever again shutting a final door between me and someone I have cared about.

Oscar was from the first completely open with me. Anita didn't mind this sort of thing as long as she didn't have to know about it. His relationship with me was restricted to Saturday nights and would be as entirely private as mine with Wilson had been entirely public. It would end with summer when he was free of his university teaching responsibilities to concentrate on his work. By then I should have become a competent sexual being ready for the open market. No, he didn't put it that way. He was never again as blunt as he had been about Wilson. Oscar knew how to be kind and funny about not quite savory arrangements so that raising any objection seemed a regression to grammar school morality.

Used to Wilson's spartan taste in food, I was unprepared for Oscar's appetite, and he did not expect to help me in the kitchen or with any other domestic problem. He wanted to leave all husbandly and fatherly responsibilities behind him. He left whatever personal problems he might have had behind him, too. I've never known anyone as resolutely and often maddeningly cheerful as Oscar.

"I made a bargain," he told me once. "If I made it through the war, I'd spend the rest of my life celebrating it."

As he pointed out to me, I could have done worse than to offer my overdue virginity to Oscar. He did not rush me, and he was patient with my timidity and squeamishness. I felt rather like a child being taught to ride a bicycle, that is until *he* mounted *me*, and then I became my father's violin, a thing seemingly of wood and strings, that charged Oscar with crazed energy. I did not know whether I was terrified of him or myself for the power I apparently had to call up such a rutting.

He did not neglect my 'pleasure,' as he called it, so much as never clearly locate it. From his caresses, I thought I should gradually learn to purr like a cat, but I was too tense in my ignorance to feel the heat he called up as anything more than flashes of ambiguous feeling somewhere between pleasure and pain.

After he left, I often cried hysterically, a response that misled me to think I was in love with Oscar in a way I didn't consciously comprehend, for I also came to dread his arrival on Saturday night, and I was giddy with freedom the few times he was unable to get away.

I did have the sense to refuse Anita's invitation to spend Christmas day with the family. Wilson and I had always planned something to circumvent rather than celebrate that holiday, he not wishing to be politely tolerated in the house where he had grown up, I not wanting to be reminded of the central delight I had been to my parents on such occasions. I had never even explored the cupboard where I supposed the Christmas decorations were stored.

I did what I had wanted to do when I first came home. I went to the Animal Shelter and picked out an already housebroken and spayed young dog, short-haired and black but not as large as a Lab. Then on whim I picked up a black kitten as well. The major part of my Christmas buying, after I'd chosen extravagant presents for Oscar's children (nothing for Oscar at his request), was done in a pet shop.

The dog already had a name, "Rocket," suggesting a male child's brief infatuation with a puppy. I didn't like it, but she was old enough to be used to it. The kitten I named Maud, as all vain, bright and beguiling females should be. From the first night they slept together in the laundry room by the back door.

Rocket's occasional growl and brief, sharp bark woke me several times during the night. Only someone who has lived years alone can know the absolute pleasure of those animal sounds in the no longer empty house.

"What's this, Dulce?" Oscar exclaimed when Rocket raised her hackles and growled at him and Maud clawed to her highest perch on the bookcase. "A zoo?"

Oscar didn't seem able to like an animal he didn't own. Either Rocket had been abused by a male or she was jealous because, even when I insisted on her good manners, she was sullen about them. She tried to keep herself between me and Oscar, and his slightest affectionate gesture started up a hostile singing in her throat. I finally had to tie her up on the back porch, but just as Oscar went into his fit of passion, Rocket began to howl. I had to disengage myself and go speak to her in my firmest tones.

When Oscar left that night, I had hysterical giggles.

"You're turning yourself into a witch," Oscar decided. "Next it will be a black minah bird."

Neither the image nor the idea of the bird was distasteful to me. But Rocket's continued hostility was becoming a real problem.

"Look, Dulce, you have to get rid of her before you become too attached to her. You can't have a dog around that doesn't like people."

I did not tell him that Rocket was not only polite but quite friendly with the friends I occasionally had in for drinks or dinner, but I did not take Oscar's advice.

Finally he laid down his ultimatum, "Me or that dog."

When I chose the dog, he thought I was joking.

"I know it's shameful to admit it, Oscar, but what I need are pets, not a lover."

"But that's crazy."

I did not argue with him though I knew Rocket and Maud were my first investments in sanity, creatures with whom I could exchange affection and loyalty, about whom I could be ordinarily responsible. How many bad whims and potential disasters can be more simply avoided than with the words, "I have to go home to feed the animals?"

Later I understood that Oscar didn't have the time or energy for more than one woman a winter, and he had to sulk through the rest of that one until he could return to sculpting and to being my friend.

That summer he introduced into his group of huge phallic and pregnant shapes some less voluptuous figures, empty at the center. I bought one and placed it in the garden by the roses where Wilson had once pitched his impregnable tent.

I would have liked to declare my independence of Wilson's influence by dropping out of the PhD program since there was no longer any point in winning his approval. I was, I think, worried that having such a degree might intimidate another more ordinary sort of man who might make friends with my animals, like my view and marry me. I began research for my thesis simply because I didn't know what else to do.

Conception and development of character fascinated me in Shakespeare where in the early plays crude models of the later great characters could be found. Left to myself, I would not have spent months locating other scholars who had noted and explored that subject to see if there were any observations left to be made. But it was a more humane topic than many with teasing application to life.

I wondered if Wilson and Oscar were early, crude models of extremes of male influence in my life or the great characters before whom others would pale. I waffled between a sense that my life was already over and that it had not really begun. I was so much more settled than most of the other people I knew, yet my commitments seemed to have dwindled rather than increased.

My fellow students worried about money and pregnancy and the constant irritation of intimacy in ugly surroundings. My artist friends were old enough not to have outgrown those concerns but to simplify the last of them to the constant irritation of intimacy anywhere.

I didn't have to keep late hours to get my work done, and Rocket encouraged me to take long walks on the beach, which have always been one of my greatest pleasures. With her protective company I was also free to explore the university grant land bush, trails intersecting for miles through scrub forest edged with berries and wild flowers. At home Maud's antics often made me laugh aloud, and her warmth in my lap as I sat reading was a simple comfort.

After Oscar, I didn't encourage already attached men to come to call without their wives or girl friends. I deflected any domestic complaints offered over public coffee at the university or a glass of wine at an opening. I did sometimes listen to their wives as an antidote to my envy. Very few of them seemed content with their lives. In those old days I thought, though never said, that they should be. I was surprised at how many of them envied me.

"You're the only one of us the men ever listen to," one wife observed, a woman both brighter and more committed to her own mind than I was, but she was delayed in her studies by two small children and her husband's academic needs.

The men did listen to me for the simple reason that I asked good questions. Their wives wanted equal time for giving answers. Even quiet men can't tolerate that; they stop listening.

Men married to artistic rather than academic women fared little better. To the complaint that time at home was eaten up with everyone else's needs, husbands were apt to shout, "God, if I had some time at home, I'd have a poem to show for it!" This was before the time that men did stay home, even the best of them, more than once a week. Though some did laundromat duty and food shopping, they thought of these tasks as interim measures until they could make enough money not to feel humble in their expectations of service. Yet their wives also looked forward to a time when life would be made more tolerable with money.

Only one out of all those graduate school marriages survives into the 80s. Among male artists and their wives, the odds are better (or worse, of course, depending on one's point of view). I speculate that wives of artists don't expect life to get better, early on resign themselves to or embrace a role of cherishing genius without rationalization. My mother lived that way with my father, not expecting diamonds or a plumber either.

"If only men *were* superior," wailed one young wife, "it would make life so much easier."

For all their difficulties, for their envy of my freedom and serenity, I knew those women also pitied me, particularly on those occasions when I needed an escort, the more for their remembering the years of Wilson. I tried not to feel sorry for myself. I knew the Oscars of this world are worse than nothing. About the Wilsons of this world I wasn't entirely sure.

As a young woman of the 80s I might not have waited until I was thirty to consider what my own sexual tastes actually were. Perhaps I was backward even for my own generation. I didn't give friends the opportunity to tell me so. Lee Fair was the first person, aside from my mother, in whom I ever confided. The impulse took me by surprise, for she was not only younger than I but one of my students.

Like Wilson, Lee had published a book of poems in her early twenties. Unlike him, she had then married and had a child, a choice no wiser for her than it would have been for him. Yet she defended what she had done on the grounds that motherhood is central to the female vision. No woman without that experience could have very much to say. She was too fiercely vulnerable for me to point out how few of our well known women writers had children. The Brontës, Jane Austen, George Eliot, Emily Dickinson, Willa Cather, Gertrude Stein were all childless.

I had assumed rather than thought about children myself. I was not particularly interested in those belonging to my friends, but I did not read that as a dislike of children. Mine would be well brought up as I had been.

Lee's child, Carol, was both remarkably quiet and watchful compared to other five-year-olds I had known. I did not actively dislike her, but I was unnerved by the critical appraisal in her gaze. Any time she was due to arrive with her mother, I took as much care about my appearance as I would for a lover.

She asked odd questions, too, like "Were you a sad little girl?" She was attracted to sorrow, as Wilson had been. She told me, "My daddie didn't die. He just went away."

Some of my childhood books were still on the shelves, and I found some of my old dolls, stuffed animals, and games in the cupboard with the neglected Christmas ornaments. As Carol became accustomed to the place, she spent less time suspiciously staring, though she went on asking questions.

"Did you always play by yourself?"

"A lot of the time," I said. "I liked to. I liked to play in the garden."

Sometimes I stood by the window watching her climb among the rocks as I had done, and I supposed my mother often watched me when I was unaware of it. Then Carol would turn, look up and wave. I waved back and turned away, not wanting to seem to spy.

"You should have a child," Lee said. "Why don't you have one?"

"I manage better with animals," I replied, wondering for how many years I'd used self deprecation as a way to defend myself against personal questions.

"You mother your students."

"Do I mother you? You don't seem to me that much younger than I am."

"I'm not," Lee said. "And at the rate I'm going, I'll be twenty years older than you are by the time I finish my MA."

Lee's face was dark and strained, and there was already a lot of grey in her mane of black hair. She was always exhausted, working as a cocktail waitress on week-ends, studying late into week nights, finding time for Carol.

"I don't have your stamina," I said.

"I don't have it either. I just don't have any choice . . . now."

Like so many other women I knew, Lee made me feel guilty, but the others all had men to stand between them and any altruism I felt. Lee was alone, and I did want to do things for her to make her life easier.

"Don't offer to do things for me," she warned, "because I'll let you."

"Is there anything immoral about doing your laundry here while you have a meal rather than down at the laundromat?"

"Not yet," Lee said.

Her guardedness, her fear of dependence, made me at first more careful of her feelings than I would otherwise have been and perhaps less aware of my own.

One afternoon, when I offered to pick Carol up at

kindergarten to give Lee an extra hour at the library, she said, "Don't get indispensible."

"Oh, sometimes you seem to me as impossible as a man," I said in sudden irritation.

"Sometimes you seem as insensitive as one," she retorted.

That exchange, as I thought about it, seemed to me basically funny.

"Does neither of us like men very much?" I asked her over coffee, after Carol had been settled in my study with some books.

"I don't have anything against them as long as they leave me alone," Lee said.

"You don't want to remarry ever?"

"No," she said. "Why do I seem to you impossible?"

"You don't. It's only that I don't expect to have to be as careful with you as . . ."

"With a man?"

"The men I've cared about anyway."

Then for the first time I tried to describe my years with Wilson to the final distress of having destroyed whatever it was between us by one fatal question. I talked about Oscar, too, the rigid, the controlling structures men made in which there was never simply room to be.

"Why did you choose men who didn't want you?" Lee asked.

"I wasn't aware . . . with Wilson anyway . . . that I had," I answered, but, as I saw the doubt in her expression, I supposed I wasn't telling the truth. "I don't know."

"Do you really not know now either that you're choosing a woman who does want you?" Lee asked quietly, and, when I did not respond, she said, "Is that to be my fatal question?"

"It mustn't be," I finally managed to say.

"You may not be able to help that," Lee said, and then she called Carol to her and went home.

Again I was faced with my peculiar blindness to my own motives. For months I had been courting Lee in the ways traditional to a lover rerouting myself on campus on the off chance of meeting her, stupidly disappointed when a similar head of hair revealed a much older and less appealing face. I had brought her small presents, even flowers, and taken her to restaurants and the theatre. I had taken advantage of a convention of physical affection between women to take her arm as we walked along together, to hug and even sometimes kiss her.

When Lee warned me off, there was always also an invitation in it as there had never been with Wilson, and my impatience with her caution was my desire to set no limits on my love, to let it open and flower as it would, at last.

I had never been able to tolerate Oscar's charge that Wilson was a homosexual. It was with perverse relief that I could now exonerate him with my own sexuality, at least the possibility of it.

If I were, in fact, a lesbian, there did not have to be any limits set with Lee, who by now was no longer my student. I might even propose that she move in with me. Who could criticize such an arrangement, one woman helping another? Carol. Well, Carol could be my child, too. I had already begun to give her my childhood. Lee could give up her hideous job, even finally have time to write again. She could have my study. I did most of my work at the university anyway. And Carol could have my old room which I now used as a guest room.

So I sat happily rearranging the uses of the furniture without a single moral or emotional apprehension.

When I saw Lee the next day, I embraced her joyfully. Then I looked into her uncertain face and said, "Don't you see? It makes everything so much easier."

Lee laughed in disbelief.

"Tonight you won't have to wake Carol and take her home."

I felt neither shy nor frightened. Lee and I had been casually naked together in the changing room at the pool. I already knew a delight in the shape of her breasts, the curve of her back, the length of her thighs. And I knew how tender and sure her hands were, tending her child. I also knew she wanted me and had wanted me for a long time.

When we finally lay together in absolute intimacy, all my sexual bewilderment and constraint left me. I understood my power because I could feel it in a singing heat to be fed to a roaring. I was hardly aware of Rocket's one howl which soon faded into resignation.

"Rocket, you beast," Lee said to the dog in the morning, fondling her ears. "Did you have to make a public announcement?"

Carol said, "I had a funny dream, that I could float . . . in the air."

I was having the same sensation awake, a combination of euphoria and lack of sleep.

For Lee our love-making did not clear away all the obstacles. When I proposed that she give her landlord notice and move in with me, she wanted to know if I'd really thought about living not only with her but with Carol.

"She's not always an easy child."

"It isn't as if I didn't know her. Carol and I like each other."

"But you'll have to love her," Lee said.

"I do," I protested. "Why don't we ask her if she'd like it?"

"And if she says no?"

I realized I was not prepared to put my fate quite so simply at the whim of a five-year-old.

Lee was embarrassed when I talked about money.

"You don't create a problem," I tried to explain. "You solve one."

With Lee and Carol to support there was a practical reason for me to take my academic career seriously, accept a full time appointment the following term and have a real use for my salary. Lee could go on with her MA or not. Maybe it would be better for her to stay home, write, and have more time for Carol.

"Even men resent dependents. Wouldn't you?" Lee asked.

"Why should I? You're the point of my life."

For a month Lee and Carol spent three or four nights a week with me, and we all grew increasingly tired and strained. Carol began to have unsympathetic dreams, woke needing her mother's attention.

One night I heard her say to Lee, "You smell funny."

After that Lee left a basin of water on my dresser and washed her face and hands quickly before going to Carol. I did not quote, "Will these hands ne'er be clean?"

One morning after a particularly unsettled night, Lee said, "It isn't going to work. Carol just can't handle it."

"She simply can't handle living in two different places. Half the time she doesn't know where she is when she wakes up. If you moved in, she'd be able to settle down."

"Why don't you ever go in to her?" Lee asked.

"Well, I will from now on. It didn't occur to me," I admitted.

Of course, when I did, Carol bellowed, "I want my mother."

We decided that I should keep Carol on my own over the week-end when she saw very little of her mother anyway. It would also give Lee a chance to get the rest she badly needed. It worked because I devoted myself to Carol. I took her to the zoo. We went to a toy shop and bought new books and some doll furniture which we set up together in her room. I fixed her her favorite macaroni and cheese, and then read to her.

The effect of such attention backfired when Lee came home. Carol simply became as demanding of me as she was of her mother, behaving very like Rocket in her attempts to keep between us, making herself the center of attention even at the price of our irritation. Again Lee's solution was to move out, mine for them to move in, and Carol was now on my side.

Lee did not so much change her mind as give in. All in

one day, she gave her notice, quit her job and dropped out of the university. Then all the nervous energy which had kept her going through her impossible schedule drained from her, and she slept like a patient after major surgery.

For several weeks, I got up if Carol called in the night, got up in the morning to get her off to kindergarten and myself to UBC, collected her and brought her home to Lee who increasingly often had not bothered to dress. I did the shopping, the cooking, the laundry, the cleaning, exercised the dog, mowed the lawn, electric with energy to be all things for Lee, provider, mother, lover, for Lee was filled with sleepy gratitude and sexual sweetness.

"Are you sick, Mommy?" Carol finally asked her.

"I suppose so," I heard Lee reply.

"Are you going to get well?"

"I suppose so,"she said again, but the listlessness in her voice suddenly alarmed me.

"Are you all right?" I asked her later that night. "Are you getting rested?"

She only murmured and kissed me.

Early in the morning she was restless, got up, went to the bathroom, came back into the bedroom and stood by the window.

"Are you all right?" I asked again.

For an answer she came back to bed and held me in her arms.

When I woke again, her breathing was unnaturally heavy. I tried to wake her and couldn't. The empty bottle of pills was in the bathroom for me to find. I phoned the doctor who phoned an ambulance.

When Lee had recovered enough to talk, she said, "I should have told you. I was trying to find someone to love Carol . . ."

"But how could you not want to live?" I asked. "We've been so happy."

She turned her face away from me and closed her eyes.

Hysterical crying or giggling are the luxuries of a woman

who lives alone. I had Carol to take care of, comfort, reassure. When she had gone to sleep, I hardly had time to note my own exhaustion before I was asleep myself.

When I woke to the new, requiring day and tried to think about Lee, I could not. I moved automatically through my appointments until lunch time when I could spend a few minutes with her in the hospital.

"No Visitors" was posted on her shut door.

I went to find a nurse.

The nurse took me to a waiting room. "Her mother's here. She's been trying to reach you."

"Her mother?"

I did know Lee had a mother and a father. She spoke of them very little, as little as she spoke of her ex-husband or anything else about her past. She came from Winnipeg and said that even the name of the city made her teeth hurt.

A woman with pure white hair and eyes even more exhausted than Lee's came into the room.

"Dulce?"

"Yes," I said.

"I must thank you for being so kind to Lee and Carol through this distressing time."

Kind? I could not imagine what Lee had told her mother.

"I'm making arrangements to take them back to Winnipeg with me tomorrow. Would it be convenient if I came and packed their things tonight?"

"Is that what Lee wants to do?"

"I'm afraid she doesn't have much choice. She can't simply be a burden to strangers."

"She's been no burden," I protested. "She was simply terribly tired . . ."

"Perhaps she hasn't told you," her mother said. "She has a history of . . .this."

"But Carol has just really settled in and started to feel at home."

"She hasn't had an easy life," Lee's mother said.

It wasn't exactly lack of sympathy for her own daughter

which she expressed in concern for Carol; she seemed simply saddened and resigned.

"If Lee wanted to come home to me, I'd . . ." I began.

"I'm so sorry. She doesn't want to see you. I'm sure she's . . . well . . . ashamed of all the trouble she's caused."

When I picked up Carol that afternoon, I looked at her soft dark cap of hair, her watchful dark eyes and could no more bear the thought of losing her than of losing Lee. What craziness was it in Lee to have thought I would be allowed Carol?

"Your grandmother's here," I said. "She's going to take you and your mother home to Winnipeg until she's better."

"Then do we get to come back here to be with you?"

"I honestly don't know. I hope so."

Carol was quiet then until we got home. She came with me, as was now her habit, to walk Rocket, who did not take her customary long circlings in the bush but stayed with us, bumping clumsily and persistently against us on the narrow path.

Over dinner Carol said, "Mommy said you'd take care of me if anything happened to her."

"She's going to be fine."

"You should make her go to school. Even kids have to go to school."

"She was only having a rest."

"That's when she always gets sick."

First her mother and now her child were tattling on Lee, for whom I felt a pointless, painful loyalty.

"Can I take my doll furniture?"

The next day there was no trace left of either Lee or Carol. I did not even think to ask for their Winnipeg address. Lee had taken my life, if not her own, in a way that I had never meant to give her.

Though it has often seemed obvious to me that troubled friends are in need of psychiatric attention, I have never known what I would say to one about myself, except perhaps that I have too often been mistaken and don't seem able to learn from life as I believe I sometimes do from paintings and poems, even occasionally from a novel.

Lee Fair wrote a novel, part of which is based on or takes off from those brief passionate months we spent together. It is always difficult to know, even when one is not personally involved, how much feeling and judgment really reflect on the raw material of life. Perhaps I would more easily and resignedly accept the portrait of me in it as Lee's real view of me if she hadn't also dedicated the book to me. Am I a muse or a villain? For the artist there may be no clear distinction. My name as a character is Swete, and I am very like the other preying lesbians about whom I compulsively read for several years after Lee left me. Swete seduces the main character and robs her of her child's affection, then of her financial independence, and finally of her will to study and write until finally her only way to regain her own life is to take it. The main character recovers to marry her psychiatrist, as Lee also did, though she divorced him not long after the book was published.

Lee is now one of Canada's best known lesbians, that first novel something of an embarrassment to her. To her credit, she used it as an example of how we have been raised to trash each other and seek our salvation in men. Carol's two sons keep Lee from the extremes of separatism. Lee and I exchange Christmas cards, and we have dinner together occasionally when she is in Vancouver to give a reading or lecture. I don't ever attend them, and she has never asked for an explanation. Perhaps she remembers that I don't go to Wilson's either.

I have long since given up fantasies of nursing either one of them in old age. In any case, I will sooner need that attention than either of them will whose bones are not so well acquainted with sea mists as mine are.

What I have come to understand about myself is that I am interested in art rather than artists. Those who blundered into my life under the mistaken impression that

I had either something to give or be given have only threatened my pleasure in their very real accomplishments.

So many people seem to draw their nourishment directly from passion as plants take nourishment directly from the sun. I have been only badly burned by such heat. Yet the art that has been made from it has sustained me all my solitary life.

I still prefer those arts which don't require the presence of human beings: literature, painting, sculpture. Films are less threatening to me than live theatre, and I prefer my music canned.

After Lee, I encouraged neither men nor women in any sort of intimacy; yet I have gone on being for one artist or another a symbol until I've become something of a legend myself. It is not really respectable, in western Canada anyway, for a poet to pass thirty without having written a poem to me. I have been muse, witch, preying lesbian. I have also been devouring mother, whore, Diana, spirit of Vancouver, daughter of the tides.

In a sense my life has been lived for me in the imaginations of other people, and there is nothing dangerous about that if I don't try to participate, for in that way disaster lies. My real companions, in my imagination, are my counterparts throughout history and the world who, whatever names they are given, are women very like myself, who holds the shell of a poem to her ear and hears the mighty sea at a safe and sorrowing distance.

# HIS NOR HERS

The virtue of a reclusive husband is the illusion of freedom he may provide for his wife once the children are old enough for school and social lives of their own. Gillian's husband did not like her to be out as many evenings as she was, raising money and/or enthusiasm for one good cause or another. She irritated him also when she was at home, either being far too noisy and playful with their two daughters, already inclined to giggle, or busy at her typewriter clacking out right-minded letters to the editor, to her Member of the Legislative Assembly, to the Prime Minister himself. But, when she asked him what he wanted her to do, he couldn't say. Gillian suggested that his image of a wife was a warm statue, breathing quietly in the corner of the couch, not even turning her own pages to disturb his reading. It was a far less offensive image to him than it was to her. A quiet presence was what a wife should be, but increasingly he had to settle for a quiet absence.

"Do you know where your daughters are half the time?" he asked her.

"Yes," Gillian answered, for she knew what homes of friends they'd found more hospitable to their taste in music, their interest in their hair, their bursts of high-humored silliness.

"Well, I don't. I don't know where you are half the time."

33

"Only because you don't listen."

How could he pay attention through all their mindless morning gossip simply for casually dropped clues to their whereabouts, he wanted to know.

"You can't, darling," Gillian replied. "And if we're all resigned to that, why can't you be?"

Sometimes, when he remembered to, he studied Gillian's clothes to decide whether or not she was dressing appropriately for where she said she was going. Since she inclined to suits without more adornment than a bright scarf at her throat, he thought it only fair to dismiss the idea of her being unfaithful to him. She was co-operative enough when it occurred to him to make love to her, and she had no cause to complain, as some women did, about an overly demanding husband. He had never been suspicious enough to try to check up on her. It would have seemed to him also somehow beneath him. He was not the kind of man to have married a woman he couldn't trust.

He wondered occasionally if he shouldn't have allowed her to take some sort of part time job, something dignified and clearly low paying to indicate that it was an interest rather than a necessity. It might have used up some of her tireless and tiresome energy and made her more content to stay at home in the evening. But he was not the kind of man to marry a woman who wanted to work, and Gillian had never been forceful in such suggestions.

"It's good for your company image to have a wife active in the community," Gillian reminded him.

Gillian had the taste to do nothing strident, like marching for abortion or peace. She raised money for the art gallery, lobbied for better education for handicapped children, for scholarships for the gifted, and she supported the little theatres. She never asked him for unreasonable donations, nor did she drag him, as so many other husbands were dragged, to the symphony or gallery openings.

"With your interest in the arts, why don't you want to stay home and read a good book?"

"I'm a people person, darling. That's all."

Clearly "people" could not include him, the singular and solitary man that he was. But he had to admit that she never discouraged him from fishing or hunting, even encouraged him to take longer and more expensive sporting holidays than he could make up his mind about for himself since he did not like the idea of being selfish.

"You're not selfish. You're a very generous man. Why not occasionally be generous to yourself?"

Away from his wife and daughters, he could stop brooding about them, stop feeling left out of their lives, for which he had no taste to be included. Sometimes he wondered what it would have been like to have a son, but he was even less easy in the company of men if there were no business topic to preoccupy them. He fished and hunted alone. What he would have enjoyed was knowing that Gillian was back at whatever lodge or cabin waiting for him. Yet that sort of wife might complain about being lonely.

Sometimes when Gillian grew impatient with his complaints, she said to him, "You have a good marriage and two lovely children. Why can't you just relax and be satisfied?"

Gillian believed what she said. Long suffering was not on her list of virtues, nor did she think it should be. She complained neither to her husband nor about him. When she said of him, "He has a difficult temperament; he's reclusive," she was simply describing him to excuse his absence from plays, gallery openings—husbands weren't expected to be on committees. Gillian considered herself as good a wife as her husband could reasonably expect and a good deal better than he might have had.

He did not know that Gillian was not extravagant with his money because she had some of her own. She didn't think of herself as secretive about it so much as keeping her own counsel. There was no need for him to appropriate what was hers as if it were some sort of dowry. She didn't ask him the particulars of his financial life, about which he was also inclined to keep his counsel. Unlike him, she never suspected that he might be unfaithful. She knew that he wasn't. He was far too fastidious a man to be involved in anything he would think of as messy.

Gillian's conscience about him was perfectly clear. She did do good works. She was a good mother. And she knew more clearly than he did that he would be just as irritated with her at home as he was with her for not being there, not because she was an irritating woman but because he was an irritable man.

Gillian did not know how long ago it had first occurred to her that she would one day leave him, after the girls were raised and safely settled. Simply gradually her illusion of freedom made her feel she would one day enjoy the real thing. Gillian would not leave him for anyone else. It would be unfair to involve a third party in divorce. Therefore, whenever a third party became at all pressing about time Gillian did not have, emotional support she could not offer, long before there was any question of commitment, Gillian retreated into being a wife and mother with, yes, some feeling of guilt about the deserted lover but with a sense, too, that it was for the best since she refused to burden any lover with the guilt of feeling responsible for a broken marriage. When Gillian decided to leave, she would deal with the problem of her outraged husband by herself, for outraged she knew he would be, no matter how much he complained about her inadequacies.

"Duplicity" was not the word Gillian would have used to describe her life, perhaps because she could move quite openly with a lover, go out to dinner, go to the theatre without causing a flicker of gossip. She could even invite one home, though she didn't very often, out of loyalty to her husband really because invariably a lover asked, "How can you live with him?" For Gillian it wasn't all that difficult. She knew women who stayed with husbands who drank, who beat them, who didn't pay the bills. Her marriage in comparison was a solid, sane arrangement in which to raise children.

"But he's such an impossible person!" came the protest.

"Aren't we all," Gillian would ask, "one way or another?"

But she liked to avoid such discussions when she could. Her lovers almost always befriended her daughters, sometimes even became their confidantes. Gillian enjoyed being able to include the girls in her happiness. Sometimes she even took them with her on a holiday with a lover, for their father couldn't abide traveling with children but wouldn't begrudge them the experience. Occasionally, Gillian thought, the girls mourned the loss of a lover even more than she did, but the period between lost love and restored intimate friendship usually didn't last long. By now Gillian had what might almost be described as a community of ex-lovers who had become friends.

With men such an arrangement would not have been possible. If Gillian had been attracted to men, her life might have been full of tension and deceit. As it was, she never had to lie to her husband about whom she was with and only very occasionally about where she was going.

Only once her husband said, "That friend of yours, Joan, I think she's a lesbian."

"She may be," Gillian said lightly, "but she's great, good fun."

"Doesn't your own reputation concern you?"

"Of course, but I'm not a bigot, and neither are you."

In fact, Joan was only a good friend. Gillian's taste in women was for the feminine and sensitive. Her husband would never have suspected any of her lovers of being a lesbian. The idea would have offended his whole concept of womanhood. Her lovers might seem to him "flighty" or "neurotic" but never perverse.

It was Gillian's own behavior he would have suspected if he had ever seen her among her ex-lovers, for her bright scarf became an ascot, and she held her cigarette between her teeth when she lighted it. Her laughter was bold, and her eyes were direct and suggestive. Even the way she downed her beer, which she didn't touch at home, would have shocked him.

In this role, her daughters loved her best, for she was full of fun and daring. No matter what they were doing, there was the tension of excitement, which made them prance and whinny. They knew their mother was never like that around their father. They associated their mother's mood with themselves away from him rather than with her friends.

Gillian acknowledged the latent eroticism she felt for her daughters and they for her. It was one of the joys of mothering daughters. She would brook no criticism from her friends about it.

"Why should I mind if they grow up to be lesbians?"

But they were both growing up to be even crazier about boys than they were about their mother and her exciting friends. Gillian didn't worry about that either, though it made her sometimes restless, aware of how empty her particular nest would be when they were gone and she had no buffer between her and her irritable and isolated husband. For, though he was critical of the girls, they had grown very good at teasing and cajoling him when it was necessary.

Was it about this time, too, that the pattern of her relationships with other women shifted? Lynn, who had to be called Lynn Number Two or Lynn R.—it had gotten that bad, her friends teased her, such a string of women she'd had—instead of beginning to make unreasonable demands, was simply drifting away, busy when Gillian had a free night, not home at the hour she knew Gillian habitually called. Lynn finally confessed that there was someone else.

Gillian felt both bereft and betrayed. She had never left a lover for someone else, as she wouldn't leave her husband. There was something immoral about inflicting jealous pain.

"Pain is pain," Lynn Number One, who resented this new designation, said to her. "Don't you think I was jealous of your husband?"

"But why would you be?"

"You sleep with him, don't you?"

"Once a month."

"You stay with him."

"The children," Gillian responded automatically.

"Gillian, you've always wanted your cake and to eat it, too. Face it: you're not getting any younger. What was in it for Lynn R.?"

"That's awfully calculating," Gillian said.

She began to drink too much, to get maudlin with old lovers about the past beauty of their relationships, their lasting loyalty. (She wasn't speaking to Lynn R.) She often had to be forcibly sobered up before she was sent home, and she was later getting there than she had ever risked, even at the passionate height of an affair. The security of home, which she had never lost sight of in delight, seemed less meaningful to her in sorrow. Before, she could bring all her own nourished happiness in to brighten the gloom. Now, far more particularly miserable than her husband, she could not endure his bleak moods. When he approached her sexually, she turned him harshly away.

"You are *my wife*," he said, more shocked than angry.

Gillian was shocked herself at how without generosity she was for him, how reckless of him. For she let him see how angry and out of control she was. She snatched up her coat and left the house.

She went to a lesbian bar where her friends had sometimes gone, a place too public for the way she arranged her life. There she picked up a young girl, hardly older than her own daughters, and took her to a hotel for the night.

"Won't you even tell me your name?" her young lover pleaded in the morning.

Gillian's terror overcame her remorse. She fled as cruelly as she had from her husband, revolting from what she had done. She was not that kind of woman, to take advantage of a mere child and to compound it with deserting her. If Gillian had had the presence of mind, she would have left money on the dresser.

Arriving home, Gillian expected to have the day to pull herself together and to figure out how to get back from the too far she had gone. Her husband had not gone to work. He sat in his chair in the living room waiting for her. She put a surprised and guilty hand to her mouth. She had not made up her face, and his eyes were appraising her sternly.

"That is never to happen again," he said, a thought-out new confidence in his voice. "Nor are you ever going to go out in the evening more than one night a week. I have been a patient man, a far too patient man, and I've been taken advantage of."

"I want a divorce," Gillian said in a calm tone that masked hysteria.

"Don't be silly," he said, as if she'd suggested something like a drink before breakfast.

"I'm not being silly. I've come to my senses," Gillian said, first wondering what on earth that phrase meant, then frightened that she knew.

"If you call flinging yourself out of the houee in the middle of the night . . ."

"Ten o'clock."

". . . sensible . . ."

"This is a discussion that is now finally over," Gillian said. "Our lawyers can deal with the details."

"Gillian, we have been married for nineteen years. We have two still dependent children. What are you talking about? What's happened to you?"

"Because of the girls, I think you'd better be the one to move out," Gillian said in a practical tone.

"This is *my* house!"

"It's *our* house, according to the law."

"I will not tolerate this, Gillian!"

"I suggest you talk it over with your lawyer. That's

what I'm going to do," she said and turned to leave the room.

"Gillian!"

Half way up the stairs, she heard the front door slam, and she sank right there, suddenly too weak to take another step. Though she had entertained the idea of leaving him for years, she had never considered the means of doing so. His lawyer was hers in so far as she had one. Legally, she didn't know what "marriage breakdown" was. She did know that humanly hers had, and whatever irrationality and self-destructiveness had led her into this circumstance, there was now no going back.

Slowly Gillian got up and went to the phone in their bedroom. The first call she made was to a locksmith, ordering the locks on all the doors to be changed by four o'clock.

At six o'clock that evening, Gillian and her daughters sat at the dinner table, listening to a pounding fist on the front door, then on the back, not speaking to each other until they heard the slamming of the car door and the starting up of an engine.

"Are you afraid of him, Mother?" her youngest daughter asked timidly.

"I never have been," Gillian said.

"Is it legal?" her older daughter asked.

"It will be," Gillian said. "This evening you can play any music you want as loudly as you want, and you can invite your friends over."

But that evening the house was quieter than it would have been if the master of gloom had been home, his forced absence even more palpable than his presence.

Gillian overheard her younger daughter say, "I don't really like Daddy, but I'm used to him."

"He's our father," the older replied, but casually.

Ugly days stretched into ugly weeks in which Gillian often felt a prisoner in her own fortress. She had given up all her committees since her real interest in them had never been strong. They had been little more than a screen behind which she could lead her personal life. Now she had neither a personal life nor a husband to deceive, for he was now nothing but an enemy into whose hands she was determined not to fall. She saw none of the women who had been her intimates for so many years. Any hint of impropriety now would irreparably damage her case in court, leave her not only without a fair financial settlement but even without her daughters.

In the end, her husband behaved as Gillian had counted on him to, not generously but with scrupulous fairness. She could live in the house until the girls left home, at which time it would be sold, the proceeds divided between them. There was generous child support until the girls either reached twenty-one or finished college. For her own support, Gillian was responsible. The money her husband had never known she had made looking for a job less urgent than it should have been for Gillian's state of mind.

"Mother," her oldest daughter finally said to her, "even when Daddy was around, you used to have fun."

"You're right," Gillian admitted.

"Well, it's time you started having fun again."

It wasn't that simple. Gillian was more than ever at risk, the custody of her daughters the price she could pay for any visibility in the bars. The cohesiveness of her old friends, which she had once prized, excluded her as long as she could not behave as she'd expected others to behave, resigned to loss and open to new adventures of the heart. Gillian simply could not forgive Lynn Number Two her betrayal. There was something else, too. As long as she had been married, the limitations of any other relationship were clear. Now, when she tired of someone—supposing that woman were not as untrustworthy as Lynn Number Two—Gillian could see no way out, no iron-clad and moral excuse for waning interest. Could there be a woman so remarkable as to hold Gillian's interest for the rest of her life? She had never thought of a woman in those terms.

Gillian's husband enjoyed his perfect solitude no more than Gillian enjoyed her freedom. After his outrage had worn itself out, erupting only occasionally at some convenience or familiar object lost to him, he suffered from simple loneliness, which he had no social skills to combat. Even his sporting trips, which he had made sure he could still afford, were not the escapes from domestic irritation which they had once been and lost their savor.

His daughters dutifully lunched with him, but he knew he bored them with his complaints, which would be repeated to their mother in a tone not sympathetic to him. He was not even sure what kind of sympathy he was asking for. He had been too deeply humiliated by Gillian's treatment of him to imagine that he wanted her back even on his own terms, which she would never agree to. He wanted back what he could not have, the illusion of Gillian as his wife.

And Gillian also wanted back what she could not have, not her husband, but the illusion of freedom he had given her.

# THE REAL WORLD

"There's no reason, just because she's eighty, that she shouldn't live in the real world," Tess complained, flinging a long trousered leg over the arm of her father's chair which she had appropriated even before he died for reasons which had been obvious to her mother and obscure to herself until very recently.

"You don't think she should join you in cross country skiing," Margaret said mildly, "or go to a rock concert or try pot . . ."

"Might help her arthritis," Tess said.

"The point is that her world is just as real as yours, and, if you love her, you should want her to live comfortably in it."

"Even if I have to turn into a hypocrite and a liar, Mother? Even if I have to deny the most important thing in my life?"

"In your *private* life," Margaret said.

"What *private* life?" Tess demanded. "If Gram knew, then maybe I could have a private life."

"There will be time enough for that when you can afford your own place."

"But Annie has a whole year to go in school, and the way things are now, who knows when she'll get a job? I could pay for her board here."

"No," Margaret said, getting up. "When you're ready to live your own life, you have to have your own space for it."

"Wait a minute," Tess said. "Don't just walk off . . ."

"I have to get dinner. You need to clean up and bring your grandmother downstairs."

"Mother, all sorts of people live together now. Nobody my age can afford to do anything else."

"Then move in with other people your own age," Margaret said.

"You want to cope with Gram on your own? Who'd cut the grass? Who'd fix the furnace? You don't even know how to use a screwdriver."

"I hope Annie knows how to cook and do the laundry and clean house."

"Oh, Mother, those aren't hard things to learn. You said yourself anyone who can read can cook."

"Well, I'll just get on with my simple task," Margaret said.

As she fixed the salad, weighed out the noodles, and tasted the stew for its final seasoning, Margaret let Lou admonish her from his by-now-accustomed grave. Surely, if Annie had been Andrew and they wanted to begin their married life in this house, Margaret would not have objected. In ways, it would be easier to welcome another daughter rather than an unaccustomed son into the house. Lou had anticipated this turn of events by the time Tess was twelve, had read and read to Margaret everything he could find to shed positive light on their daughter's masculine tastes and behavior.

"Couldn't this become a self-fulfilling prophecy?" Margaret had asked. "It's one thing to accept an accomplished fact, quite another to encourage a tendency. Why can't I teach her to cook and to sew?"

"Because she doesn't want to learn," Lou pointed out reasonably. "And she does want to learn about tools and fixing the car."

"Why does that have to mean she'll be a lesbian?"

"It doesn't," Lou said. "It only means we have to be open to that possibility."

He had kept his foot in the door of Margaret's conscience even for the five years since he'd died: "Let her be who she is."

But that was before Margaret's mother had moved in, and surely her mother had some right to be who she was as well, though Margaret admitted to herself that her mother's views were often both alien and offensive to Margaret.

Only this morning her mother had said, "This letter from my sister took three weeks from Toronto. It's all those coloreds at the post office, that's what it is."

"How so?" Tess asked, amiably enough.

"They can't read English," her grandmother replied.

"The ones I know can," Tess said.

"Well, you just must know a better class of them than I do."

Tess had grinned, hugged her grandmother, and gone cheerfully off to work. It was Margaret who flinched at her mother's bigotry, who was shamed by it.

How on earth Tess then could expect her grandmother, church-going, snobbish and sheltered, to accept something entirely outside her own experience, not to mention her moral universe? Even now, she told people that Tess worked for Toyota but would never allow Margaret to say to anyone that her daughter was an auto mechanic. Fortunately Tess cleaned up and changed at work and was miraculously grease-free. She said being greasy was just an unnecessary macho trip.

Lou, rational, kind, impractical Lou, would probably have settled down to educating his mother-in-law if he'd lived long enough to know that it was necessary. Margaret simply couldn't do that. She even allowed her mother to think that she'd stayed away from church all her married life out of respect for Lou's atheism and now had happily returned to the fold. Since Margaret had to take her there and fetch her, it was easier to go to the service than to make a point of not going.

Margaret heard the voices of her mother and daughter in the dining room, drained the noodles, tossed the salad, and carried them both to the table.

"Will you get the stew, Tess?"

"Sure thing," Tess answered, and Margaret was pleased, as she was every evening, to see her daughter in a skirt.

"How about a game of Scrabble tonight after supper?" Margaret's mother suggested.

"All right," Margaret said, though she knew she'd have to call the game short in order to get the last of her book-keeping done.

"Sorry, Gram, I've got a date," Tess said.

"Why don't we ever see any of these dates of yours at the house?"

Tess threw a glance at her mother and said, "Wouldn't be considered proper, Gram."

"Well, in my day it wasn't considered proper unless they came to the house. Is everything just turned upside down in your generation?"

"We don't stand on our heads after all," Tess said in a tone that always managed to make her grandmother in-dulgent rather than cross, which gave Tess the illusion that her grandmother was indulgent.

Once Tess had gone up to her room to change again into jeans and then take the stairs two or three at a time in her rush to be with Annie, Margaret's mother registered her complaints.

"She's too old to behave like that and dress like that. What kind of a man has a date with a girl in blue jeans, dashing around like a basketball player?"

"Nearly everyone her age dresses like that," Margaret would answer, over and over again, to reassure rather than contradict her mother, for, though she was critical of Tess, it was more out of puzzlement than lack of affection.

"Well, maybe one of these days she'll fall in love and turn into a young lady."

"Let's enjoy her the way she is while we can," Margaret said.

"This house would be a tomb, wouldn't it, without her?"

Margaret felt the coldness around her heart which was the climate she had lived in since Lou died and knew that without Tess the house would, indeed, be as cheerless as the grave.

"Still, I'd like to see her married before I go. Might even hang on for a great-grandchild."

Margaret spelled "child" on the Scrabble board, but it was her own she was imagining, her mind flipping back through twenty-one years as if she had a photograph album before her: Tess as bold as brass from the time she could crawl, up in trees, on skates, on skis. The level blue gaze that looked up at her from her breast had never faltered. They were Lou's eyes, and Margaret was glad he could be looked at as he looked at the world though she had thought both child and man daft in their persistent rationality which imposed so much irrational hope on the world around them.

"What will the world do to her?" Margaret had asked Lou.

"Let her be strong," Lou answered. "Let her trust herself."

"But how will she trust other people?"

"She can start with us. That's a good beginning."

"It's your turn again," Margaret's mother said.

"Sorry. This better be the last game. I still have work to do."

Margaret was doing the books for a local dress shop, one of a couple of dozen accounts she had gradually taken on after Lou died, work that paid reasonably well and kept her at home for her mother and daughter. If her mother hadn't been able to contribute quite generously to the household, Margaret would have had to sell the house and go out to work. Now that Tess also insisted on making her own contribution as well as buying her own clothes and paying her own car installments, Margaret had a sense of near affluence, but she put money aside rather than getting used to spending it. When Tess did decide to move out, she might need a bit of help for a while.

She heard Tess come in and waited for her to tilt her fine mane of tan hair around the office door on her way to the fridg for a beer or a glass of milk.

"Want anything?" Tess asked.

"Piece of cheese and an apple."

Tess brought her in a plate, knife and napkin to go with her order, signs of shy but growing domesticity which touched Margaret unreasonably now that they were obviously not belated signs of heterosexuality but simply indication of Annie's good influence.

"How's Annie?"

"Depressed," Tess said. "She thinks her parents are beginning to suspect and will kill her. Why are some people so awful?"

"They're ignorant, that's all," Margaret said.

"What she needs is to move out of there."

Margaret sighed.

"You do like Annie, don't you?"

"Of course I do, darling. It's just that you both are young enough to think that every problem has to have an immediate solution. Annie needs her parents until she finishes school. Time enough then to think about what you'll do."

"You think I don't want to leave home because I can't take care of myself," Tess said.

"Well, you are a bit of a domestic retard, you know."

"I can *fix* the washer and dryer."

"And it probably wouldn't take you more than fifteen minutes to figure out how to use them."

"Yeah," Tess said, "But don't you have to know all sorts of stuff like which pile what ought to go into and what can't go in at all? Remember the year we all had red underwear because Dad decided to help you out?"

Margaret laughed. Tess couldn't have been more than thirteen, but her underwear had been a mortification to her and probably still would be.

"Maybe some people just don't have the knack," Tess said.

"Shall I give you some of your father's bad advice? Don't learn to do anything you don't want to do because you'll probably be stuck with doing it all your life."

"You don't much like bookkeeping, do you?" Tess asked.

"Oh, I don't mind. It's not very exciting, but it's nice to do something you know can come out right."

"You'd better teach me to do the laundry, and maybe I ought to know how to cook, just a little bit anyway. Just don't tell anybody, all right?"

"Not even Gram?"

"Especially not Gram!"

It was convenient for both Tess and Margaret that her mother needed help negotiating the stairs and rarely left her room before dinner unless a special outing had been proposed. In three weeks, Tess was as comfortable with the washing cycle as she was with the motor of the washing machine, and it became her habit to spend an hour with Margaret a couple of times a week in the kitchen.

Margaret, an intuitive and inventive cook, quickly learned that, if Tess was going to develop beyond boiling an egg, grilling a steak and making salad, Margaret would have to give up words like "dollop," "bloop," and "pinch," directions like "season to taste" or "stir until it thickens." Tess needed standard measurements as well as some reassuring notion that stirring would take three or five minutes since, for all she knew, cream sauce might need three hours of her attention. She had an absolute aversion to tasting anything out of a pot, afraid of burning her mouth. Unlike most new cooks, she grasped the idea of getting things done at the same time very quickly and was more particular about that than Margaret had ever been. Tess was quick, too, to veto any menu that took nervous rushing at the end.

On Friday of a week for which Tess had prepared every

dinner with nothing but reassurance from Margaret, she was very pleased with herself.

"These beans are a bit overdone, I'd say," Tess observed, more to preserve a sense of modesty than because there was anything seriously wrong with the vegetable.

"It's not like you to criticize your mother's cooking," her grandmother said.

"I'm not," Tess admitted. "It's my own. Has been all week. What do you think?"

"Is it true?"

Margaret nodded, smiling.

"Well, maybe I'll see a great-grandchild before I die after all!"

Tess scowled at her mother and said, "That's not for me, Gram."

"Ah, but that's what you said about cooking, and look at you."

"Nobody said anything in my sex education class about cooking making anybody pregnant."

"Well, it's certainly a step in the right direction."

As Margaret anticipated, Tess surrendered the kitchen at once. Though Margaret was irritated with her mother, she was relieved to have the kitchen again to herself, her own vocabulary and methods restored to her. At least, the mystery of cooking had been dispelled for Tess. She could do it now when she wanted or needed to.

Margaret did take the opportunity to say to her mother, "Don't be on at Tess about having children. She may really not want them, ever."

"Wait until she falls in love!"

It was odd to Margaret that her mother didn't realize Tess was in love. Oh, she supposed the signs were not all conventional though Tess did have long telephone conversations with Annie on evenings they didn't meet. What made it so obvious to Margaret was not only Tess' eager happiness when she went off to meet Annie or brought her home for a meal but her increased sense of responsibility. It was not only the laundry and the cooking. She was being more careful about money as well as more interested in it.

"I like my job well enough," Tess said, "but, you know, it's not going to go anywhere."

"What else do you think you'd like to do?"

"I'm a pretty good carpenter, and I like electricity. What I might really like to do is learn to be a contractor. You can start out doing renovations and work up to building whole houses. There's a guy I work with who says there's good money in it, just too much hassle. I don't think I'd mind the hassle."

"How do you go about learning?"

As Tess outlined the options, Margaret realized that she must have been thinking about it for a long time.

"It would be a drop in salary at first, but I don't think it would take me very long to catch up."

Though "my granddaughter, the contractor" would suit Margaret's mother no better than "my granddaughter, the grease monkey," Margaret trusted Tess to find her own way. She had always been someone to learn by doing. Though she'd outgrown a stubborn prejudice against books as "all a pack of lies," Tess would always trust a teacher more than a set of instructions to acquire a new skill. Margaret had the belated pleasure of learning that about her daughter first hand, when before she had had to trust Lou's testimony, for Tess had worked with him in his basement shop since she was a small child.

It was not many weeks before Tess had found a tolerant contractor who hired her as an apprentice carpenter, and Tess woke each morning as excited as a child anticipating a special treat.

"There are always new problems to solve," she said. "You'd never really run out of them."

Then one night Tess was out unusually late. Margaret was already in bed with her light out when she heard Tess come in. She didn't go to the kitchen but went straight to her room. The next morning all her sunny energy was gone.

"I'll take that up to your grandmother," Margaret offered about the breakfast tray Tess normally delivered.

When she returned to the breakfast table, Tess had not begun to eat.

"Aren't you feeling well?"

Tess shook her head.

"Fever?"

Tess shook her head.

"What is it, darling?"

"We broke up last night," Tess said quietly.

"Why?"

"Her parents, mostly. They came out and said they were sure I was a lesbian, that she hadn't been dating since she met me. They've forbidden her to see me."

"Well, in that case," Margaret said indignantly, "she can certainly move in here!"

"It's not that simple. She won't be twenty-one until August. I could be charged with corrupting a minor. I suppose you could, too."

"That's ridiculous!"

"Anyway, Annie is pretty scared, and, you know, she's not as sure about all this as I am. She says, what if she wanted a baby, and maybe this was sort of kid stuff . . ."

Margaret's first reaction was fury at herself for not making Annie welcome all those months ago. Then she reflected that, if Annie's parents indeed felt the way they did, such a move would only have invited their wrath much sooner.

"I really love Annie, Mother."

"I know you do."

"So I have to let her go."

Tess got up from the table, put on her jacket, and picked up her tool kit.

"There's a plumbing course that starts tonight. I wasn't going to sign up for it because it's every night for three weeks. Now I guess I will."

Margaret was furious with Annie's parents, furious with

Annie. If she hadn't been sure of her own feelings, why had she strung Tess along all these months? Who were any of them to question the validity and strength of Tess' love?

"Lou?" she demanded out loud. "Now do you see? Who can she ever trust?"

Though Tess was subdued and absorbed in her work, she didn't withdraw from her mother and grandmother. If anything, she became even more dependable and solicitous. On week-ends she stayed at home, tried baking a cake, running the vacuum cleaner, and she bought a hideously difficult jigsaw puzzle for all of them to work on together.

Margaret wanted to suggest to Tess that she shouldn't neglect all her friends, but they had been Annie's friends, too, and it would be like Tess to leave them for Annie. In time, Tess would find other people though once her class was over, she saw only her work crew, and they were all men.

"I think Tess is getting too serious," Margaret's mother remarked. "She doesn't ever go out any more. And what's happened to Annie?"

"Exams, I suppose," Margaret answered.

"I always liked Annie, such an affectionate child."

Margaret was tempted to a negative remark about Annie, but she refrained, out of loyalty to Tess, she supposed, who never spoke of Annie except with tenderness. It was as if a loved friend had died. Sometimes Margaret wanted to snap, "Did it ever occur to you what a bitch she's been?" But she knew it to be a furious lack of generosity to someone who had hurt her child. In fairness to Annie, Margaret tried to believe that she hadn't had much of a choice.

Then Margaret's mother asked Tess herself, "Whatever's happened to Annie?"

Tess turned her level gaze to her grandmother and said, "I wanted more than she could handle. I loved her."

Margaret braced herself.

"Well, I'm sorry, dear," her grandmother said. "That

can't have been easy for you."

When Tess left for yet another series of classes, Margaret's mother turned to her and asked, "Did you know that?"

"Yes."

"But the poor child! That must have been terrible for her."

"Yes."

Margaret could not be sure how much her mother actually understood of the relationship between Tess and Annie. Perhaps as long as no one put any name to it but love, her mother had the heart to understand. It occurred to Margaret that Tess had a surer estimation of her grandmother than Margaret did. For, however bad her mother was with generalities, she was pretty good with particulars.

Through the summer Tess' hair bleached, and her skin turned honey color.

"The only bad thing about being a woman on this job is that I can't take my shirt off."

She had begun occasionally to go to the beach. She had found some new friends to sail with, but Margaret saw a new reserve in her face which made her look older and less sure of herself. She was happier coming home from work or a class than she was from an outing.

One late evening in the fall, when Margaret and Tess were having a beer together in her office and discussing how Tess might learn to set up books for a business of her own, there was an urgent knocking at the door. Tess went to it, and Margaret followed, concerned by the lateness of the hour. Only because the person who had come in was folded in her daughter's arms did Margaret know it must be Annie. She stepped back into her office and shut the door.

Nearly an hour later, wondering if she could decently get past the living room and up to bed, Margaret heard Tess' light rap.

"She's staying the night," Tess said, the expression on her face concerned, her eyes washed with wonder. "We can talk in the morning."

"Is she all right?"

"I think she will be."

"Where . . . ?"

"With me," Tess said.

She'd never before even asked to have Annie for the night as though she had felt anything less than Annie's living there would be improper.

Margaret wanted to ask Tess if she were sure, if this was what she wanted after all these months, but to ask was to pretend she couldn't read Tess' face.

Tess laid the facts before Margaret at breakfast before Annie was up. Annie had been made pregnant by a friend of her father's who had been encouraged to "straighten her out." This result, far from pleasing her father, gave him the excuse to throw her out of the house. Trash.

"What about the man?"

"He's married, and anyway Annie doesn't want anything to do with him. She doesn't want anything more to do with men."

"And the baby?"

"She thinks she ought to have an abortion," Tess said, her eyes steadily on her mother, "but she doesn't want one."

Margaret who had wanted children so very badly and finally had managed only Tess knew that her own prejudice against abortion was irrational, and she tried now to keep it under control.

"It would be her one chance to have a child," Tess said.

"What are you thinking it has to do with you?"

"Everything," Tess said. "I want most to have her move in here because you and Gram would be company and help for her and because I could go on saving money, but, if you still don't like that idea, I can find us a place of our own."

"Do you want a baby?"

"I want Annie's."

"Will her father call the police when he finds out where she is?"

"Annie's twenty-one now. Nobody can touch us."

"Let me think about it all," Margaret said. "Right now, tell Annie she's welcome, and I'll talk to her when she feels like getting up."

"Mother, if you think we might do it, I'd like to ask Gram about it myself."

"All right."

Because Tess had volunteered to take on the problem of her grandmother herself, Margaret didn't let consideration of her mother stop her thoughts. In fact, when she entered them at all, Margaret saw her mother's expression of amused tenderness at the sight of a baby being carried into the house.

But was Annie old enough, sure enough of herself to take on the responsibility of a child even in the shelter of Tess' love and support, which only a few months ago she was persuaded to spurn as "kid stuff?" Then she heard Tess say, those months ago, "I really love Annie, Mother." Whatever the eventual outcome, decisions had to be made in terms of that fact. Tess and Annie would live here, if Margaret's mother could be persuaded, or somewhere nearby together.

When Annie did get up just before lunch, the sight of her pale and distressed young face dispelled the doubts it might have supported in Margaret. Who could refuse to shelter and help someone as abjectly vulnerable, so brutally used by parents in the name of protecting her?

"Oh, Annie, I'm so glad you're here with us."

Tess came home early from work to find Annie in the kitchen helping Margaret, both of them deep in plans for the baby's coming.

"You two certainly aren't wasting any time," Tess commented, and then she deliberately and formally kissed Annie.

"You need to talk with your grandmother," Margaret said, "the sooner the better so that she won't feel left out."

"Right," Tess said. "I'll just change."

"I don't have any clothes," Annie confessed.

"We'll soon take care of that," Margaret said.

Their easy flow of talk was somewhat inhibited now, for

Annie probably in shyness over Tess's direct behavior, for Margaret because she was suddenly apprehensive about her mother. It was nearly an hour before Tess came downstairs with her grandmother.

"I can hardly believe it!" the old woman exclaimed. "A baby in the house! Annie, I'm so glad you've come back to us. Tess wasn't the only one who missed you."

Then they were all talking, full of practical questions, plans, sudden bursts of laughter.

"Never mind about months from now," Margaret announced. "We've got jobs to do right away, this evening. We need to move me out of my bedroom and you two into it."

Against protests from both Tess and Annie, Margaret was firm. She would miss the luxury of her own bathroom, but private and comfortable space for the children was far more important. Her mother was surprisingly on her side, and, rather than stay down in the living room alone, she went back upstairs where she could watch and supervise the move.

When it was accomplished, Tess and Annie needed no encouragement to go to their own new room. Margaret offered her mother a glass of port and joined her in her bedroom where she imagined they might more often be now last thing before bed. Margaret was newly grateful for her mother's company.

"This is really all right with you?" Margaret asked.

"I wish the poor child had a father for her baby, but under the circumstances the only real disgrace is her own family behaving that way! I can't imagine it. They can't be Christians, can they? Why, they might even have forced her into having an abortion like those awful 'pro choice' people!"

Ordinarily Margaret would have flinched the more surely for hearing her own prejudice elevated into a moral principle, but at that moment she relaxed instead into the knowledge that she and her mother were on the same side, pro this particular life anyway, which did so clearly establish that they all could live in the same real world, whatever the difficulties it might pose among its certain pleasures.

# JOY

I'm divorced and Derek's never been married, but this isn't a story about us so much as it is a story about Joy, who has by now acted out so many of our uncommitted errors that she is the only plot of our otherwise static relationship, if it can be called a relationship at all; neither of us has had the courage or the ignorance to be engaged. And so it is not our game. It is Joy's game. We are simply Joy's kibitzers.

She and I had both arrived much too early at the Vancouver Airport to meet the same plane coming in from California. Dressed in a pale linen suit and a thin summer coat in the middle of November, she sat on one side of the customs shed waiting room right next to the steam radiator. I stood on the other side of the room in sneakers, wool trousers and a duffle coat. She was no more than nineteen; I was no less than twenty-nine. But we had each dressed with our own kind of care for the same kind of waiting. I probably spoke first. I usually do, to animals, children, and all sorts of women. It's one of the many things about me that Derek thinks he likes but might not like to live with. He speaks to no one, being a Canadian just one generation away from England. And he likes me to come to the airport in trousers, too, because it means that I am not making a special occasion of either his leaving or his coming back.

Joy, who gave me her name at once as if it explained as much about her as any of the other facts, was, yes, meeting someone, her fiance. She hadn't been in Vancouver long herself, just one night, and she hadn't slept much, even though she'd been on her way the two nights before that, flying from Australia. She just couldn't sleep; she was that excited. It was cold, wasn't it? She hadn't expected it to be cold, but somebody at the hotel had explained it was the beginning of winter here.

"Do you know, can a person get married here on Sunday?"

"I don't know why not."

"It is Sunday tomorrow, isn't it? I'm that confused." She laughed, which made her cough, a rotten cough, deep in her chest and obviously familiar to her.

"Have you got a license?"

"Not yet. Maybe Wally will have one with him. He's coming up from San Diego. We have to be married before I can get into the States. He said it was Mexico or Canada, and he liked Canada better and so would I. So he sent me a ticket to Canada." She laughed again and coughed again. "It's my chest. I was that scared when I had to have a medical, but it turned out all right. It's nothing really, only my cough medicine spilled, spilled all over my wedding dress, this big stain all down the back of it. I took it right to the cleaners when I got here. They want to fix it for me. I hope they can. I want to be married in a church. I think it's nice to be married in a church, don't you? I don't know much about it, not when people are all alone, I mean. Wally's folks wanted to come up, but it would cost too much. It's awfully expensive, isn't it? Traveling. I would have had to wait another year to save up for a ticket. Wally didn't want to wait that long. We've already waited a year. I'm that excited!"

As she chattered and laughed and coughed, I grew concerned about her. If her Wally had no more grasp of the practical problems than she had, they'd be days trying to get married. They couldn't get a license on Sunday. She couldn't get her dress out of the cleaners on Sunday. A minister, a church, witnesses: she hadn't a clue how to arrange any of these things.

"Where are you staying?" I asked.

She couldn't remember either the name of the hotel or the name of the street, but she knew the place when she saw it. Alarmed at the prospect of her giving such directions to a cab driver, I almost offered to take them downtown; but Derek would be tired. He wouldn't want to be troubled with strangers, particularly this kind of muddle-headed child whose needs multiplied with every sentence.

"How old is Wally?"

"He's twenty-one, two years older than me." She hesitated. "He's a sailor, but he's not just an ordinary sailor. I mean, he's not like a sailor. You'll like him, Ruth. I know you will."

The waiting room had gradually filled with people, and through the glass doors I could see the first passengers standing at the immigration desk.

"Here they are," I said.

"I'm that excited!"

And she was. She had no real reluctance or doubt or fear. Her nervous touching of her hair, her throat, the seam in her stocking was only a taking of basic inventory which had already been approved. She was lovely. She was ready.

I was so busy looking for her Wally that I didn't see Derek until he stood right before us, half amused, half irritated. I kissed him with more energy than I intended, then turned away from his embarrassment to introduce him to Joy.

"Was there an American sailor on the plane?" I asked.

"No."

"He must be in civilian clothes," I said. "Shall we just wait to say hello?"

Derek hesitated. "You wait. I'll take my bag to the car

and meet you there. Where is it?"

I handed him the keys, knowing I ought to go with him, but I wanted to see Joy safely in Wally's hands before I left her. And I wanted to give them my phone number at least. I stood by her, watching the passengers claim their luggage, go through customs, and then come through the doors to be greeted or to hurry alone through the crowd to bus or taxi.

"Maybe he's been held up at the immigration desk," I said, as the waiting room emptied, leaving us once more alone together. "Shall I go see?"

All the passengers had been cleared, but the immigration officials were glad to hear that Joy was still in the waiting room. They wanted to see her.

"He must have missed the plane," she said.

"Are you sure he was to be on this plane?" the immigration officer asked, not unkindly.

"When is the next plane?" I asked.

"At eleven." It was only six-thirty. "Another at one, and that's it for the night."

"Do you want to come home with me?" I asked. "I could bring you back to meet the late planes."

"She can stay here," the officer said. "We'd rather she stayed here."

"But you haven't had any dinner, have you?"

"She can get dinner at the cafeteria."

"Don't stay," Joy said. "Derek's waiting. I'm all right."

"Have you enough money?"

"Yes, yes, I have plenty of money," she answered nervously.

"Well, look, take my phone number and call me if you need anything. Call me anyway. Will you call me?"

"We'll take care of her," the officer said, in a tone meant to be reassuring, but I didn't like it.

"I'll call," Joy said. "You go on now."

I tried to make an amusing story of it. It was always

better to break through Derek's irritation by ignoring it; but his uninvolved silence, as we drove back to the city, began to irritate me. We arrived at my apartment so unadmittedly out of sorts with each other that it was only half way through the second martini that we began to be more than civil. Even then, as he told me about the problems of his trip, his whole account was designed to make me feel guilty at having kept him waiting. I wondered, as I stood in the kitchen making the salad, how it was that we had skipped both the period of romantic passion and violent quarrels and had settled into the subtle tensions of married life without either being married or seriously playing at it. Probably it's my fault. My first marriage taught me not to expect much or at least not to ask for it, and Derek's cautious intelligence makes it honorable to give no more than is asked.

At dinner he settled to one of his favorite topics, the peculiar shallowness of the American character, using his business contacts and this "no-show sailor" as good examples. He didn't include me. One of his greatest compliments has always been that I don't seem like an American at all. But the dinner was good, and by the time we had finished the bottle of wine he was feeling genuinely fond of me. He reached into his briefcase for a small box. They were very pretty earrings. Derek has excellent taste.

"I missed you," he said.

"I missed you, too." It was true. Whenever we're apart, I think Derek and I both spend a lot of time trying to decide whether or not we should marry. It's exhausting. When we're together, the question doesn't seem to come up. It's more peaceful.

"Coffee?"

I couldn't keep my mind on him. I looked at my watch so often that he finally asked if I was tired and wanted him to go home.

"It's not that," I said. "It's Joy."

"Who?"

"The Australian girl. I keep wondering if Wally is on the eleven o'clock plane."

"I doubt it," Derek said. "An American sailor? I doubt it."

"You know, you're wrong about Americans. They have a romantic streak."

"Well then, sailor. All sailors are alike. Even the Australians. Haven't you ever heard of the English girl who fell in love with an Australian sailor? He promised her he'd come back and marry her. He said his name was Sidney Harbor."

"But Wally sent her a ticket. He wouldn't have sent her a ticket . . ."

"Ruth, why do you have to get so involved? You don't even know these people."

"Because they don't know anybody else. Joy's all on her own, thousands of miles from home, and she's only nineteen."

"More fool she," he said, but with some sympathy.

"I'm going to phone the airport."

No, the immigration officials said, the sailor had not been on the eleven o'clock plane. The young lady was still waiting. They didn't think it was necessary for me to speak with her. She was perfectly all right. I wasn't an old friend, was I? They'd give her any message. I said I'd call back at one.

"I don't like the sound of it at all," I said. "They're acting as if they had her in custody."

"They probably do. After all, if the sailor doesn't show, she becomes a problem for Canada. She may not have any money."

"I think we better go back out there."

"To do what?"

"To be with her. To vouch for her."

"Honey, you can't just take the responsibility for a stray Australian."

"Why not?"

"Oh well, why not? As you say. I suppose I'm just tired."

"You don't need to come with me," I said. "I'll drop you off at your place on the way."

Wally wasn't on the one o'clock plane either. I sat with Joy in the immigration office.

"When's the next plane?" I asked.

"Nine-thirty in the morning."

"Why don't we go home then?" I suggested. "You come home with me, and I'll bring you back in the morning."

Joy looked up at the immigration officer. She was too tired to think what to do. She waited to be told.

"Have you decided what you'll do if he doesn't come?" the immigration officer asked.

"I won't talk about it," she said quietly, without any anger. "He's coming. Something's just gone wrong."

"But what if he doesn't come at all?"

"I won't talk about it."

"Let me take her home," I said. "It's too late to do anything tonight."

"Are you willing to take full responsibility for her?"

"Of course. What time do you want her back in the morning?"

He looked down at Joy who seemed to have lost all interest in the conversation. "Oh, let her sleep. Just phone us when she wakes up."

Joy was glad to go back to my apartment with me, but she asked to stop at her hotel to pick up her things. I made her describe the street and the hotel as best she could, but I did not recognize either. I simply drove up and down the main streets of the city, but it was dark and it had begun to rain. Nothing looked familiar to her. She was cold and coughing.

"We'll find it tomorrow," I said. "You have to get some sleep."

Tired as she was, she couldn't rest. She had been without anyone to confide in as long as she'd been without sleep. I made up her bed, gave her a glass of sherry, then a bowl of soup, and finally a sleeping pill. It was five o'clock in the morning before she closed her eyes and slept suddenly like a child, leaving me wide awake and helplessly parental.

Derek was quite right. Joy was a fool. She had known Wally only five days! And that was over a year ago. On the strength of them, she'd broken her engagement to a settled Australian who could have provided her with a security she'd never really known, having left her own casual home at fourteen to make room for a stepfather and more children. "Security isn't everything," she said hopefully. "I feel comfortable with Wally, you know. I like him that much." Oh, her friends had tried to reason with her. Nobody trusts a sailor. And everyone knew that American sailors, even if they were as white as milk, often had black babies. Joy didn't really believe that, she said, but, even if it were true, did it really matter? She knew he would not stand her up; it was that simple. Once, when they were supposed to meet, each waited in the wrong place all day long. By the time they did discover each other, Wally had to be back to the ship, but neither one had doubted the other for a moment.

Five days! Yes, he had sent her a ticket, but he might have panicked then, only twenty-one years old, about to marry a girl he didn't even know. And she had confessed that she had only eleven dollars and twenty cents. She'd spent the rest of her savings on clothes and luggage and presents for Wally's family. What would she do? Even if he did turn up finally, what kind of a marriage was this, based on the fact that each of them had been willing to stand on the wrong street corner all day long? Fools, a couple of silly fools! Wally, if you don't turn up to marry this girl, I'll wring your neck. I'll personally hang you on our mutual flag pole. If you don't turn up . . . I lay in the weak light of the winter morning, watching the hands of the clock edge toward nine while Joy slept soundly, not even disturbed by the single ring of the telephone.

"This is the Immigration Office at the airport."

"Yes?"

"We have a young American sailor here who wants to know what we've done with his girl."

"We'll be right out," I said. "Joy! Joy! Joy!"

She dressed slowly and then wanted something to eat. I tried to hurry her, but it did no good. Was she finally having second thoughts of her own? Dressed in the same clothes, but wearing a sweater of mine under her coat, she sat next to me in the car with nothing to say. As I pulled into the parking place opposite the customs shed, I saw her sailor standing on the sidewalk.

"There he is," I said.

"Yes," she agreed, but she made no move to get out of the car. "Let's have a cigarette."

"Joy, what would he think if he saw you just sitting here?"

"But I don't know what to say to him, Ruth. What shall I say to him?"

"Just get out of the car, walk over there, and say anything you want. Say 'hello.' "

"But then what?"

"That'll take care of itself. Just try it . . . now, go on."

She opened the car door, but then she turned to me again. "I'm that scared. What if he doesn't recognize me?"

"You can't sit here all day," I said, exasperated.

She started across the street very slowly. Wally was busy brushing lint off his uniform but suddenly he looked up and saw her. I don't think she ever did say hello. There in the middle of the street, holding up traffic, she was lifted into his arms and whirled round and round. Then he set her down again, kissed her, stared at her, kissed her again. It took both horns and shouting drivers to make them at last aware that they were standing in the middle of the street.

I put them both in the back seat. Wally had begun to explain what had happened. His three week leave had been canceled at the last minute. He'd gone to his superior officer, to the chaplain, finally to the captain. He was given mercy leave, only ten days, and by that time he'd missed three planes. He didn't know where she was, of course. He didn't know how to reach her, but he knew she'd be here when he arrived. The story came in sentence fragments interrupted by long silences in which they did nothing but drown in each other's eyes.

It was like that all day long. Both of them, at my insistence, would try to concentrate on the practical problems that confronted them: finding Joy's hotel and her belongings, getting a license, checking with American Immigration to see how soon Joy could enter the United States. It was clear that Wally had had all these things in mind before he arrived, but, just as he was about to make a normal and intelligent decision, he would look at Joy again, and that would be that for another half hour. In the end, I gave up and simply told them what they were going to do. I found Joy's hotel, installed Wally in her room, and brought her things back to my apartment. I called a minister. I called a friend in Victoria who knew how to get them a license in three days. I called myself a romantic fool because I knew they were going to have a wedding, a church wedding, with a reception afterwards, wedding cake, champagne and all.

Derek thought I was absolutely out of my mind. No, he would not be best man. No, he certainly could not persuade people in his office to take time off to help fill the church, but on Tuesday night he arrived with a case of champagne, and on Wednesday afternoon he was at the wedding himself with his camera. I'd persuaded my landlord, who was growing a beard to support a centennial and to irritate his wife, to stand as best man. His wife helped me shame the local baker into making what he called wryly a "last minute, well seasoned fruit cake," which is the sort of wedding cake anybody in the Commonwealth expects. He never did send me a bill, and he and his wife and all their children came to the wedding. The stain had come out of Joy's wedding dress, which she had made herself of white satin with a short skirt and fitted bodice onto which she'd sewn sprays of seed pearls. The landlord, with manly embarrassment but no prompting, helped Wally choose flowers for both Joy and me, and they had white carnations in the buttonholes of their blue suits. The minister's wife had put flowers on the altar. Thirty people stood as Joy and I moved from the front pew to take our places before the altar and as Wally, the bearded landlord, and the minister came in from the vestry.

The minister began: "As we gather here today to join these two young people in holy matrimony, we are mindful of all those friends and family across seas and continents who are also with us now in spirit."

It was the happiest wedding I've ever been to, and the reception afterwards had a natural gaiety, inspired by the enthusiasm of the bride and groom. They had never seen a prettier church. The wedding cake was delicious, and the champagne, which they had never tasted before, was much better than beer or gingerale. Wally kept saying, "Gee, this is great! Man, the fellas back at the ship will never believe this!" Joy could not bear to take off her wedding dress; it was that beautiful. She decided to wear it back to the hotel. Derek and I drove them downtown.

"Now, Wally, you give this girl a good dinner," Derek said firmly. "You both need real food after all that champagne."

"Man, wasn't that a great wedding?" Wally demanded.

"It's the prettiest wedding I've ever been to," Joy agreed. "It's the only one I've ever been to."

"I went once before." Wally said. "To my brother's. But that was so serious. My mother was crying, and, you know, for a while I thought my dad was crying, too; he wasn't. It was a real hot day and it was just his Vitalis melting and running down his face. It wasn't anywhere near as good as this. Hey, I like champagne."

We let them out in front of their hotel and watched them go up the steps hand in hand.

"Man," Derek said, imitating Wally as he brushed the

rice off his own shoulders, "this isn't Vitalis."

"I don't suppose it really matters that they don't know each other," I said tentatively. "They're so young they don't even really know themselves."

"I wonder if any of us ever do," Derek said, a momentary sadness in his voice. "Shall I take you out for dinner?"

I wanted to be dewy-eyed about this marriage. I've had enough reality to know I have to live in it; but, if I can't daydream about myself, I still like to daydream about other people. If Joy had been able to go back to San Diego with Wally, they might have remained for me a harmless, romantic indulgence. Nobody I know, however, could manage American Immigration authorities as we'd been able to manage everything else. When Wally's leave ran out, Joy's papers had still not arrived. She moved back into the apartment with me to wait.

Oh, it wasn't that their brief honeymoon had been dreadful. It was real and it was funny. Wally had apparently taken Derek's advice about dinner, but he had also, in his enthusiasm, ordered yet another bottle of champagne with the result that, when they finally arrived in their room, he passed out cold and slept peacefully, in the middle of the bed, all night long. The following night he'd had a nightmare, bashed Joy in the eye with his elbow and said sharply, "Get out of my bed, Joanne!" Joy was obviously not disturbed so much as curious about everything that was happening to her.

"Ruth, do American girls shave their legs?"

"Lots of them."

"But do nice girls? Do you?"

"Yes, I do," I answered, unaccountably embarrassed as I wasn't by a good many much more intimate questions.

Why did I worry? Wally seemed to me a good sort of boy with comfortable, homely notions about love that had to do with remembering to leave his wife enough money and to write to her every day. But Joy knew so little about the world she was going into, and Wally knew so little about her, so incredibly little.

"Ruth, have you noticed anything about my teeth?"
"What do you mean?" I said, knowing perfectly well
what she meant.
"I never meant to lie to Wally. I really didn't. But the
first night I met him, how was I to know I was going to
marry him? He'd never been to Australia before, and he was
talking about all the crazy stories the other sailors had told
him just to scare him off: like all the young girls having
false teeth. I didn't lie to him. I just didn't say anything."
"Does he mind?"
"He still doesn't know."
I tried to make her understand that the United States
was very much like Canada, not all mansions with swimming
pools and Disneyland, and I tried to explain to her how
little money Wally earned. It was difficult, for, while I
wanted her to realize that her taste for two pound steaks and
half a dozen chops at a time would be a hopeless extrava-
gance, I didn't want her to think that I was complaining
about my own meat bill, which was five times as large as
usual.
"Are there any vegetables you really like?" I asked,
after watching her struggle with any that I served.
"Potatoes," she answered cheerfully.
She lived on meat, potatoes, bread, H.P. sauce and
strawberry jam. And dreams. Great dreams of the United
States where refrigerators and washing machines and automobiles were given away with breakfast cereal. She did not
know she was being unrealistic. She was perfectly willing
to learn everything. She kept THE JOY OF COOKING and
LADY CHATTERLEY'S LOVER by her bed. And she loved
my steam iron so much that I finally gave her one to take
south with her.
Against my worry, I set her capacity to make everyone
love her. The landlord took her rollerskating. His wife, a
hairdresser, gave her an American styling to go south. Even
Derek, who admits that it takes him five years to make
friends with anyone, took her to the movies a couple of

times when I had to work late.

"Are you ever going to marry Derek?"

"I don't know," I said.

"How long will it take you to know?"

"At least ten minutes longer than it takes him."

"You ought to marry him right away and have at least six kids."

"How many do you want?" I asked.

"I'm easy. I think I'm pregnant already. I'd be that pleased!"

Those three weeks probably seemed very long to Joy, but the day her papers arrived I had to hide real disappointment. I was used to having her around. I knew I'd miss her.

"I've decided," she announced, coming away from her packing into the kitchen where I was cooking vast amounts of steak.

"Decided what?"

"To shave my legs as a very special present for Wally."

Right after dinner, I went into my bedroom and got her my electric razor. She didn't want to do it alone, and so she used the outlet on the stove, setting herself up while I began the dinner dishes.

"It's grown there nineteen years," she shouted wistfully above the buzzing razor and running water. "It tickles."

I turned to look. There she sat, one long, bare leg braced against the oven door, her young face intent, her secret false teeth set.

"Look, Ruth. Look at that scar! That scar is ten years old."

Gradually, as she shaved each leg, she rediscovered her whole childhood, a long, slow exposition of her life. Finally she was finished. She looked up with real wonder.

"I feel as if I'd just got to know myself for the first time. Like drowning. Wait till I tell Wally. He'll be that amazed!"

I imagine that he was. I've imagined a lot of things about both of them in these last years. Joy was pregnant. They sent the birth announcement to both Derek and me. They had named their son "Derricke."

"Good grief! And they can't even spell it," he moaned. "If you tell this to anyone, I'm done for. They'll think I'm the father!"

Then we both laughed as we hadn't laughed since Joy was here.

That was the last of the good news. They were sent overseas. Joy wasn't very well. I remembered her cough. When Wally went back to the States to get out of the Navy, Joy and Derricke were not with him. We had a note from him, saying that Joy had taken the baby back to Australia. She was homesick. Homesick for what, I wondered: for steak, for a mother she hadn't seen in years, for her settled Australian, or for the dream she had had of America?

"It's a shame," Derek said, "but they didn't have much of a chance, did they?"

I think it troubled him as much as it troubled me. Neither of us was much encouraged when Wally's Christmas card arrived. He had a job as a mechanic. Joy thought she might, after all, like to come back. He was saving everything he could, but he also had to send money for her to live on. It was going to take a long time, which was why he was asking us if we saved Green Stamps. He did. He had discovered it was possible to buy a plane ticket with Green Stamps. Already some of his friends were helping him.

"Green Stamps!" Derek groaned. He'd been involved in the fight to keep trading stamps out of British Columbia. "The poor, young fool. She doesn't deserve him, you know. Green Stamps!"

"He'll never get enough," I said. "It'll take years."

Three days ago, there was another card which said, "Be sure to watch FACT OR FORFEIT on Channel 10 Wednesday night. Wally."

I don't own a television set, and Derek's won't get Channel 10, so I phoned the landlord, who invited us both over this evening to watch.

"Probably he's going to try to win some money," the landlord's wife said.

"Poor cluck," the landlord said, clean-shaven so long now I'd almost forgotten his beard. "He should never have let her go home."

We were all tense and sad, that "great wedding," that "prettiest wedding" a weight on all our consciences because we'd known at the time it was foolish and had gone ahead anyway to be accomplices against any probable future. But what else could we have done? Even Derek, with all his caution and reserve, had given in. One of the pictures he had taken was framed on the mantlepiece above the television set.

The program began. Three little girls were asked three silly questions and then given a set of automobile tires each. A woman came up from the audience to take part in a drawing. A little boy won a hair dryer and a vacuum cleaner. It was terribly depressing and stupid. I imagined Wally winning a free trip to Disneyland or a home permanent. We sat through the commercial. No one said a word.

Then there Wally was, stainding on the stage with the announcer. He looked older, thinner in the face, but his grin was steady. The "facts" he had to supply were more difficult than those for the other contestants, but he knew them and answered with a voice as confident and enthusiastic as it had been on the day of his wedding.

"We understand, Wally, that you're saving Green Stamps," the announcer said.

"That's right."

"How many books have you got so far?"

"Just over 100."

"How many do you need, Wally?"

"Five hundred and fourteen."

"That's a lot of Green Stamps. Would you tell the audience what you want them for?"

For a moment, Wally hesitated. The landlord's wife said afterwards she was sure there had been tears in his eyes.

There may have been. I was aware only of the rage in me. I didn't think I could bear to watch another minute of it, even if he did get the Green Stamps he needed. It wasn't as simple as that. It had never been as simple as that. How did he know, how did anybody know, whether or not Joy would make the trip a second time, Green Stamps or not? One fairy tale a lifetime is all most of us can stand.

"To bring my wife and baby back from Australia," he finally answered.

The announcer signaled, and a huge board, as big as a garage door, was lowered to the stage. Pasted on it were hundreds of books of Green Stamps.

"Gee, isn't that great?" Wally demanded. "Man, isn't that marvelous!"

"And, Wally, because we happened to know what you were saving stamps for, we decided we'd just go ahead and cash these in for the ticket."

The announcer signaled again. The board was raised. There behind it was Joy.

*"But I don't know what to say to him, Ruth. What shall I say to him?"*

She didn't say anything. Wally walked over to her, picked her up in his arms, whirled her round and round, set her down again, kissed her, stared at her, kissed her again. For a moment the camera switched to the side of the stage where a small child stood watching.

"Turn the ruddy thing off!" the landlord said. "I can't stand one more minute of it."

"All we need's champagne," his wife said, wiping her eyes.

"That program ought to be called FICTION AND FORTUNE," Derek said. "I wonder if he knows yet that she's got false teeth."

"And a bad chest," I began, obsessively co-operative, "and an appetite for steak and a firm conviction that in the United States they give away automobiles and refrigerators and airplane tickets with breakfast cereal."

"For Green Stamps," the landlord said. "What *is* the matter with Green Stamps, Derek? I always meant to ask you."

"You're paying double for what you think is free."

"That's what he's done all right," the landlord said, nodding his clean-shaven chin.

"Nothing is free," I agreed, for, after all, I came to Canada to get away from Green Stamps and all they represent, but I am still American enough in secret to be glad that Wally can't admit Joy is too expensive, even the second time round. Nothing is free.

# A MATTER OF NUMBERS

If this were a good magazine story, I would be a twenty-five-year-old widow and Frank would be a twenty-three-and-a-half-year-old graduate student. We'd struggle through twelve columns of my qualms until that eighteen month gap between our ages became a problem we were big enough and in love enough to live with. Some kind of gimmick—an ideally married Dean and his wife could confess to the same circumstance?—in column number eleven would do it. We'd carefully not walk off hand in hand into the classroom together since I'd still be on one side of the desk and he on the other, but the chalk dust would turn to stardust just the same. Probably there are such stories to be told, but mine isn't that kind.

I am a thirty-eight-year-old divorcée and Frank is a twenty-year-old undergraduate. I don't like the implications of that any more than an editor would. It's not just bad for the ads (Think how sinister that dreamy bubble becomes: "He forgets that I'm fifty" or even "Buy him a *Webster's Collegiate*"); it's immoral. And I wouldn't have read any farther either if I'd been reading at all, but I wasn't.

A mathematics lecturer, whose skill with figures has nothing to do with her own, worries about students falling asleep, not in love. Any student who lingers at the end of a lecture is either afraid of the exam or as hypnotized by

79

numbers as I am. It is even safe to go out for coffee or beer. A woman mathematician is, after all, one of the boys. Add to these general observations my specific attitude toward students: my interest in them has always been strictly academic. Theoretically, I understand that they, like other members of the human race, have colds, girls, breakdowns, and mothers: practically I am concerned with their brains in relation to mathematics. I know that makes me sound limited as a teacher, but I have found that students learn more from being taken seriously than they do from being treated with personal sympathy, except in extreme cases.

Frank was not an extreme case. I was aware of his test results long before I was aware of his face. Brilliance in mathematics is not extraordinary, but there is beauty in it about which I always feel relief. I have the same response to Bach and to some of Stella's paintings. So, marking papers, I soon learned to anticipate Frank's, to rest through it before going on to the complex and irrational mistakes of other students. He was not the sort of student to ask questions in class, nor did he stay after class to argue. The first time he spoke, polite but not quite diffident, was to point out an error I had made and was already frantically looking for. Certainly I couldn't have detected then any private motive in his concern. Nor would it have been sensible for me to suspect my own gratitude. During the next class, I doubt that I would have picked him out in the crowd. I was perhaps a little more relaxed, but I always am when there are other intelligences in a room.

The second part of the course I was teaching is a matter of alternative solutions, and, when we came to it, Frank took part in discussions dutifully. He did not need to think aloud. Perhaps I should have wondered then why he came to class so regularly, but bright students often have a sense of social responsibility. It's hard to describe him as I saw him then. Colorless, I should probably say, or military color, khaki from his hair to his wash trousers. All bone, from his thin skinned skull to his long, thin legs. Even his teeth were long so that he closed his lips purposefully, but I'm sure I didn't notice that. His eyes perhaps, that somewhere between brown and green called hazel, but I would have noticed not the color but the intelligence of them. Are they intelligent eyes? I saw his mind and was relieved by it.

More and more often he joined the coffee drinkers after class. He never set himself apart from the others or called particular attention to himself. His intelligence didn't shine so much as glow like the live light of a fire. That I did feel, and I responded to it with insensitive pleasure. There was nothing personal about it for me, at least not in the ordinary sense. I never thought how proud his mother must be of him. I never wondered at all about his private life, the friends he had or the girls he went out with, if he went out. I did begin to wonder what he planned to do, and one day I asked him. I liked what I heard, the certainty in him about an academic career. After that it seemed natural enough for him to come to the office occasionally to talk about fellowships at other universities, the men he might study under. Never in any of those discussions did we exchange personal information. I suppose I treated him more as an equal than as a student, but it would have been foolish not to. It would not be long before he was my superior.

Perhaps nearly anyone else would have begun to notice little things, the careful courtesies, the book left occasionally on my desk, the sometimes odd nervousness. I didn't, or, if I did, I dismissed them all as pleasant but unimportant idiosyncrasies of the brightest student I had ever had. What I didn't notice in him I might have noticed in myself. I began to think about Frank. I even began to talk about him, but nearly every teacher talks about good students. When did I really begin to notice that purposeful closing of mouth, the long shape of his fingernails, the habit he had of thumbing his shirt cuff? When did I begin to recognize him in the coffee shop just by the tender back of his neck? I don't know. I had had one very long and very bad bout of love from which I had recovered. I so firmly believed I was now immune that it never occurred to me to consider I would fall in love again. And certainly falling in love with a twenty-year-old student was so far from a possibility that it couldn't even seem ridiculous.

On a wet spring afternoon, Frank walked me to my car under his umbrella. I was talking more than usual, vaguely aware, I suppose, that he was unusually quiet, but I didn't worry about that. I never worried about Frank. He opened the door of the car and dropped my books behind the driver's seat. I was standing close to him under the umbrella when he straightened his boy's body to his man's height and looked down at me.

"What are we going to do?" he asked.

There was no intimate gesture. Even the expression on his face was familiar, the deliberate mouth, the concerned eyes. For me, it was as if a hand had reached to the center and torn me loose from myself. But I imagine my face changed no more for him than his had for me.

"I don't know," I said, and I got into the car and drove away.

At first I did not think at all. I moved around my apartment, fixing supper, with the same automatic defenses I might have had if I'd just been in an automobile accident or heard that my father was dead. Then, when I sat down to eat, I couldn't. I stared at the adequate meal I had made for myself and asked aloud the melodramatic and pointless question of all hideous errors, "What have I done?" The answer is always so grossly obvious. But pain of certain sorts tries to perpetuate itself. I reviewed every moment until I had collected all the innocent past into present guilt. And then I admitted, again aloud, the two important facts: "Frank is in love with me, and I am in love with him." I was appalled. I called myself names. I paced. I wept. I thought of his mouth, his eyes, his long boy's body, the thumb on his shirt cuff. And I waited for him to telephone or to arrive at the door so that I could hold him against the damage I had done to him. Caught in that absurdity, I wept again, but I was still waiting, and I went on waiting until after two in the morning.

I did not know how I would get through my lecture the next day. I dreaded seeing him again, but I hurried to class. He wasn't there. I turned my back on my students and filled three boards with figures. He couldn't have done anything foolish, not Frank. But how did I know? He might be sick. He might simply be embarrassed, regretting what he had said. He was not in the coffee shop either nor in any of the crowds of students I watched all day, realizing that at some time I must have memorized his traffic pattern.

At home that night, I wondered if I should telephone him. I did not know where he lived, whether with his parents or in a dormitory or in an apartment of his own off campus. At any other time, I would not have hesitated to call university information. Now, I was suddenly afraid of what might be said. It was ridiculous. Two days ago, I didn't count the number of times I spoke his name quite openly to other students and to colleagues. Now I worried about getting his number from a girl in information. What would I say if I did telephone him? Perhaps I would have to speak to his mother. I couldn't ask him to my apartment. Someone might see him. But I couldn't meet him in the coffee shop or any other public place. Perhaps we could go for a drive. But that was dangerous, too. And what did I intend to say or do?

I intended, until I had admitted it at least twenty times to myself, to take a boy half my age into my arms and then figure out later, too late, what I should have done instead. Why not? The French did it. It was ordinary for an older woman to have an affair with a young man—boy, I corrected myself. Marriage didn't have to have anything to do with it. He could be free later, when he was ready, to marry. I looked at myself, the extra ten pounds that testified to my long indifference, but, if I dieted, if I let my hair grow a little, I still had some time, two or three years, perhaps even five. More than I needed. Frank would go somewhere else to graduate school in eighteen months.

"This is not France. You are not Simone Signoret in a Colette movie."

No, I was a mathematician in the moral wheat belt, already divorced and old enough to be Frank's mother. It was necessary to drive fifty miles to see a foreign film. We would have to drive a hundred and fifty, still unsafe, my job and his degree at stake. And for what? That was not a good question to ask. Why didn't he telephone? Why didn't he pound down the door?

He did not attend class all week, nor did I see him anywhere else on campus. What if he'd dropped out? Frank couldn't do a thing like that, not with his mind, not with his certainty. But, if he had, where was my argument for protecting him from possible expulsion? Denying him, I might still be to blame.

At no point in that long week or the week that followed would I have used any argument at all. If Frank had appeared anywhere, I would have gone to him and stayed with him, whatever the cost. I knew that; therefore I couldn't phone him. I lost five pounds without dieting. It was not becoming. I looked a year older for each pound.

Then early in the third week I did see him, far off, going up the steps of the library, just a tall, thin, khaki colored boy; but he was golden to me. He was all right. I did not even mind his absence in class that day because I knew he was somewhere, getting on with his own work and his own life. I looked at my students again with real academic interest. There were one or two not as bright as Frank but quite bright enough, and there were all the others, needing help. Perhaps in another week, he'd be able to come back. We could have coffee together . . .

I had gradually lost hope with pounds. That night I felt shamefully and bitterly reduced, not because for three weeks I had wanted Frank out of all reason but because now I could hope we might some day have coffee together. I never wanted to see him again like that. If I couldn't love him—if I couldn't tell him I loved him, at least I would refuse to pretend not to.

I began to take different paths from the library to my office, from my office to class, for, of course, he had known my pattern as well as I knew his. I wanted to see him, not to speak to him, just to see him. And occasionally I did, always at a distance, the strong boned forehead, the boy's neck. And each time I had the same sense of relief. But in the evening I suffered from that luxury.

A thirty-eight-year-old woman in love with a twenty-year-old boy is a fool. Perhaps all women in love are fools; a thirty-eight-year-old simply knows it. Such knowledge does nothing but intensify the suffering. The rationalizing and daydreaming don't stop for all the self-mockery. How did the end of *Candida* go? "Say to yourself, 'when I am thirty, she'll be forty-eight.'" Absurd.

And, of course, I wondered what Frank was thinking and feeling. Was he angry with me? Or had he decided from the moment I said, "I don't know," that he must take responsibility? I wondered if he was protecting me or himself. Why should I want to be protected? I could lose a job. I could get another. It was a seller's market. I wondered if he knew enough to protect himself.

Then, after a month, there he sat in class. I was in the middle of a long proof, which, after half an hour, did not work out. I did not feel the usual interested panic, but I could not simply stop in front of fifty students and burst into tears or swear and walk out. I began to check back through the steps. Then Frank spoke in that familiar tone, polite and protective.

"There was an error in the first part of the problem," he explained, "the part you did on Wednesday."

The students all turned back in their notes to find the error and correct it. For a moment I looked directly at Frank, his golden eyes, his carefully shut mouth. He must have been studying the notes all along, seen what would happen today, and come knowing I would need him.

"Thank you," I said.

He looked down at his hand, the thumb carefully rubbing the cuff of his shirt.

He did not join the group for coffee, but at the end of the day, as I was gathering up books and papers to go home, he knocked on my office door.

"I'd like to apologize," he said, awkward in his height, as if he'd grown another inch in the month he'd been away.

"Apologize? Why?"

"For being such a fool," he said. "I suppose you must get a lot of that sort of thing. I mean, I suppose a lot of guys like me think that . . ."

"There aren't a lot of people like you, Frank," I said, but quietly so that it might even have been taken as a mild reproof.

"I hope not," he said. "For your sake. Would it be all right with you if I did come back to class now? If I had coffee occasionally?"

"I don't see why you shouldn't," I said.

He smiled then with an embarrassment of long teeth and held out his hands for my books. On the way to the car, he told me about new fellowships, about the average he thought he would have at the end of the year, about his schedule for next year. I didn't say much, but I doubt that he noticed. When we stood by the car, I did not ask him, "What are we going to do?" I knew.

I cooked myself a marvelous meal that night with rich sauces and I enjoyed it. For the first time in a month I did not have to imagine myself with only eighteen months to live, under the love-death sentence of my thirty-eight years. Nor did I have to imagine Frank, his young bones burdened with so grotesque a loving mistake. We were free, two bright cornbelt mathematicians, to talk together, to drink coffee together without addresses or personal histories. It was simply a matter of numbers, eighteen years or eighteen months. And Frank was already my superior, having both defined the problem and worked out the solution. Loving like that is a relief; it doesn't end.

# ONE CAN OF SOUP AT A TIME

"It's nothing personal. I just don't like being married,"
she said, lying next to him in the dark.

"Nothing personal?" She felt him sit up, dragging the
blankets away from her shoulders as well. "What do you
mean, 'nothing personal?' "

"Just that. I like you fine. I just don't like being married."

"Like?"

"That's a compliment," she said, reproof in her voice.

"Thanks."

"Oh, how can we talk about it if you start out taking it
all personally and getting your feelings hurt?"

"All right. Okay. Let's start this again." He was reaching
for a cigarette. "Shall I turn on the light? Do you want a
cup of soup?"

"I'll get it," she said.

"No, I'll get it."

"I'm tired of this particular argument."

"What argument?" he asked, the light blooming behind
his head.

"About the soup."

"You know what I'm tired of?" he asked, and his voice
was simply tired.

"I know what you ought to be tired of."

"Just that," he said. "And it's been getting worse. There is nothing I can do, no minor, automatic, mindless, little gesture . . ."

"The minor, mindless automatic little gestures are just where the trap is," she said, relaxing now that the real argument was getting underway.

"I understand you. I know what you're saying, the daily fabric of life and all that. Okay. But when a man can't even offer to get his wife a cup of soup when she's at the point of asking him for a divorce without first consulting the principles of women's liberation . . ."

"It's degrading," she said.

"What's degrading?"

"Feeling obliged to get me a cup of soup."

"I don't feel *obliged*. I would genuinely enjoy getting you a cup of soup. What in hell's the matter with that?"

"You're trying to set me an example," she said.

He groaned.

"I know you don't mean to, but you are," she said more gently.

"If I don't offer to get you a cup of soup, I'm a male chauvinist pig. If I do, I'm trying to set an example."

"That's right."

"Then how can I win?"

"You can't."

"And that's a male chauvinist's fantasy in the first place," he said, his face in his hands.

"Do you know why it's easy for you?"

"What's easy?"

"Getting me a cup of soup?"

"Weren't you the one who said you were tired of this particular argument? Fuck the cup of soup!"

"Because you only have to do it for a year or two, and just over 800 cups of soup is possible to imagine, for someone as good natured as you. But once you get your degree, once your paycheck starts coming in, how many cups of soup am I going to be obliged to make?"

"Well, let's see," he said. "I'm twenty-four now. It's going to start when I'm twenty-six. I'm not sure what the life expectancy of a man is now. Around seventy? Seventy from twenty-six is . . . ah . . ."

"Forty-four years."

"Times three hundred and sixty-five . . . What makes you think I'd suddenly stop getting the soup? By then we'll be able to afford beer, and I'll put a fridg in the bedroom. Why don't we buy a hot plate now?"

"Are you asking my permission?"

"Well, damn it, darling, it is your money," he said, a plea for understanding in his voice.

"And then it will be yours."

"You think I'll make you ask permission for every stupid little thing? Don't you know me better than that?"

"Then why do you feel you have to ask my permission?"

"I really need that cup of soup," he said.

"I'll get it."

She was just pouring the soup into the saucepan when he came into the kitchen, lighting another cigarette.

"I smoke too damned much," he said.

"Too expensive?"

"You are a relentless woman without an ounce of nagging love for my lungs."

"They're your lungs."

"I didn't know you were thinking of quitting work once I'm through," he said, a careful, crafty neutrality in his voice.

"I'm not."

"Then what's the problem about asking permission? You don't ever plan to go through what I'm going through. You don't ever intend to be humiliated by being dependent."

"Do you feel humiliated?"

"I have to work damned hard not to be sometimes. And conversations like this don't help much when you make me see myself as some sort of groveling, unliberated little house-wife. I need to be reassured that I'm really just a guy learning to live without false pride, doing enough of the housekeeping to learn permanent instead of temporary lessons."

"So that you'd never, under any circumstances, do to me what you're doing to yourself."

"Yeah. I guess."

"Even when you start making more money than I do. Even when I take a year off to have a baby."

"That's right."

She put a cup of soup down in front of him and sat down on the other side of the table. They looked at each other.

"But *I'm* not doing it to you," she said. "You're doing it to yourself. I don't have to say, 'It's my money,' for you to think it's my money. *You* won't have to do it to me. I'll do it to myself, thinking he was so good natured, so unselfish, so thoughtful; he didn't even make a martyr of himself."

"You'd have better sense."

"Why? Do you think a woman who's supposed to be dependent and like it is going to have more sense than a man who only tries it for a couple of years?"

He bent down and sipped his soup without lifting it from the table. "I want a separate bank account."

"What?"

"I want a separate bank account," he repeated. "And, since I do the shopping and pay the bills, I want all but fifty dollars deposited in it every month."

"There's no more than fifty dollars' spending money between us."

"All right," he agreed. "All but twenty-five."

"I really do like you."

"I like you, too," he said.

"Do you think it's as simple as that? Lots of husbands do that for their wives."

"Yeah, well, you're not really my husband," he said. "I'd like to handle the problem a bit more personally anyway. I'd like to take it very personally, on a day-to-day basis, one can of soup at a time."

"When I said I didn't like being married, I didn't mean I was thinking of leaving you."

"Couldn't very well while I was a helpless dependent," he agreed.

"And now that I've got only $25, I can't afford to."

"Surely a woman who's only going to be in that trap a couple of years can figure it out as well or better than a man who's supposed to be in it for life and like it."

"I don't even want to set you a good example," she said through a yawn.

"You'd better not. I couldn't stand it either."

# A CHAIR FOR GEORGE

What put the idea in Harry's head was the fight his neighbor had had with a visiting mother-in-law. Harry found her in the middle of the street with her luggage at eight o'clock in the morning; so, as much for his neighbor as for the poor woman, Harry drove her to the airport, listening all the way to her indignant descriptions of domestic practices easier to credit to transient baboons than to those seemingly normal people next door. On his way back downtown to cheer himself up, Harry imagined what a visit from his mother-in-law would have been like. She'd been dead for fourteen years, a year longer than he'd been married to Anna, and Harry had never met her. He assumed, because he loved and admired his wife, that her mother would have had the same resourcefulness and humor, but perhaps tempered by a white-haired, totally uncritical devotion to him and, of course, the children. The image of this aging, loving woman, called up to comfort and reassure Harry, made him sad instead, for he realized how much he and Anna and the children had been deprived of the reality of her care. His poor motherless wife, his poor grandmotherless children. Harry's own mother lived somewhere in South America with a third husband and sent a Christmas check once every two or three years.

Harry's sorrow was made so real to him that he spoke to Ray about it during their morning coffee break.

93

Ray, who didn't have a mother-in-law either, agreed that you certainly did read a lot about the deprivations of the nuclear family, such a narrow unit of loyalty in a hostile urban environment. It was no wonder women turned to drink and children were too much influenced by peer values. Back at work over specifications for the new hospital annex, Harry was not only sad but beginning to be anxious. Anna was making twice the blackberry wine she had last year. It was true the crop was better than it had been in two years, and she'd already made more jelly and frozen more berries than they could use. Then there was Joey's refusal to pick because "none of the other kids had to." Anna had pointed out to him that none of the other kids had a mother with an Irish temper who had inherited the secret of the Chinese water torture; so he'd picked, eighty pounds Anna said, and ruined only two shirts. Not bad for a nine-year-old. But, if Joey had had a grandmother . . . Here Harry's imagination went vague, perhaps distracted by his work, perhaps simply unable, in the circumstance of the blackberries, to see what joy she might add to an enterprise everyone else in the neighborhood already considered quaintly archaic. But still she was rocking in an as yet unpurchased rocking chair, maybe just keeping Anna from sampling too much of the wine or discouraging Sally from wearing one of Anna's discarded bras on her head. When Harry sometimes registered mild complaints about such antics in his six-year-old daughter, Anna chided him for projected vanity. Sally was a pretty child, but she looked more like Anna than like Harry. Anna's mother would have taken a natural pride in her, taught her that a little vanity is not a fault in a woman or a little girl.

The article in the paper that night was not, therefore, as Anna suggested, another of his instant pudding ideas but simply a marvelous solution to the problem that had been troubling him all day. The next Sunday, the YWCA was going to gather all the grandchildless grandparents and all the grandparentless grandchildren together for an adopt-agrandparent tea, and Harry was determined that they would all go and come home with a grandmother of all their dreams.

"I've been thinking about this for a long time," he said earnestly.

"How long?" Anna asked. "Since this morning when you drove that old harpy out to the airport? I've spent the day drinking with her poor daughter."

"Drinking?"

"Yeah, drinking."

"They were drinking coffee," Joey put in.

"That's not drinking?" his mother asked.

"It's not what Dad means, I don't think," Joey said, a bit uncertain.

"Grandmothers make people cry," Sally observed.

"Not all grandmothers, Sally," Harry corrected. "It's limited experience that leads to bigotry, Anna, don't you see? We don't want the kids to be culturally and emotionally deprived."

"Learning to read has turned Sally into a bigot. She generalizes about everything."

"Did you people ever have a grandmother?" Joey asked.

Anna and Harry stopped to consider. Harry had a faint memory of his mother's mother, crying over the word 'divorce,' but that information would simply serve to confuse Sally further.

"I had a grandmother," Anna admitted, and her face softened. "She was a handsome old lady with sharp thighbones. The most uncomfortable lap I ever sat in, but she had a wonderful hole in her neck, right here, where her skin draped, just the size of an egg. I always wanted to fit an egg into it."

"Did you ever?" Sally asked.

"No, I never did."

That bit of Anna's past didn't set exactly the tone of nostalgia Harry might have wished for, but in it he felt the first weakening of her resistance. After the children had gone to bed, he raised the subject again when he could elaborate on the dangers of a grandmotherless childhood without giving Sally nightmares or Joey ideas.

"I don't know," Anna said even then, "grandmother shopping at the Y just doesn't have much appeal for me."

"If you can get the kids' winter coats at the Sally Ann, what's the matter with getting them a grandmother at the Y?"

"I think it may be carrying recycling too far."

"She might even enjoy baby-sitting occasionally."

"*That's* exploitation," Anna said fiercely. "I've been wondering all along why this grandmother obsession. Why not a grandfather while we're at it?"

"Grandfather?" Harry repeated.

"Sure. We might find one who could fix the plumbing and do other little odd jobs around the house."

Harry was ashamed of himself, not because he had a secret plot to exploit a lonely old woman but because he had suddenly discovered a real prejudice in himself against lonely old men who were sad on public benches feeding the pigeons but who would not do at all in Harry's about-to-be purchased rocking chair. Granted not all old men would lust after Anna or Sally, but the plumbing didn't really need fixing. Anna was very good at that herself. And most children just didn't have grandfathers, did they? Grandfathers, by definition, were dead. His were anyway and always had been.

"Just to begin with," Harry said cautiously, "I think a grandmother would be easier since we're all pretty much amateurs at this sort of thing. I mean, we haven't had any practice at being relatives for years."

"We haven't had to live through a lot of other natural disasters either, floods, earthquakes, fires. Some people would think we were just plain lucky."

"Then later," Harry conceded generously, "we might think about a grandfather as well."

Harry and Ray had a really good discussion over coffee the next day about the potential human resources right out there in the urban jungle, which once tamed . . .

"Become a zoo," Anna said, taking her less enthusiastic part when Harry tried to repeat the experience with her that night. "Warning: don't feed the grandmothers."

Harry brought home the rocker on Friday night. The cane seat had broken through, but Ray had told him the blind repaired caning very reasonably and very well.

"*I* can repair caning," Anna said, the lines of the chair too handsome for her to be distracted right away by its implications.

It occurred to Harry that one of the reasons they didn't take more advantage of urban resources was that Anna was a city of resources in herself. Though Harry sometimes regretted that most of his solutions were for problems they didn't have, he couldn't regret his wife who saved them money for the fun of it and therefore never objected to his spending for the fun of it.

"Are we going to get a grandmother this Sunday?" Sally asked.

"It's beginning to look that way," Anna said.

"Do we have to wear shoes?" Joey asked.

"The way we did when we bought the house?" Sally added.

"Real shoes," Harry said, "not sneakers."

Joey even put on a bow tie, the sort that snapped on with an elastic band so that he could pull it out and shoot himself with it and practice dying on the back seat all the way down to the YWCA. Anna threatened his real life if he did it once they got there, a mortal vocabulary he cheerfully understood. Sally had a real ribbon in her hair and was trying to remember not to stand with one foot on top of the other in her patent leather shoes, but one of Joey's more energetic expirings had already outlined in brown the sole of his shoe on her white knee socks.

"Do grandmothers speak English?" Sally wanted to know.

"Of course," Harry said, his nervousness making him impatient with her.

"Well, not all of them," Anna reasoned, "but a lot of them do."

"Joey said grandmothers . . ." Sally began and stopped abruptly.

"Grandmothers what?" Anna asked, turning to look at the children.

"Nothing," Sally said, responding to some secretly delivered threat from Joey, and then both children began to giggle.

Grandmothers what? Harry wondered and then began to catalogue in his mind the frailties of age which might inspire his children's primitive humor. Should he have talked more realistically about old people, about failing memory and eyesight and hearing and digestive systems? He hadn't wanted to put them off an enterprise so much his responsibility, and anyway surely at the YWCA there wouldn't be anyone who was . . . old. The sweat began to trickle down Harry's back.

"Now we don't have to make any big decisions today," Harry instructed his family as they bunched along the sidewalk from the parking lot.

"Like when you bought a car and were sorry?" Sally asked.

Harry did not know why the whole project was beginning to seem to him too much like a commercial enterprise, too, and he resented Sally's sharing his sentiments, but he couldn't muster the haughtiness to say, "We are not *buying* a grandmother," perhaps for fear that Anna would simply point out that instead they were trying to get one for free. She was, for the moment quiet, broodingly quiet, but quiet.

There were far more grandparents than there were grandchildren in the large reception room, and they behaved like people waiting for a chartered flight or tour bus, chatting cheerfully among themselves to display their talents as genial companions. Several of them even had cameras. What surprised Harry was the average age, particularly of the women. Either grandparents were getting younger or he was getting older. The women who approached him behaved just as his own mother did, flirting with him as if no one, least of all Harry, should assume they were old enough to be his mother. Few of them seemed to be. Harry, long ago resigned to his mother as an exception, one of those rare women who simply shouldn't have had children, had the uncomfortable impression that she might not be as odd as he had thought. Then across the room he saw Anna talking to a woman with genuinely grey hair whose intent expression suggested that she might be slightly hard of hearing. Relieved and hopeful, he excused himself from his several admirers and went to join his wife, who was listing the ingredients for her blackberry wine.

"I'm teetotal myself, and I don't believe in having drink in a house with children," the woman said loudly, and with a glare at Harry she turned on her tennis shoes and walked off.

"The shoes misled me," Anna said with a shrug. "I usually get along with little old ladies in tennis shoes. How are you making out?"

"The ones I've been talking to are more indifferent to children than to drink," Harry admitted. "Maybe this wasn't such a good idea after all. Why don't we get the kids and go to the zoo?"

At that moment it seemed to Harry it would be easier to teach the children kinship with all of nature than with their own species, a cynicism he would turn into a sentimental revelation once they were out of this terrible place and actually with grandmother seal and grandfather bear.

Sally and Joey were, however, absolutely absorbed, along with several other children, with a dozen small sets of magnets made to look like lady bugs and spiders and bees. They were rather absent-mindedly attended by a woman who was reading Loren Eiseley's *Immense Journey*. She looked up and smiled a greeting to Harry and Anna.

"Children don't want too much attention paid to them. It just makes them silly," she said.

Harry would have observed that it was, nevertheless, sad that none of the potential grandparents seemed to have any interest in the children and left them to the professionals, but he didn't want to be rude, and the book she was reading had fascinated him.

"That man's marvelous," he said.

"Yes. It takes a lonely man to have that kind of kinship with life, but it's a big compensation."

Anna had squatted down to take a closer look at the magnets.

"They're funny stones," Sally said. "They can walk. They're maggots."

"Magnets," Joey corrected. Then he turned to his mother and jerked his head back toward the woman. "Could we have her?"

Harry laughed, embarrassed. "I guess all the children would like to take you home."

"Could we?" Sally asked. "She has all kinds more maggots in her purse. Her name's Mary."

"You'd better give them back to her now so that some other children can have a turn," Anna said.

"She *gave* them to us," Joey said.

"That's right," Mary agreed. "I didn't think it would do any harm, just to bring along a few little gifts."

"Don't you work here then?" Harry asked.

"Heavens no. I just came to meet some children."

"Would you like to go to the zoo?" Anna asked. "We thought we'd all go to the zoo."

Mary smiled and shook her head. "I don't really like to see all those animals behind bars."

"We could go to the beach instead," Joey said. "Couldn't we?"

"Sure," Harry said. "Of course we could."

Standing on the shore, tearing up bread for the seagulls, Harry said conversationally, "I see your point about the zoo, but it can be educational."

"Not for the animals," Mary said.

Anna laughed and took Mary's arm.

"Is she going to come home for dinner?" Sally asked. "Do grandmothers come home for dinner?"

"Not when they have a grandfather at home waiting for his dinner," Mary said.

"He could come, too," Joey said. "Couldn't he?"

"Sometime, certainly," Harry said in his hardiest tone.

"Like tonight," Anna said.

If Harry had any objection to his wife, it might have been that she sometimes took him more seriously than he took himself. She sometimes didn't know the difference between giving in and taking over.

"He wouldn't come," Mary said. "He said since God didn't see fit to make him a grandfather, he didn't see what business it was of the YWCA."

"It's a Christian organization," Harry said, suddenly indignant.

Anna burst out laughing.

"Why is Daddy mad?" Sally asked.

"Because he's having an argument with somebody who isn't here, and that's frustrating," Mary explained. "I didn't mean to hurt your feelings, Harry, but there'd be no way to lie about how George feels. I told him nobody owns children in the first place, but he went on about what sort of a rummage sale it would turn out to be."

"How can he talk about children like that?" Harry demanded.

"Oh, he likes children well enough."

"I understand exactly how he feels," Anna said. "I thought Harry was crazy. A ready made grandmother appealed to me about as much as a tv dinner."

"I like tv dinners," Sally said. "I have them at Linda's."

The following Sunday, George and Mary came to dinner. Mary sat in the rocker and looked right in place there. George sat stiffly in Harry's chair while Harry prowled in and out of the room on errands, unable to think what else to do with his displaced body.

"You'll have to buy a chair for George," Joey confided as he dragged his box of sea shells along the hall on his way to show them off to his new grandparents.

"No doubt," Harry said.

After several glasses of Anna's wine, George had Sally on his lap and was teaching both children a variety of hand tricks which Harry himself had known years ago and could have taught the children himself if he'd thought of it.

"Come over here and talk to me, Harry," Mary said. "You and I were right, and I think we should be able to gloat about it a little. Anna won't let me help in the kitchen."

"There's a grandmother labor law," Anna said on her way out of the room, "No exploitation."

"The children get their humor from Anna, and they get their trust from you. It's a happy combination in them."

With that compliment, Harry had to take his suspicious eyes off George and concentrate on Mary, who thought so many of the same things he did about human resources and the urban question that she kept him entertained until it was time for dinner.

"Leg of lamb?" Harry asked, looking down at the platter as if his sight betrayed him.

"Oh, Harry, you carve it perfectly well," Anna said. "He always threatens to take a leg of lamb down and have it x-rayed."

"Would you like me to have a go at it, Son?" George asked. "I used to be a butcher."

Harry felt the protest at being again displaced rise and stop at the word "Son." "Why . . . thanks. That would be great."

Sitting down next to Anna, Harry had the odd sensation of being like a child at his own table. He did not feel reduced so much as relieved, as if the whole weight of the evening no longer rested on his reluctant shoulders, and maybe, if he watched carefully enough George's aging, deft hands, he might learn to carve a leg of lamb himself. To be

called "son," which he never had been before in his life, was
to be given time between himself and all he still had to learn.

"Grandfathers are daddies, too," Sally announced. "Are
grandmothers mommies?"

"Don't generalize," Anna said.

"That takes a little more time," Mary said to Sally.
"We'll see if your mother will let me help with the dishes."

"I don't have to dry! I don't have to dry!" Joey shouted
and pulled out his tie in preparation for a fine fall off his
chair.

"Son!" Harry said, as Mary laid a quieting hand on Joey's
head so that for once Anna didn't have to threaten to kill
him, too.

"Woman came into my shop once," George said, not
looking up from his task, "and asked for the left leg of
lamb. 'Left?' I said, and she said, 'that's the one that always
has the tail on it.' "

"Is that true?" Anna asked amused.

"Nope," George said, "but the one she got did. So does
this."

"Is it a left leg?" Joey asked.

"Yep."

"You're going to confuse the children, George," Mary
said.

"Well, you can't trust a good idea, but you can still enjoy
it when it works out," George said. "Don't you think that's
so, Harry?"

# SEAWEED AND SONG

"I don't care how many strays you bring home as long as they're human," Anna said, not once but any time either of the children or Harry was tempted by a cat in the back alley or a puppy in a pet shop window.

"Maybe it will die out there in the rain," Sally tried.

"Nonsense. That's why cats have fur coats."

"I could buy that dog with my own money," Joey said, "and pay for the food."

"I don't get up at five in the morning to deliver papers for a dog!" Anna replied energetically. "If you want to give your money away, send it to Oxfam."

"Pets can teach kids responsibility," Harry suggested tentatively when the children were out of earshot.

"What does it teach the animals?"

"That's not as important, is it?"

"My point exactly," Anna said firmly. "People are more important. Do you know how much North Americans spend on pets every year?"

"Second only to atomic weapons, I suppose," Harry answered glumly.

Anna didn't have many moral passions, was rather of a temperament to indulge convictions and whims in other people.

Right after they moved from an apartment into their

own house, she let Sally tie string from her bed to her dresser to her door and down the stairs and back again. To Harry's and Joey's complaint that someone was going to break a leg, Anna replied, "So watch your step." Day after day Sally slowly tied her way through the house and even out into the yard, the house and grounds an elaborate web until she slowly unmade it all on her way to bed.

"Are you sure she's all right?" Harry asked, never having heard of a five-year-old having a nervous breakdown.

"Sure," Anna said. "You and I can knock down walls and dig up flower beds to lay hands on the place. It's just her way of claiming it."

Only days after Sally suddenly gave up her spidery ways, Joey decided on his paper route which got Anna up at five a.m. to be sure he had his breakfast. She encouraged his obsessions, saving money and *National Geographics.*

Even, Harry had to admit, his own weakness for fad diets didn't prompt nutritional sermons, perhaps because his interest in them never lasted more than a week.

Anna was a reasonable woman, except when it came to pets.

"I don't care how many strays you bring home . . ."

"As long as they're human," her husband and children chorused.

Occasionally walking down the Granville Mall, Harry had fantasies about a positive testing of his wife's dictum. But whether he chose a forlorn drunk or aggressive young prostitute, he suspected he'd have a harder time passing the test than Anna would. It did not occur to him that Anna had stirred up the same fantasies in their children who were not yet old enough to have developed critical foresight.

Those kids must have been combing the beach below their house not for shells or bits of tackle, not for an aimless dog or crippled seagull but for a stray to suit their mother's definition.

"That's human?" Harry whispered to Anna in the kitchen

right after he'd got home from work to be confronted in his own living room with the children's "stray."

"He's perfectly all right, only a bit damp," Anna said, softly but cheerfully.

"How long is he going to stay?"

Anna shrugged. "Until it stops raining, I guess. Sally says his newspaper house on the beach leaks."

"But in Vancouver it can rain for weeks!" Harry protested. "Anyway, it's illegal to camp on the beach."

"All the more reason for him to stay here," Anna said.

"He's a grown man," Harry said. "What kind of a man would follow a couple of young kids home?"

"Shh . . ." Anna warned him. "He's no more than a boy."

"Is he old enough for me to have to offer him a glass of wine?" Harry asked, as he poured himself and Anna one.

"I think so."

Harry sauntered back into the living room, fighting the instinctive mistrust he felt for this scarecrow with an ample head of seaweed who sat in Harry's chair, the children at his feet, as intent upon him as if he'd been an alligator or monkey or other exotic nonhuman Harry had been tempted by all through his own pet-deprived childhood. It was the only time in his life Harry saw a sudden, profoundly distasteful parallel between his wife and his mother, who had also collected strays, several of whom she'd married.

"A glass of wine?" Harry said slowly, as if the creature were deaf or didn't speak English.

"Poison."

"I beg your pardon?"

"Poison," it said again, still in a faint, sinister whisper.

"No it's not," Sally said. "Mom makes it herself."

"It's all right, Sally," Harry said, reassured at this indication that she was not in thrall. "Lots of cats don't like milk."

"Xgo's on a vision quest," Joey said. "Sometimes he doesn't eat anything for days."

"Xgo . . . What kind of a name is that?" Harry asked.

"From numbers," Joey said. "He made it up from numbers."

"Xgo, you'd better get off Dad's chair now," Sally said, a friendly authority in her voice. "That's where he sits."

Xgo, like a sullen, untrained dog, didn't move.

"Come on," Sally said.

She and Joey together half hoisted Xgo out of the chair and steered him to the couch.

Harry sat down with the glass of wine he might have given to Xgo and picked up his evening paper.

"Male chauvinist," he thought he heard, but it was faint enough for him to ignore it, the paper hiding his increasing agitation.

"You're going to sleep in the guest room," Sally was explaining. "That's really my room, but I don't sleep there. I sleep with Joey."

"Incest."

Harry knew he couldn't actually be hearing what this sea oracle was saying. It must be Harry's own paranoia inventing these responses.

"She's afraid of the dark," Joey said, a kindly contempt in his voice.

Harry skipped an article about a bear mauling a child near a garbage dump in North Vancouver and went on to read about the failure of institutions of higher learning to teach people to read and write.

Called to dinner, Harry momentarily regretted that they had broken down the wall between the dining room and the kitchen for a sense of space and friendliness. He would have liked to impose as much intimidating formality as possible to make it as clear to the rest of the family as it already was to Harry that Xgo was a creature meant to live out of doors. On this week night there wasn't even anything to carve. Anna was serving meat loaf from the stove.

When everyone had a plate, Xgo bowed his head and said something that sounded to Harry like, "Cannibals," then picked up a small portion of mashed potatoes in his fingers.

"Oh, no!" Sally said, scandalized. "Watch me."

Sally still held her fork like a shovel, and her elbow did a lot of high work. Xgo imitated her exactly. She looked doubtful.

"Maybe you'd better watch Dad," she suggested.

Xgo dutifully stared at Harry through the rest of the meal.

"I think he's a vegetarian," Joey murmured to his mother.

"Speak up, son," Harry commanded. "Or am I going deaf?"

"I don't think he eats meat."

"Surely Xgo can speak for himself?" Harry suggested.

"Woof," Xgo said.

Joey laughed.

"You have to eat a little of everything," Sally explained to their guest, "even if you don't like it. Meat's good for you. Even dogs like meat. And this isn't hard to cut or chew or anything."

She was busy demonstrating by wiggling her fork in her own meatloaf and chewing with exaggerated ease. Xgo took a bite and made a noise that could have been a suppressed word or a sob. He reached for his glass of milk.

"No," Joey checked him. "You have to swallow first. Then you can have a drink."

Harry was fascinated at Xgo's obedience to the children. He was sure that, if either he or Anna had corrected him, Xgo would have defied or ignored them. Anna sat serenely as if what happened at the table was not a bizarre inverted Rousseauian experiment, civilized innocence ascendant over natural man.

Did Harry hear the words, "Junk food," as Anna put dessert in front of Xgo?

"Now, watch Dad. He's the champion ice cream eater round here," Joey said proudly.

Harry stifled a noise in his own throat as he demonstrated

his prowess under that bright, malignant stare.

"Dad and I are going to have coffee in the living room tonight," Anna explained. "You kids can show Xgo how to help with the dishes."

"I stand on a chair," Sally said, getting up to demonstrate.

Harry made his escape before he could observe more.

"You can't be serious about letting him stay," he whispered urgently as soon as he and Anna were in the living room.

"He's perfectly harmless," Anna whispered back. "And aren't the kids good with him!"

"They're treating him like a moron or a tame bear!"

"They seem to be treating him very much the way we treat them," Anna said, amused.

"But he's not a child. And he's anything but harmless. He's downright hostile."

"Oh, Harry, he's only shy." Anna said. "And adolescent. Think how worried his parents must be. If when Joey's sixteen, he decides to do something crazy, I hope there are people around to take him out of the rain."

"Joey has more sense!"

"Now," Anna said as if she looked forward to an inevitable and dreadful metamorphosis of her beloved son.

"Well, if he's going to take up with every beach bum who comes along . . ."

"The kids are being kind," Anna said.

And Harry wasn't There was no point in arguing that he was only fulfilling a duty to protect his family from outside threats. This creature was *inside* where the duty of nurturing took precedence. All right, Harry would be kind.

"We'd better get Xgo's room ready," he suggested when the dishes had been done.

It was a rule in the house that Anna did no more chores when dinner was over; so Harry and the children found clean sheets for the bed and made it up while Xgo sat on the hope chest like a patient in a hospital.

"Maybe you'd like a book or two," Harry suggested.

He didn't wait for the encouragement he knew would not be forthcoming but went off at once to locate Xgo something to read. The adult library was in Harry and Anna's bedroom. Anna had just finished reading Atwood's *Life Before Man,* a title so appropriate it might seem offensive. Harry was rereading Dickens, whose social conscience should be having a more profound effect on Harry's than it was. What would that piece of human driftwwod read? Harry picked books at random, knowing whatever he chose would fail Xgo's test of taste. Simple kindness must go undaunted by scorn.

"Xgo's into meditation more than books," Joey explained at Xgo's refusal even to put out a hand to accept the books.

"We're a bit short on prayer mats around here," Harry said cheerfully and went off to join Anna before his high spirits got the better of him.

"How's everything?" she asked, looking up from the paper.

"Why just fine," Harry said. "Water him regularly and he may soon cover all the walls."

All day the next day, Harry kept looking out the window, and he irritated other people in the office by turning on the radio for every weather report.

"You'd think you still had your boat and it was Friday," someone complained.

"It's going to rain for weeks," Harry said glumly.

"Well, it's March. What do you expect?"

"A break. A minor miracle. Just one day of sun."

Harry knew, no matter what Xgo did, Anna wouldn't put him out in the rain. Though Harry didn't think of himself as particularly possessive about his things, he wished he'd checked his camera, his binoculars, his fishing tackle. Less selfishly, he began to list each thing in the house Xgo might steal and sell, from Anna's mother's silver to the television set. "We hardly ever use either of them," he could hear Anna saying. Harry answered aloud, "That's not the point!"

"What's not the point?" his secretary asked.

By the time Harry got home that night, he was surprised and relieved to see the house still standing, though it couldn't have burned in this downpour. Still, he expected to discover it gutted of all valuables.

There was no one in the living room, but the furniture was still there. He could hear Anna in the kitchen.

"Hi! Everything all right?" Harry asked with false cheerfulness.

"Oh, Harry, I'm afraid not."

"What's happened?"

"Xgo's gone," Anna said.

"What did he take with him?" Harry demanded.

"Nothing but maybe my hairbrush. I haven't been able to find it all day."

"Are you sure? Did you check my camera?"

"Xgo's not a criminal. He's just an unhappy, confused kid. And he's so dumb. He broke the bedroom window to get out. I guess he couldn't open it. It was painted shut. But he could have walked out the door. We weren't exactly holding him prisoner."

"Where are the kids?"

"They've gone out to look for him. I told them there wasn't any point. He obviously didn't want to stay."

"They'll be drenched," Harry protested.

"They've got their rain gear on."

"If they bring him back, I'm not letting him into this house!" Harry said with finality.

"The kids' feelings are really hurt," Anna said. "They really were trying to help him."

There were the sounds of boots on the front porch. Harry rushed to the door to find no one but his two very wet, dejected children.

"He didn't go back to his house," Sally said.

"It isn't even there," Joey said with disgust. "Somebody took it down or it dissolved."

Dinner was a glum affair.

"It's bad enough when a dog runs away," Sally said. "When Cricket's dog ran away, she said it was because her mother made it eat cheese soufflé. We didn't make Xgo eat anything awful."

"Maybe he thought we were going to make him take a bath," Joey said sadly.

Though Harry was tempted to preach a joyful sermon about their failure, which had to do with not treating people like dogs or bums like guests, he was too touched by their grief to take advantage of it.

"Why don't I take us all to the movies tonight to get our minds off Xgo," he suggested.

"Nothing but X-rated in a ten mile radius," Joey said. "Anyway, it's a school night."

The next night the children were no more cheerful, and Anna seemed infected by depression. Every time Harry tried to lift their mood, he was treated like someone having an uncontrollable fit. No one was unkind. Even when he suggested going out for fudgesicles, Sally said in a resigned tone, "That's okay, Dad."

What his poor kids needed and had needed all along, was a pet, something small and dependent enough to be within their ability to take care of. Harry was through arguing with Anna about it. It was time to take things into his own hands.

In the pet shop, Harry studied the puppies and kittens. They seemed far too fragile to him for the circumstances. He might run over one and finally break Sally's heart. Or it might run away like Cricket's dog or Xgo. He looked at the tropical fish. Though they were beautiful, he couldn't warm to them. Then a small yellow canary began to sing, a sound as bright as sunlight in the room.

"There!" Harry said, and he bought it along with the largest cage in the store.

Harry knew what Anna would say, and he had plenty of time to rehearse his argument on his drive home. While she was absolutely right that human beings were the most important, kids couldn't start at the top like that and suffer those kinds of failures. They had to begin with something small, like this bird. Even when God was making the world, He started small . . . well, that might sound a bit pompous, particularly from an agnostic like Harry. But he'd use it if he had to.

"A *bird* in a *cage?*" Anna said, in absolute disbelief.

" 'In the prison of his days/teach a free man how to praise,' " Harry said and then added, "Auden, Freshman English."

"Is he happy in there?" Sally asked.

"Listen to him," Harry said, for the obliging bird had already begun to sing a sharp, trilling melody that went on and on.

"How do you turn it off?" Joey asked.

"You cover the cage," Harry said, very slowly.

"Well, I mean, it's okay and all," Joey said.

"I think he's beautiful," Sally said.

"And here's his seed and some cuttle fish," Harry said, "to keep him happy."

"Can we keep him, Mom?" Sally asked seriously; she knew what a concession it would be.

"Oh, well . . ." Anna said.

"Just a bit of bird seed, and it's perfectly safe in there," Harry said.

"You kids will have to take care of it," Anna said. "I'm not cleaning a bird cage."

"I will," Sally said.

"Okay, I'll take my turn," Joey said.

"But this is not the thin edge of the wedge," Anna said firmly. "There's to be nothing more. This is it."

"Then you should have got a dog, Dad," Joey said.

The bird stopped singing abruptly.

"Now look what you've done!" Sally shouted. "You've hurt his feelings."

"It's just a bird," Joey said, defending himself, but he turned to the cage and gave a long, hopeful, imitating whistle.

The bird replied.

"See?" Joey said. "That's how you turn him back on."

Harry watched Anna. He wouldn't have to start back at the beginning of creation, but he would have to say more about the nature of cages, the creatures who were at home in them, the creatures who had to break out.

# MUSICAL BEDS

Harry had a bad habit of opening his mail at the dinner table, in principle because he was an open man, in fact because he couldn't stand news—good or bad—unleavened by his wife's and children's response. Whether it was the Memorial Society announcing that they could have not only cheap funerals but also cheap charter flights or an appeal for crippled children or a cheque from the lottery, he wanted his plans for burial, holiday, charity, or riches shared. Harry got no more than half a dozen personal letters in a year, and with those particularly he did not want to find himself alone.

"It's from your mother," Anna said, setting the dinner plates under the pale blue envelope Harry dangled like a dead rodent from his reluctant index finger and thumb.

"Our grandmother," Sally said, more speculative than assertive.

"Our real grandmother," Joey added in a tone that made her sound less rather than more important. Some months ago they, as a family, had adopted a pair of grandparents at the YWCA, who suited them all very well.

"There's nothing *wrong* with real ones," Harry said, a sharpness in his tone clearly distinguishable to everyone at the table as guilt.

"Well, no," Joey conceded, "I guess not if you know them."

"I know my mother," Harry said, haughtiness turning to glum confession in the space of that short sentence.

"We don't," Sally reminded him.

"Well, are you going to open it or drop it into the stew?" Anna asked.

Harry contemplated the alternatives, sighed, and reached for his fork. Anna's stew was so tender there were no knives on the table.

"He's opening it with his fork!" Sally announced.

"He's going to eat it," Joey concluded with delight.

"I am going to read it," Harry said, and he did ... in silence.

When he had finished, he put the letter in his lap with his napkin and began to serve dinner.

"No carrots, please," Sally said.

"One carrot," Anna corrected.

"How *is* your mother?" Joey asked.

It saddened Harry that he could already guess about a nine-year-old child that he would grow up to be a used-car salesman or worse. "She's fine."

"*Where* is she?" Anna asked.

"On a cruise," Harry said, "with a friend. It ends here."

"Is she coming to stay with us?" Sally asked.

"She'd like to," Harry admitted.

"What about George and Mary?" Joey asked. "Won't they be mad?"

"Why would they be mad?" Harry demanded. "It hasn't anything to do with them."

"I thought real grandparents were like Santa Claus and the Easter Bunny," Sally said, "only they turned out to be George and Mary instead of you and Mommy."

"Look," Harry said, "Real means *real*. We went to find George and Mary because most of your real grandparents are dead, but you have one real grandmother who is very much alive. Only she happens to live in South America, which is very far away."

"Who's her friend?" Joey asked.

Maybe Joey would be a lawyer . . . for the prosecution.

"His name's José," Harry confessed quietly.

"Hose Hey?" Sally repeated.

"It's Spanish," Anna explained.

"Do real grandmothers speak English?" Sally asked. She'd wanted to know the same thing about adopted grandmothers before they met George and Mary.

"Of course, my mother speaks English," Harry said.

"What about him?" Joey asked.

"Well, I don't know."

"Where are she . . . and him going to sleep?" Sally wanted to know.

" 'He,' " Anna corrected, "as long as granddaughters are supposed to speak English."

"I speak English," Sally answered angrily. "Where are they going to sleep?"

"We haven't even decided to invite them yet," Harry said.

"Your own mother?" Anna asked in surprise.

"It's Hose Hey," Joey decided. "He's the problem."

"One of them," Harry agreed.

"Do they sleep together?" Sally asked.

"How should I know?" Harry shouted.

"It's time we talked about something else," Anna said.

"What a thing for a six-year-old kid to ask!" Harry said, as he and Anna were getting ready for bed that night. "What a thing for her to *have* to ask about her grandmother."

"She didn't mean anything by it," Anna said. "She probably just wanted to know if she and Joey were going to have to give up their room."

"It's time they stopped sharing a room. It's time she got over being frightened of the dark."

"Harry, most of the kids in this world not only sleep in

the same room but in the same bed with their parents and all the animals."

"We're not peasants."

"Are you going to show me the letter?"

He dug it out of the pocket of the trousers he'd just slung over the chair, handed it to her and watched her read it, sitting on the bed, her long, dark hair falling forward over her breasts. She still had on her trousers and one shoe. She was as proud and careless about her body as a child, and it was that Harry wanted for Sally instead of the glamourous artificiality of his own mother, who had been collecting husbands and 'friends' as long as Harry could remember.

"Rid of husband number four," Anna mused as she read. "So nice to be traveling again with someone *completely* congenial."

"Read either 'rich' or 'docile,' probably both."

"She has plenty of money of her own," Anna said.

"From our point of view."

"Well, where *are* they going to sleep?"

"How about the Bayshore Inn?" Harry suggested.

"Harry . . ."

"I'll pay for it," he hurriedly added. "Anna, you've never met my mother. She wouldn't be comfortable here. She's used to being waited on . . ."

"We could give them this room; it's just as comfortable as the Bayshore."

Harry looked around at the room, which they'd made by bashing down the wall between two small rooms so that their queen-sized bed did not crowd either Anna's sewing table or Harry's desk. It was a sanctuary not only for sexual privacy but for projects, for plans, for hilarious late night arguments.

"It would take a month to clear it out," he objected.

"It's as good a time to spring clean it as any."

"But where would we sleep?"

"You could have the single bed in the guest room, and I could put up the camp cot in Sally's room." Sally's room had no furniture in it, waiting for a time when she consented to occupy it.

"We have to sleep in separate rooms so that my mother can consort with this gigolo, this . . . Hose Hey?"

"It's only for a couple of nights," Anna said reasonably.

"It's immoral!"

"Don't be a prude. As far as the kids are concerned, you couldn't persuade them anything of interest goes on in our bed, never mind your mother's."

"You haven't met my mother."

"I'm looking forward to it."

"Why the devil, after all these years, is she coming?"

"Mortal curiosity," Anna suggested, "or maybe just because the cruise ends here."

Harry, having resigned himself to Anna's decision, helped her reorganize their room for his mother's comfort, and, while he was at it, he also tried to make the guest room as comfortable for himself as he could. He arranged a new book on Frank Lloyd Wright, some political interviews, a book on organic gardening on the shelf by the bed, and then he tucked in *Fanny Hill*. He fixed the reading lamp, which hadn't before ever stayed on for more than five minutes without turning itself off like an institutional chaperone. Anna brought in a tin of cookies and a glass jar of dried fruit. He added a bottle of brandy and two glasses. They might get a late night drink together, and, after all, they'd managed to sleep in a single bed more than once before. He wouldn't suggest it beforehand . . .

"They're sleeping in your room then," Joey said, interrupting Harry's comforting reverie.

"That's right."

"You better tell Sally not to mention that when we have dinner with George and Mary tomorrow night."

"Joey," Harry said, sitting down on the bed and folding his hands low between his knees, "Your grandmother, your *real* grandmother, is not your ordinary YWCA grandmother, I'll grant you that. She's always been a very independent sort of person, and she's a very attractive woman; so it's not surprising that she's had a number of men . . . friends. But it's not George and Mary's job or my job or *your* job to criticize the way she lives. She's your grandmother, and you're to respect her."

"Gotcha. So tell Sally," Joey said and wandered off down the hall, leaving Harry with his folded hands nearly touching the floor.

Perhaps because he simply couldn't think of the right way of putting it, Harry said nothing to Sally. He, therefore, had to suffer the I-told-you-so despair in his son's eyes on the following evening as Sally graphically rendered the preparations being made for her grandmother and José. Mary and George were a model audience, neither shockable nor encouraging, so that Sally finally dropped the subject for schoolyard scandals less close to home.

After dinner, however, George said, "That's a peculiar first name. How does Mr. Hey spell 'Hose?' " Only Anna thought it was simply funny.

"Harry," Mary said, as she and he were doing the dishes, George, Anna and the children happily settled in the living room for a game of monopoly, "I don't want to sound like a mother to you, particularly since you've got a mother of your own, but I don't think it's right for a married couple to give up their bed to anybody, and I'm sure your mother would agree with me."

Harry wanted to say, petulantly, that it was all Anna's idea, that he'd wanted to put them up at the Bayshore, but there was no point, particularly with Mary, in pretending the problem was a disagreement between himself and Anna, who was being, under the circumstances, a better and kinder wife than he had any right to expect.

"The truth is," Harry said instead, "I don't think she'll even notice she has our room. She's not a . . . domestic sort, or she wasn't when I last saw her about fifteen years ago."

"It's a lot to ask of Anna."

"She asked it of me," Harry could finally say.

"That Anna," Mary said, shaking her head.

They went back into the living room together, and for a moment Harry could enjoy the scene before him, his wife and children in the warm protection of grandparental welcome, but it was shaded with nostalgia as if it had taken place years ago against the imminent arrival of his mother and José.

Usually the one to complain about the casual attitude Anna and the children had about clothes, Harry was the most reluctant to dress for the occasion, reminded of his governess and boarding school dominated childhood when dressing up for his mother was a rare and extremely embarrassing occurrence, that glamorous stranger always greeting him with surprise and disappointment, a plain little boy whose ears stuck out, whose eyes watered, bunched into his clothes like a bag of dirty laundry on legs. What was the opposite of an Oedipus complex, he wondered, as he adjusted his most conservative tie. He had never wanted to be his mother's suitor, the only role she could assign to a male.

His own children looked beautiful to him as they stared up at the big cruise ship, docile with wonder, Joey's bow tie neat under his chin, both Sally's socks riding high and trim. He realized he didn't care at all what his mother thought of them. Anna took his arm and with her other hand hooked Joey gently by the collar. Harry reached for Sally, who took his free hand and swung and skipped along beside him.

"Harry, dear Harry." There she was at the top of the gangplank, surprisingly unchanged, the same trim and expensive figure he had always looked up to, but, when he reached her, he was looking down, and in that close second her face suddenly blurred like an old photograph. When he stepped back to introduce her to his wife and children, Harry saw that his mother was, in fact, fifteen years older.

"Do call me Rose," she was saying to Anna. "Everyone calls me Rose. I never let Harry call me Mother."

José, a tall, rather frail man in his sixties, stepped forward to be presented.

"You speak English," Sally said with approval, and Joey bumped into her, as if by accident.

"What an adorable little car!" Rose said as they arrived with a worrisome amount of luggage at the Austin. "Will we all fit?"

"I can sit on Hose Hey's lap," Sally said, and, once she'd settled herself comfortably on his surprised knees, she asked sociably, "Do people on a big boat like that ever throw up?"

"Adorable," Rose said again.

Joey's ears were so red they had begun to pulse.

The house was adorable, too, and so, when they finally got there, was the master bedroom. Was it the way José hesitated in the hall? Was it the way Rose flung her coat across the whole bed? Nothing was said, but it was perfectly clear to both Harry and Anna that Rose had no intention of sharing the room with anyone.

"And José," Anna said, "let's show you to your room."

This time Joey tripped Sally before she could say anything, and she followed him down the hall, punching at his back, as Anna offered José the room Harry had so comfortably prepared for himself. He remembered *Fanny Hill* and thought of it resignedly as some compensation for the old fellow. It wasn't as easy to feel generous about the brandy. It didn't occur to Harry until some time later that he, himself, had nowhere to sleep.

Rose held court in her room for what was left of the afternoon. Out of her suitcase came exotic weapons for Joey, ethnic dolls for Sally, jewels for Anna, and so many alligator wallets, belts, bookends, and desk sets for Harry that he began to mourn the creature skinned. At the end of this unseasonal Christmas, Rose's face was as empty as her suitcase.

"Come along," Anna said, "give your grandmother a chance to rest before dinner."

His mother probably didn't visibly flinch at the title. Harry was working to be insensitive and kind, and he was surprised to feel sorry for her, age beginning to defeat all her careful disguises.

"She's pretty," Joey said, his new dagger strapped onto his new belt, leaning on a spear.

"I like the way she smells," Sally said.

"The spear doesn't come into the kitchen," Anna said. "She *is* pretty."

"But can Hose Hey read to us tonight?" Sally asked. "I want to look at his teeth."

"We'll ask him," Anna said, "but just don't talk about his teeth, all right?"

"What are they made of?"

"Plastic," Joey said knowledgeably, "That's why they make that funny noise."

"Why don't they sleep together?"

"Maybe because of his teeth," Joey said. "Where are you going to sleep, Dad?"

"I haven't really had time to figure that out," Harry admitted, "but I think I'd better borrow your sleeping bag, if you don't mind."

So it was late that night Harry found himself blowing up an air mattress he'd discovered in the basement and laying out Joey's sleeping bag on top of it on the floor next to Anna's cot.

"Reminds me of week-ends on the boat," he said. "That was a great boat."

"Well, we'd outgrown it really," Anna said, yawning. "I'm glad we bought this house."

"Do you suppose he really is going to sleep in there?"

"I think Joey's right about his teeth," Anna said. "Anyway, she strikes me as the sort of woman who always sleeps alone." She put her arms around Harry. "It's a miracle you're here."

Harry looked down at his wife, but the image in his mind was of his mother, seeing her really for the first time as a man does see a woman, and as a woman she wasn't real. Her surface would come off on your hands, and underneath those expensive clothes would be nothing but a series of carefully constructed wire shapes. He shivered slightly, then realized that the woman in his arms was his very real wife who was shaking with laughter.

"What's so funny?" he whispered, suddenly fearful of being overheard.

"Everything," she whispered back.

"It's ridiculous!" he said, and he was laughing, too.

But Harry aged forty years in that night, and he was aware of every ancient bone as he hobbled down the stairs to breakfast. His mother had suggested she needed only a bit of tea and toast after nine in the morning, served in her room, and there had been no sign of life behind José's door; so Harry's crippled entry into breakfast was observed only by Anna and the children.

"You better have my bed tonight, Dad," Joey suggested.

Harry straightened up and shook his head. "We've played enough musical beds around here. I'll make it for one more night."

"Do you know why they don't sleep together?" Sally asked.

"I thought we'd already worked that one to death, Sally," Anna said, the sharpness in her voice suggesting that the cot hadn't been an ideal resting place either.

"Well, but I asked Hose Hey. He said they weren't married. He said only married people sleep together."

"Now why hadn't that occurred to me?" Harry asked, looking at Anna.

"Well, now you know," Sally said.

"Can I take my spear to school?" Joey asked.

"It's a dangerous weapon, son. Ask your friends home to see it tomorrow after your grandmother's gone."

"And after she's gone," Sally said, "and you guys get to go back to your room, I think I'd better move into mine."

"It's all right by me," Joey said, who had wanted his own room for a long time but now was not certain how to react to Sally's declaration of independence.

After the children had grabbed their lunch pails and their coats, admonished to be quiet leaving the house, Harry and Anna were left to their coffee.

"Do you think she really will go into her own room?" Harry asked.

"I think she's decided the old arrangement is indecent."

"Well," they said to each other, "now you know," and the long day and the long night ahead would not be difficult in that new knowledge.

# A MIGRANT CHRISTMAS

Harry wasn't the one in the family who had a principle against doing what everyone else did. It was his wife, Anna, who liked to be out of sync with everyone else, whether for buying a house or starting a family; so Harry never seemed to have either the problems or the pleasures his friends did, both his children and his mortgage years younger. Mike's son was dealing dope before Joey had tried a cigarette behind the garage, and Al's daughter was in danger of pregnancy before Sally learned to read.

"Well, it gets worse before it gets better," Al philosophized. "The best thing about kids is that they grow up and leave home."

"Joyce and I have an even better solution. We're growing up and leaving home first. We're going to Mexico for January," Mike announced.

It wasn't just that Joey and Sally were too young to leave alone. Harry frankly couldn't imagine a holiday without them. Even the year Anna had talked them into going to Europe, Joey was less than a year old and went everywhere on Harry's back. Harry still couldn't eat an ice cream cone without expecting a second tongue to help. He and Anna were far too old to take a holiday on their own and still be able to stop at every advertised snake pit and haunted house along the way. Harry would feel like a fool going into one of

129

those child-sized motel swimming pools by himself, and he
didn't suppose you ever took just your wife out for a hamburger even if, like Anna, she happened to love them.

No, he didn't envy Mike and Joyce their freedom from
the children for a month, but he did envy them their winter
holiday. Wouldn't it be really good for Anna and the kids
to have at least a couple of weeks out of the rain sometimes
tipping to snow, in the winter sun? They wouldn't have to
drive all the way to Mexico. Anna was good with languages,
so good it had been sometimes hard for Harry not to feel
unmanned by her confident handling of their lives all the
time they were on the continent. Her stomach was as
admirable as her tongue. She hadn't taken one Lomatil in
the months they were in Europe. There were weeks when
Harry ate nothing else. Montezuma's revenge, and therefore Mexico, had no part in Harry's daydream.

"People in wheelchairs take winter holidays," Anna said
over after-dinner coffee at the kitchen table while the
children made a quarrelsome game of the dishes.

"Mike and Joyce don't even have a golf cart," Harry
protested.

"Oh, it's because Mike and Joyce . . ."

"It is not. It is nothing of the kind. I want to do just
what they're not doing. I want to take the kids along, go
when we can all enjoy it together."

"What about school?" Joey asked.

"Might keep you out of trouble for a while after you got
back," Anna suggested.

Their problem with Joey was that he was too good in
school, his patience more often tested than either his mind
or imagination.

"Then you like the idea?" Harry asked, encouraged.

"Could I take Petey?" Sally asked.

"I don't think birds are allowed to cross the border,"
Harry said.

It was one of those remarks that sent all three others into
rounds of laughter which mildly puzzled Harry.

"It's—like—birds, Dad," Joey then said kindly. "Going south. Petey could migrate in his cage."

Mike had already taken January, and the office was too short-staffed for Harry to have a holiday at the same time.

"Go for Christmas," his boss said.

"All right," Anna agreed.

"We aren't going to miss Christmas, Sally," Harry explained. "Everywhere is Christmas."

"Will it snow?"

"No. We'll probably go swimming on Christmas day, just the way they do in Australia."

"Can we cut our own tree?"

"It will be a cactus. Now, look, you guys, the point is something different, all right?"

"Christmas isn't exactly boring the way it is," Joey said.

"It's time they traveled," Harry said later when the children had gone to bed. "They're in a rut already."

"Well, kids are conservative about greed, that's all," Anna said. "They don't want to get out of the range of Santa Claus. You can understand that."

"Since it's Christmas, do you think, just this once, we might try for reservations?"

"No," Anna said. What she had refused to do all through crowded Europe, she was not about to agree to in the sparsely populated southern desert.

"If there's no room at the inn?"

"We stay in the stable. Anyway, who but a family of nuts goes away for Christmas?"

"Jews. Every Jew I know is trying to get his kids away from Christmas."

"Happy Hanukkah," Anna said and yawned.

The only elaborate preparations Harry tried to make were those for Sally's canary, but, though he called every office from embassy to customs, he could get neither Canada nor the United States to object to taking Petey with them.

The bird had as much right to go south as they did.

"You don't even want a certificate from the vet?" Harry asked, incredulous.

"Not even proof of citizenship."

Harry finally resorted to reasoning with Sally. "What if the weather confuses him? What if he begins to molt?"

But Sally, at five, could be as implacable as her mother.

"The bird," Anna reminded Harry, "was your idea in the first place."

Harry had one of those clairvoyant moments about the trip, his idea in the first place, during which impossible-to-imagine responsibilities and problems would fall to him to bear and solve. How he wished it had been Anna's suggestion against which he could raise all that might be impractical and ominous.

Joey, once he'd brought home his first book about the desert, was Harry's enthusiastic ally.

"There are rattlesnakes and flash floods," Joey promised them all. "And much better earthquakes than we ever have."

He didn't scare Anna, who was a fatalist, but he terrified Sally with stories of carnivorous birds and aggressive cacti.

"You know, you can't treat a cactus like a tree, Dad," Joey explained. "They're more like porcupines," and to Sally he said, "You don't even have to touch some of them to make them shoot their quills at you."

"We're going to be picking grapefruit and oranges off the trees," Harry said. "We're going to be lying in the sun. We're going to be swimming and playing golf and tennis."

"I don't know how, most of those," Sally said.

"I'll teach you."

In the spirit of their escape from winter, Harry tried to curse their first snow, which fell only several days before they were to leave, but with the new snow tires he'd bought for mountain driving, he had no trouble getting home, and the kids were out on the hill with garbage can lids having a lovely time.

"This is going to be cake-and-eat-it year," Harry said confidently.

"It's hard to look out the window and then pack shorts and bathing suits," Anna said.

She did not go on to compare the experience with daffodils on the Christmas dinner table, of which she didn't approve.

"I've told them we're not hauling all our presents down there and back. We'll have a second Christmas when we get home, all right?"

"I guess so," Harry said.

It was not practical, of course, with limited room in the car, with customs, but he was not sure, come the day itself, how he'd be Santa Claus without presents.

"Well, one each," Anna said, modestly relenting.

Petey was the only one to get his present early, a traveling cage a foot square with a light-tight cover.

"It's not just to shut him up at night," Anna explained. "It's to keep him from getting car sick."

"Do birds get car sick?" Harry asked, incredulous.

"They don't get seasick," Joey said, "or gulls wouldn't ride on the ferry boats."

"Is Petey going to throw up?" Sally asked.

"How about leaving him home?"

"Just because I get car sick, you don't leave me home," Sally answered indignantly.

It snowed again the morning they were to leave, but nobody minded, and Harry presented them all with new plaid laprobes for the occasion.

"I wanted to get beach towels," he confessed, "but there weren't any around this time of year."

The children were warmly settled in the back seat, cool can between them in which Anna had packed all they needed for breakfasts and lunches along the way, Petey in his covered cage on top of that. Anna was in front with her knitting.

"We're off," Harry said, as the wheels spun for a second before the new tires grabbed and sent them in a jolt out of the driveway.

Harry had planned three days for the trip. At the end of the first, he wondered if they'd ever get there at all. It had taken them twelve hours to get to Portland. He sometimes hadn't been able to see more than fifteen feet in front of him, and patches of ice made braking no option, as the huge double trailer trucks jack-knifed across the road testified.

"Wow, look at that!" Joey would exclaim, peering through the snow veil. "Is it going to blow up, do you think, Dad?"

Sally thought it wasn't fair not to let Petey see something of the trip, but, when she uncovered him and found him huddled in the corner of the tiny cage, his feathers fluffed out like a winter overcoat, she didn't have to be told to cover him again.

"Is he going to die?" she asked every fifteen or twenty minutes.

They hadn't dared to stop for lunch not only because they might have frozen to death but because there was no sure way off the road. The others ate, but Harry managed no more than half a sandwich and a couple of swigs of Anna's vegetable soup which sat, a sour fist of fear, in his stomach for the rest of the day. He couldn't even eat the hamburgers he finally managed to buy them after they were safely installed in a Portland motel.

If the heat had worked, if the ice machine hadn't kept him awake most of the night, Harry might have been tempted to suggest they hole in there until the storm—or winter was over.

"We ought to be out of this in another day," Anna said reassuringly.

"Mike and Joyce *fly* to Mexico," Harry said grimly.

"We're doing what they're not doing," Anna reminded him.

Half way through Oregon, the snow turned to rain, but at Grant's Pass it was snowing again, and Harry was told by the motel manager that both roads into California were closed.

"For how long?"

There was no way of telling. This motel room was, at least, warm, but it wasn't until the next afternoon during the seventh game of monopoly that the sun finally came out and Petey began to sing. Though they had paid for a second night, Harry decided right after dinner, when he heard the roads were open, to leave at once. It would be the hardest part of the trip for Sally, the road twisting down out of the mountains, and this way she might sleep through it. After she threw up her dinner at a snow-narrowed turn out, she did, and Harry resisted taking up her question about the distressed bird. As they crossed the California border, they slowed to go through the inspection station where they had to give up the mandarin oranges they'd forgotten to declare at the international border. It seemed to Harry another symbolic deprivation of their Canadian Christmas.

"I thought there were orange and grapefruit trees in California," Joey said, peering out at the dark evergreen forests so like what they had left behind.

"There will be, son," Harry said determinedly.

At dawn, the first miracle of the trip occurred. There on either side of the road were the promised orange and grapefruit groves, bright with fruit lovelier than ornaments on a Christmas tree, acres and acres of them.

"Look," Joey said, "there's fruit on the ground. Could we . . . ?"

"Waste not, want not," Anna said to Harry who was always dubious about anything that might not be law abiding.

So he stopped, and they all got out and picked up oranges which were more fragrant and tasted sweeter than any Harry remembered since his childhood. So peacefully euphoric was he to have brought his family safely out of the winter storms of the north to this amazing morning that he said aloud what he had nearly decided not to mention.

"Old Carl lives in Bakersfield."

Anna did not respond.

"Who's old Carl?" Sally asked.

"A friend of mine," Harry said, preparing to regret his remark.

Carl was the sort of friend you had until you got seriously enough involved with a woman to introduce them and within moments of seeing Carl in a woman's eyes, even the most tolerant sort of woman, you wondered what you had ever seen in him at all, for he was fat, loud, and stupid. Yet, because Harry hadn't seen Carl in ten years, his memory went back to those times before Anna when Carl had been one of Harry's gang of to-hell-with-it college buddies, willing to go to any game, movie, night club, on any drunk, willing to take his car and spend his money.

"He's married now. He's got kids," Harry said. "Might just give him a call, stop for a drink on our way through, since it's Christmas time."

Anna still didn't comment. Joey was watching her; then he turned to his father and shrugged. "It's okay with me."

Carl was, indeed, delighted to hear Harry's voice on the phone, gave him instructions in confused detail about how to get to the house, told him to come for a drink, come for dinner, spend the night, whatever.

"We are not going to impose on that man's poor wife," Anna began.

"Of course not," Harry agreed. "We'll just drop in and say hello."

"Could we have a cookie?" Sally asked.

"If you're offered one," Anna said.

"They'll probably be coconut," Joey suggested brightly; he loved coconut, and Sally wouldn't touch it.

It was one of the dozen times a day the strategically placed cool can kept marginal peace with Petey functioning as a sort of one-bird UN force.

When they arrived at the door, Carl opened it and said, much less enthusiastically than on the phone, "Come in and all, but my wife says to tell you the boy has mumps, so if your kids . . ."

"I've had the mumps," Joey said.

"Sally, darling," Anna said. "You'll have to wait in the car. We'll only be a few minutes."

Sally's face filled up with tears like a glass at a tap.

"You don't want to be sick for Christmas."

"There isn't going to be any Christmas," she wailed.

"Look, maybe we better make it another time," Harry began.

"At least, come in and see the tree," Carl said. "Otherwise, I'm stuck here with my mother-in-law all afternoon."

"I heard that, Carl!" shouted a deep, sexless voice from inside the room. "It's a question of who's stuck with who."

At the sound of that voice, the tears began to drain out of Sally's face.

"I *think* I've had mumps," Joey said.

"Look," Harry said, "both of you go back to the car, all right? We won't be long."

He and Anna were back in twenty minutes.

"What did the tree look like?" Sally demanded.

"Just like a tree," Harry said, "cluttering up the living room."

"Were there presents?"

"Were there cookies?"

"Mostly there were sick kids and crabby relatives."

"Was the lady inside a witch?"

"More or less," Harry said. "Now, aren't you glad we're not having a Christmas like that?"

"We don't have crabby relatives," Sally said.

"How fat do you suppose that guy is?" Joey said.

"Even fatter than I remembered," Harry said.

Though he was promising himself not to remember anything on his own before Anna again ever, he was also feeling modestly smug about his own decent shape, his good-looking and agreeable wife, his healthy children. "Poor old Carl. Some people are born to make other people feel good."

"Good?" Anna asked.

"Well, better," Harry clarified.

On the outskirts of town, he found a motel with a kidney-shaped pool, and he slept in the California sun while Anna and the children played in the water.

The next day in Palm Springs, they all did some secretive Christmas shopping.

"Let's get the kids a piñata," Anna suggested. "We're nearly at the Mexican border."

Once they had taken advantage of the stores, Harry was restless to be on their way.

"You mean, this isn't where we're going?" Anna asked.

"You don't want to stay here, do you?" Harry asked, surprised.

"Where else is there?"

"The state park. Borrego Springs. It has everything Palm Springs has except Palm Springs."

Not until they were leaving town and Anna began to sing carols did Harry realize she'd been resigning herself to a week in that rich resort town where private guard services protected the mostly deserted houses of celebrities, where the chief conversation among the locals seemed to be skin cancer, and the tourists complained about the prices of flowered trousers. Harry had not spoken of Borrego Springs before because he wanted to seem spontaneous while being prepared. They would be in the real desert in a little community with, nevertheless, plenty of tourist accommodations, well before dark on Christmas Eve.

As they all sang together "We Three Kings," Harry heard Sally's high, sweet version of "of Oreo Tar." His cookie-obsessed daughter did not get in the way of his fantasy that they could be that new breed of agnostic wise men still following a star across the badlands in the delicate winter light to a simple place, to a yearly miracle.

"Wow!" Joey said. "Did you see that sign? 'This Road Is Subject to Flash Floods!'"

Each time they dipped into a dry wash, Joey looked in vain for the rushing water. Then he saw a road runner with a snake's tail hanging out of its beak.

"Those big ones look like they're on fire," Sally said as they passed twelve-foot-high ocotillos, their bare, viciously thorned limbs tipped by fragile red bloom.

Anna's hand rested on Harry's thigh. "I like the ones with halos," she said, nodding to crowns of bright thorns.

Then there before them, nearly at the foot of western mountains, as bare of vegetation as a dinosaur's hide, was the oasis of Borrego Springs, green with golf courses, punctuated by date palms.

The two motels near the stores were full. The next three didn't take pets or children.

"No children?" Harry asked each time. "You've got to be kidding. And the bird's in a cage."

He drove them back into the center and found a real estate office.

"I'm willing to rent a house if I have to," Harry explained, trying to sound reasonable.

"To have children in it, you'd have to buy one," the sales man explained. "Even then you couldn't buy one at any of the clubs."

"What are you, paranoid about school taxes or something? Didn't Proposition Thirteen take care of that?"

"This is a retirement community and an adult resort."

"You could camp in the park," a gas station attendant suggested. "There's no objection to kids in the park."

"It gets down to forty degrees," Harry protested. "We've got nothing with us but lap robes."

"I'd say your best bet is to go back to Palm Springs or over to San Diego."

"We want to stay here."

Sally was staring out the window watching a white-haired woman pedal a giant tricycle up the street.

"This is a funny place," she said. "She isn't really children, is she?"

"There aren't any children," Joey explained.

"Did they die?"

"They aren't allowed."

Harry got a list of every place in the valley that offered accommodation. He stood putting dimes into the pay phone as if it were a slot machine.

"Surely, on Christmas Eve you'd make an exception," he'd try. Then exasperated, he'd begin to shout, "Children have rights, too, you know!"

"Harry," Anna finally said, "I think we better get out of here."

"I'm starving," Joey said. "Are kids allowed to eat here?"

"There's that little Mexican restaurant," Anna said. "How about some tacos, and then we'll drive over to the ocean."

The place was jammed. They had to stand to wait their turn and were finally seated at a table for ten, otherwise occupied by aging couples.

"What are people doing, eating out on Christmas Eve?" Harry whispered angrily to Anna. "They ought to be at home with their grandchildren."

But Anna was exchanging friendly greetings with the old man next to her.

"Nice to see a couple of kids," he was saying. "I said to my wife—this is Rachel, my wife—funny place with no kids around, quiet as the grave."

"Oh, Sam, don't exaggerate. There are children right next door to us. We're renting. We just come down from Oregon for a month," she confided to Anna, "and renters can't have children, but owners are allowed to have grandchildren visit."

"It's unnatural!" Harry said.

When Sam and Rachel heard the dilemma that faced these Canadian visitors, they were as irate as Harry and agreed that it was not only unnatural but un-American, and they would do something about it.

"Listen," Sam said. "We've got plenty of space, twin beds in the spare room, a second bathroom, big fold-out bed in the living room."

"But children aren't allowed," Harry reminded him.

"We'll just smuggle them in," Rachel decided. "When we finish here," she continued in a lowered voice, "we'll put the children in our car under a blanket. Then a little while later, you come along . . ."

"What about Petey?" Sally asked.

"We have a canary," Harry said glumly.

"If we can smuggle a couple of kids, who's worried about a canary?"

"But you could get evicted," Harry reminded them.

"So that's the end of the world?" Sam asked.

"You're wonderful," Anna said, "Thank you."

Once the plan was approved, all six of them took their parts with elaborate seriousness. Harry insisted on paying the whole bill while Rachel and Sam took the children and hid them under their own lap robes on the back seat of their large and impressive American car.

"God, I hope they're not kidnappers," Anna said suddenly as the old couple drove off.

"You're the one who agreed!" Harry shouted, rushing to their own car.

When Anna got in beside him, she was laughing. Then she said, "I'm sorry about being so dumb about making reservations."

"I would have settled for a stable if I could have found one."

They found the car parked in the carport of number one-hundred-and-thirty-one  in the mobile home park, and they found the children in the living room, eating cookies. Harry put Petey in his covered cage on top of the television set.

"They'll think it's on tv," Rachel said, "whatever noise we make. As long as we keep the curtains closed, and the kids stay off the screened porch."

Anna helped Rachel make up the guest room beds and

then settled the children while Harry accepted a drink and a look around, never having been inside these giant kleenex boxes on wheels before.

"Come say goodnight," Anna called.

"Dad," Sally said, "You said Christmas was everywhere."

"And so it is," Harry said, smiling at his clean, comfortable children as safely settled as they might have been with grandparents.

"I don't see any tree. I don't see any presents."

"Well, older people, on their own, sometimes . . ."

"The thing is, Sally," Anna interrupted. "Sam and Rachel are Jewish, and Jewish people don't celebrate Christmas."

"Jewish people don't believe in Santa Claus?" Sally asked. "I don't really either, but everybody can pretend."

"Jews don't believe in Jesus," Joey said.

"Neither exactly do we," Anna said. "There are a lot of different ways to believe in kindness and hope and love. There'll be surprises in the morning. Just don't worry about it."

Out in the living room where Rachel was making up their bed, another worried conversation had obviously taken place.

"Rachel says we can make a tree out of palm fronds," Sam explained. "And . . ."

"You mustn't go to any trouble," Anna protested. "We came away partly to get away from all the elaborate fuss Christmas gets to be. We're not really believers either."

At that moment, they heard the voices of carolers outside the door, mostly wavering old voices with one true soprano, singing of a child born to Mary, and they all went out to listen.

"We're not all that much Jews either," Sam said as they went back into the house. "Anyway, there's no real way to get away from Christmas, not with kids in the house."

The courteous argument turned into the joy of finding palm fronds in the desert moonlight for the men, baking for the women. It was nearly as late as it always got at home when Sam and Rachel finally retired to their bedroom, leaving Harry and Anna to sleep in the splendor of a room-high tree of palm fronds, decorated with dozens of freshly baked and brightly frosted cookies, presents for everyone stacked underneath it, Harry's gift to Anna and hers to him relabeled for Sam and Rachel, the piñata hanging over the breakfast table.

Harry woke at dawn, for a moment uncertain where he was until he saw the tree, and he was very glad that he had a wife who believed in miracles rather than reservations, that Christmas would be as secret and illicit as it had been in the beginning, for the sake of the children. He got up and opened the curtains just a crack. Then he took the cover off Petey and let him sing. Outside a mocking bird in the ocotillo answered that caged, illegal carol.

## YOU CANNOT JUDGE A PUMPKIN'S
## HAPPINESS BY THE SMILE UPON HIS FACE


Perhaps because Harry had not had the conventional joys of childhood himself, he was enthusiastic about them for his own children. He was so good at holidays that Anna, his wife, often thought of him as a misplaced kindergarten teacher. But she and the children humored him through Santa Claus suits, egg decorating contests and valentines enough to embarrass the most indiscriminate lover. Usually his energy could carry the day, and they ended by laughing with him instead of at him. But there was always the danger that Harry would go too far. When a full month before Hallowe'en Harry was already planning Sally's and Joey's costumes, Anna tried to apply the brakes.

"The kids like to pick out their own costumes."

"Well, I asked Sally last night what she wanted to be, and she just shrugged," Harry protested.

"Kids are getting a bit turned off by Hallowe'en. It's all those stories about razor blades in apples and poisoned cookies."

"Not in our neighborhood!" Harry exclaimed. "If Hallowe'en isn't what it used to be, all the more reason for us to get into the act and save it. Traditions are important to kids."

"I broke my ankle one Hallowe'en," Anna recalled, "running from the cops."

"What had you done?"

"I don't remember," Anna said. "I just remember the cast and the crutches."

"But I'll be with the kids."

"And what do you want to be?" Anna asked.

"Their father," Harry answered.

So Anna finally agreed to make two pairs of black, long-sleeved pajamas. When they were finished, Harry went to the library for a reference book and to a hardware store for white paint that would glow in the dark. Then he shut himself into the basement and began to work. He had thought at first to keep the costumes a surprise, but once they were finished, he was too proud of his efforts to keep them a secret.

"After dinner tonight," he announced, "we're going to have a preview of coming events."

Anna and the kids, seated in the entirely darkened living room, listened to Harry stumble and curse in the hall.

"Is it a movie?" Sally asked.

"It's a simulated air raid," Joey said and introduced a high pitched whine of a plane passing, followed by a K-BANG of a bomb exploding which threw him out of his chair.

"Are you ready?" Harry called.

"Get back in your chair, son," Anna said.

"I can't find it," Joey answered from the floor. "Hey! Look!"

"Moving into the living room were two glowing skeletons.

"Daddy?" Sally called out.

"This is you, punkin," Harry's voice replied, and the smaller skeleton wobbled violently. "And this is Joey." The other did a similar dance. "Trick or treat!"

"Neat-o!" Joey exclaimed.

"Scary," Sally decided.

"You're supposed to be scary on Hallowe'en," Harry

said, but he turned on a light so that Sally could see the two pairs of black pajamas hanging on coat hangers. "And they're accurate. This is a girl skeleton, and this is a boy skeleton."

"How do you know?" Sally asked.

"I copied them out of a medical book. Girls' bones are different there so that they can have babies."

"They really are marvelous!" Anna admitted.

"Can we sleep in them?" Joey asked.

"Can I wear mine when I stay overnight at Cricket's?"

"Well, I guess so," Harry said, "after Hallowe'en."

"Do we really have to go trick or treating?" Joey asked.

"What do you mean 'have to?'" Harry demanded. "It's supposed to be fun."

"Yeah, well, it's just that maybe I'm getting a little bit . . . old for it, you know?"

"At nine?" Harry asked, incredulous.

"Well, some of the other paperboys said maybe they'd go round and fill up their carriers, but not in costume or anything."

"Undisguised greed," Anna said.

"My friends aren't allowed," Sally said. "Cricket isn't."

"Why not?"

"Cricket's mother says children get molested."

"Do you know what that means, Sally?"

"Hurt?"

"Well, you can't be hurt when I'm right there with you. And think of all the disappointed grown-ups if nobody came for the candy and cookies. Why, it would be like kids deciding not to get up on Christmas morning. It would be like not wanting to blow out the candles on your birthday cake. Do you know something? Without kids, there probably wouldn't be any holidays at all, except maybe New Year's and Memorial Day."

"They're really great costumes, Dad," Joey said. "Can we try them on?"

"Sure."

Both children accepted their skeletons and raced up-stairs to change.

For the rest of the evening lights went off and on as two skeletons fled from room to room until Joey and Sally has scared themselves sleepy.

"No, you can't go to bed in them tonight," Anna said. "Wait until after Hallowe'en."

"We're really going to have to do that?" Joey asked.

"Do you want to disappoint your father?"

"Sometimes having to be a kid is pretty embarrassing," Joey said.

"Nobody will recognize you," Anna comforted him.

The day before Hallowe'en Harry came home from work early. Sally and Anna were in the kitchen cutting out Hal-lowe'en cookies. Joey hadn't yet got home from school.

"Say, we'll be the most popular house on the block with those," Harry said, admiring the pumpkins, cats and witches about to go into the oven.

"They're not for here," Sally said. "They're for kinder-garten tomorrow."

"All of them?"

"The teacher said to bring things to school, and then we won't have to go out after dark."

"Another killjoy!" Harry said in disgust.

"Shhhh . . ." Anna said sharply and suddenly, looking at the clock and listening.

Faintly, off in the distance, a cry could be heard. "Pepperrrrr."

"That's Joey!" Sally said with satisfaction.

"He's three blocks away," Anna said.

"What's the idea?" Harry asked.

"To see how far away he can be and we can still hear him," Sally explained.

"Who's Pepper?"

"The dog Mom won't let him have."

Joey banged into the house, shouting, "Well, did you hear me?"

"We heard you," Anna said.

"Oh, hi, Dad," Joey said.

"Pretty much of a kid game for a guy as old as you are."

"Aw, Dad . . ."

"Come on, both of you," Harry said. "There's a sale of the biggest pumpkins you ever saw."

"Can we each have one?"

"Yep, and you can pick as big a one as you can carry."

"But we don't have to carry them around, do we?" Joey asked. "They're just for the window, aren't they?"

"Dad's not going to make you wear them on your heads," Anna said.

After dinner, Joey and Sally settled at the kitchen table, a bit intimidated by the size of their enormous pumpkins.

"Its head's as big as God's," Sally said.

"Go on," Harry encouraged. "The bigger they are, the easier they are."

"Mine's going to have two teeth," Joey decided.

"Mine's going to SMILE," Sally said, drawing out the word as she traced a mouth with her knife.

Then, as she began to cut, she hummed a tune which then turned into a song with words, which ended, "You cannot judge a pumpkin's happiness by the smile upon its face."

"Where did you learn a sad song like that?" Harry asked.

"At school," Sally said. "Did Dad show you the suckers he bought to hand out at the door?"

"No," Anna said.

"I hope we like them," Joey said.

"They're not for you," Harry said.

"I mean, just in case . . ."

"In case what?"

"In case nobody comes."

"Listen, by the time those two pumpkins get into the window, they'll attract ghosts from all over town."

Though it was only five o'clock, it was already dark as Harry drove home on Hallowe'en, and it was raining. As he came off the bridge into the residential section of the city, he looked in vain for bands of small children in costume. Here and there, there was a pumpkin in the window, and, as he passed the high school, Harry spotted two patrol cars. Too early, that was all. He wasn't taking his own kids out until after dinner.

Sally didn't want anything to eat. She had a stomach ache from all the sweets she'd had at school.

"My stomach wants to throw up," she announced, "but I don't."

"Do you mind?" Joey asked sarcastically. "Some people are trying to eat."

"You could go up and put on your costume, Sally," Harry suggested. "And be all ready."

"Do you think she ought to go out on a night like this?" Anna asked. "She's already feeling sick."

"She'll be fine," Harry said firmly.

"Won't our skeletons melt?" Joey asked hopefully.

"We'll take umbrellas, and you can put sweaters on underneath."

"We'll be pretty fat skeletons," Joey said.

They, in fact, looked like skeleton brand sausages as they stood by the door, getting into their rain boots.

"Part of my bones are in my boots," Sally said.

"You man the door while we're gone," Harry instructed Anna hopefully, though there had as yet been no callers.

It was very wet, and there was no sign of anyone else out on the street. Far off they could hear an occasional fire cracker and the wail of a siren.

"We'll just go to the houses with porch lights on," Harry said in a voice more confident than his spirit, for there were very few porch lights in evidence along the block.

Harry waited on the sidewalk while Joey and Sally trudged up the first walk under a shared umbrella. When he heard the first exclamations of admiration of their fine costumes, Harry felt vindicated, and he smiled at the polite "thank yous" coming from his two small skeletons.

"You didn't sound very scary," he said to them as they joined him.

"I was scared," Sally said. "I didn't even know that lady."

"What did you get?"

"A couple of apples," Joey said.

His tone discouraged Harry. Maybe he shouldn't have given Joey permission to deliver papers, for Harry seemed to have a world weary man of independent income on his hands instead of a kid enjoying himself.

After the next call, Sally said, in surprised delight, "They gave us a couple of cigars!"

"What?" Harry demanded.

"Candy cigars," Joey explained.

At least Sally was beginning to enjoy herself. She'd forgotten about her stomach ache, and she felt quite bold at the next house where she had a friend.

"Do you both look adorable! Harry, are you out there? Come on in for a drink, why don't you?"

"No, no thanks. We've got to make the rounds," Harry called back.

"Adorable!" Joey snorted, and suddenly he turned on Sally and gave a harsh scream.

At the next walk, Joey balked. "I can't go up there. She's the old bat who doesn't pay her bills, and she says I throw her paper in the bushes."

"And we can't go in there either," Sally explained at another house.

"Why not?"

"The man acts funny all the time," Sally said.

"He's drunk all the time," Joey amplified.

"I see."

Fire crackers exploded in the next block, and a car screeched around the corner. Sally dropped back and took her father's hand.

"Not this one," Joey said, "or this one."

After explanations like "There's a vicious dog" or "Mrs.

Hale just broke her leg." Harry gave up asking why. Joey's knowledge of the neighborhood gave him an authority Harry hesitated to dispute, but he was by now thoroughly exasperated with his son and the evening.

"Look, Joey," Harry finally said, "We aren't just out for a walk in the rain. You make this neighborhood sound like a cross between the loony bin and the emergency ward at the hospital. There must be some people who aren't too dangerous or sick to call on."

"Well," Joey said, looking up at a large, brightly lighted house with some uncertainty, "I guess this one would be all right."

"It's got a lot of stairs," Sally said.

"Go!" Harry ordered.

He stood in the street, the rain drumming on his umbrella, and watched his doggedly unenthusiastic children trudge up the steps, slick with water. Where were all the other fathers and children in the world who should be filling the streets with happy calls and friendly spookiness?

The door opened. A young man seemed to stare at the children a long time, and then, instead of giving them anything, he ushered them inside. Harry dismissed a second of apprehension. They were probably being asked to show off their costumes to the other people in the house. Joey's open umbrella, like a great bat, rocked gently on the porch.

Harry looked at his watch and looked at the house again just as a number of lights went out on the main floor. He smiled. Joey and Sally were glowing for them in the dark. He wondered if anyone in there was knowledgeable enough to recognize the authenticity of his work. In his renewed pride, he chided himself for his impatience. All kids needed persistent encouragement sometimes to enter into the spirit of a thing.

Five and then ten minutes passed. The lights did not go back on. What the devil were they doing in there? Another five minutes and Harry acted. He went up the long slippery stairs two at a time and banged on the door. No one answered. He banged again. Finally, just as he had reached for the handle himself, the door opened, and the same young man stared out at him.

"Where are my kids?" Harry asked, trying to keep his voice calm.

The young man didn't answer, and Harry suddenly got a strong whiff of incense and marajuana.

"I said, where are my kids?"

"Man, I don't know," came the slow, bewildered reply.

"They came in here fifteen minutes ago," Harry said, pushing past the unhelpful, obviously stoned-out-of-his-mind man, and shouted, "Joey! Sally!"

"It's my dad," he heard Joey say somewhere in there in the dark.

Then he saw the two small skeletons moving toward him out of the murk of a room filled with smoke and the stir of people.

"It's a party," Sally explained happily. "They're telling funny ghost stories."

Harry nodded curtly to the young man still standing in the hall and pushed his children out the door.

"Why did you go in there?" Harry demanded.

"You *told* us to," Sally answered, the weather of tears in her voice.

"They're just a bit high on pot, Dad," Joey explained. "They're really okay guys. They grow it on their roof."

"But we couldn't have any brownies. They said they were only for grown-ups."

"What *did* they give you?"

"A whole bunch of suckers, just like the kind you bought," Joey said. "I sure hope we like them."

"I sure hope you do, too," Harry said. "Come on. We're going home."

"We still didn't get very much," Sally said, peering into her bag.

The damp costumes were draped over the fire screen to

dry, and Harry sat staring at them. Anna came in with a glass of her homemade blackberry wine for each of them.

"We should have moved to that island when you wanted to," Harry said bitterly.

"There's just no way for kids to be able to be kids in this city. Anyway, Joey's giving up his paper route. I'll tell him in the morning. That kid knew all those people were stoned out of their minds, and he knew what it was. He even told me where they grow it . . . on the roof!"

"They seem to have had a good time," Anna said.

"At this rate, he'll be on pot himself by the time he's ten . . . if he isn't already!"

"Joey's too tight with his money for expensive habits," Anna said. "He won't even buy himself an ice cream cone."

"The things he knows about this neighborhood," Harry said, shaking his head. "And even Sally . . ."

"We can give a Hallowe'en party at home next year."

"They knew it wasn't safe," Harry said. "I didn't."

"Harry, knowing is finally safer than not knowing, for the kids as well as for you. That's the only real protection there is."

"You think it's still all right for Joey to be out there throwing papers at all those drunks and dope fiends and vicious dogs and cripples?"

"If he wants to and thinks he can handle it."

Harry sighed. Then he got up and went over to the window to blow out the candles in the smiling pumpkins. Anna picked up the basket of unclaimed suckers and took them to the kitchen. Harry turned out the lights, and the accurate bones of his children glowed there in the dark.

## MORE THAN MONEY

"Are we really going to move?" Freddy asked, not taking the lunch box Maria was holding out for him.

"That's what your father says," she answered.

"But can we tell the kids at school?" Tad wanted to know, his lunch already safely under his arm.

"Maybe you should say 'maybe,' " Maria decided.

" 'Maybe' doesn't count," Freddy said. "Aren't we sure?"

"Well, I guess so," Maria said, hearing the problem but still reluctant.

"Don't you want to move, Mom?" Tad asked.

"Sure I do," Maria said.

"Dad said everything in an apartment would be brand new, and there might even be a swimming pool," Freddy pressed.

"Take your lunch box, dreamer, go on, and try not to make up too many whoppers between here and school."

"But he said . . ."

"He said 'maybe,' " Tad reminded his brother.

"Maybe with a high dive," Freddy said, and he spread his arms, encumbered with lunch pail and books, for a swan dive.

"Maybe with a dishwasher, Dad said," Tad offered, still watching his mother.

"And carpets so deep you'll both break your ankles, and a garbage disposal for chewing up planes and cars, and . . . " Maria paused briefly at the unchanged look of doubt on her older son's face, "high enough off the ground to think you're flying. Whatever it's like, we'll like it."

"So we can tell," Freddy said. "We can tell, We can tell."

He flapped and flew from the kitchen, through dining room and living room, and crashed into the front door before Tad got there to open it. The front porch steps trembled, and they were gone before Maria could shout any of her good natured instructions about considering the foundation of the house, the neighbors' eardrums. Well, never mind. Freddy would be silenced soon enough unless she provided ear plugs and straight jackets for everyone else in the apartment house.

"It'll kill him," she said to herself, repeating what she had said to Frank the night before.

"It will be good for him," Frank had replied. "But that's not the point."

Why had she bought that bottle of brandy? It wasn't the bottle of brandy. Frank wasn't even angry about that. He said so. He even used it in her favor, saying now she would be able to get an occasional bottle of brandy for him and not worry about it. She hadn't worried about it. Buying it had stopped the worry of frozen lobster and two cowboy hats she'd already bought. She felt cheerful then, thinking of Frank having a treat for himself. He wouldn't buy it. He wouldn't even buy himself decent shirts if he had his way about it. Thought he could go off to work as if he were on the dole.

"I will be soon," he'd say on a bad day, but he'd always relent, not for himself but for the boys, even for her. "Sure, okay, it looks cute," he'd said about her hair piece, "and I can wear it myself when my hair falls out from worry." But that was a joke. And on a really good day, he'd say, "It's a good thing I married you because I could have been a lazy man." Lots of things she had bought were to save money. She needed an extra large washing machine so that she didn't have to send out blankets and spreads. The freezer let them have lots of bargain steaks and roasts. Even the hair piece was supposed to save money at the hair dresser though it hadn't worked out quite like that. Neither had the freezer, Frank argued. "We eat better but not cheaper." What was wrong with that?

"I don't want to sell the house," she had said.

"It's the only way we can get out of debt."

"Frank, there are things more important than money."

"Honey, I don't want you ever to say that to me again, and I don't want you ever to think it again. There is nothing more important than money when you don't have it. And we don't have it. If we go on six more months like this, we'll lose the house anyway."

"Losing" the house had struck Maria as comically unlikely, but Frank wouldn't let her laugh about it. He told her she had an unrealistic sense of humor. If you were going to be realistic round the clock, you might as well be dead.

Maria wiped the jam smears off Freddy's chair, then made a pass at the nonexistent crumbs at Tad's place. Like his father, Tad was, and she mustn't let him know she didn't like what was happening. She didn't want him to know that she was to blame. "Nobody has to be blamed," Frank said, "Just punished," she had answered.

The phone rang. It would be Maria's mother. Maria sat down and stared at the phone until, after fifteen rings, it stopped. Pointless. Her mother wouldn't believe any of her lies when she did answer an hour later. Then Maria would have to tell her.

"Did I bring you up to squander? Did I bring you up to put your husband in the poor house? Do I live to see my own grandsons in rags?"

Yes. Yes. No. Maria answered each one. She loved her mother. She was like her mother. Neither one of them had any sense about money at all. The difference between them was that Maria's father was as tightfisted as Frank was generous. Her mother had never been allowed to be extravagant except in small ways; so she'd never suffered the humiliations Maria had: bounced checks, angry letters and phone calls, a truck outside to carry away repossessed furniture. Well, the bunk beds had been a bad idea anyway, Freddy either shaking Tad out of his nest or bombing him from above. There was the shame of it. She just tried not to think about that.

"The most important thing is to be cheerful," Maria said to a silent Frank, to her horrified friend, Elsie.

All very well for Elsie to be horrified. She was a vicarious spender who could be a whole day in the shops without parting from a dime as long as someone else did the buying. It wasn't a fault really. Maria loved to go shopping with Elsie because she admired everything Maria bought. She'd say, "Oh, do you think you should?" but in a way to make the purchase even more exciting. And, after Maria had made her decision, Elsie always said, "It's really such a bargain, you know; you're saving dollars."

Maria put the last of the breakfast dishes into the sink and tried to think about a dishwasher. The idea of simply using one, already there, wasn't as appealing as going out and buying one. Now, in this kitchen, a new dishwasher would be marvelous. She saw one the other day, nothing down and only about fifteen dollars a month. Practically nothing.

"That's where the money goes every month," Frank said, "on about two hundred payments on practically nothing."

Maybe tonight, when the brandy seemed familiar, the way the dining room rug and the floor polisher did even though they weren't quite paid for, Frank would be more relaxed, have some other idea. Probably they could increase the mortgage, though Maria had some memory of Frank's having done that not very long ago. And he reminded her that they had never paid the down payment back to her father. If he hadn't needed it for ten years, surely he could get along without it a little while longer. He wasn't going to retire for another year or two. She could probably get something for the stuff in the basement, Tad's old bike that hadn't really been good enough to give Freddy, the old refrigerator—except where would she keep the watermelon and soft drinks?

Maria didn't like the smell of the new soap, and the free scrubbing brush that had come with it polished rather than loosened the egg on the plate.

"Just junk!" she said. She felt very sad, sad enough to cry.

She was a fool. Everything her father said. But sometimes it was all right. She could pay attention, but then Tad would be home in bed with the flu or her mother was just low or Frank would get depressed about the news, and then Maria forgot about money and bought things. Once she started that, she'd get back into the habit, and she'd graduate from bottles of perfume and funny books to coats and couches. Once Frank sold their car. Once he had a night job. Now the car belonged to the company, and he had to work at night anyway sometimes.

The phone was ringing again, and this time Maria answered it.

"So what's the bad news?" her mother demanded.

"It's not bad news," Maria said.

But, when she had explained it to her mother making the move sound like a Hollywood success story, she got no response at all.

"Mama?"

"And so in this penthouse, what's Frank going to do with the next set of bills—jump?"

"What I'm explaining to you is we can pay our bills—all of them."

She hadn't expected to start crying, but there she was blubbering at her mother, who stopped being sarcastic right away and told her it was probably a very good idea, and, if there wasn't a dishwasher, she'd see to it Papa bought one for Maria. She said to Maria, "There are things more important than money." She said to Maria, "The most important thing is to be cheerful."

Maria hung up the phone, both comforted and resolute. She washed her face and changed her dress. Then she called Elsie. This time the penthouse had triple plumbing—carpeted—and a built-in hi fi. Maria wasn't sure the couch they already had would be big enough. Why didn't they just go out and begin to shop around?

By the time they had walked through two department stores, Maria was considering a pool table for the boys, something that would take up less space and replace the ping-pong table they would have to give up. Probably they should have their own television.

"What's Frank going to do without a garden?" Elsie asked.

Tropical fish, maybe. House plants. Games. None of them sounded very much like Frank, really. Pool and television didn't sound much like Freddy and Tad either. Maria felt guilt flip in her stomach. Buy something for them, she thought. Buy something! She hurried along the narrow corridors of space through worlds of furniture, toys, clothes. Buy something! Buy something!

"Elsie," she said, "get me out of here."

"What's the matter?" Elsie asked, taking Maria's arm. "Are you sick?"

"I'm sick," Maria said.

And she knew what her sickness was as she stood shaking and breathing deeply on the sidewalk. Her spending sprees were just like drinking sprees. Wasn't there an organization for people who couldn't handle money the way there was for people who couldn't handle drink? She'd already lost their car, the beds their children slept in, and now she had lost their house. Where would it end? In pool tables and tropical fish. How could she stand her shame without them?

"Elsie," she said, "I need help."

"Let's go treat ourselves to a nice cool drink," Elsie said. "That will make you feel better. Then we'll just take a cab home."

Oh, that was what Maria wanted, something with five flavors of ice cream in so tall a glass she had to tip it to drink, then a cool, luxurious ride home. She hadn't, after all, spent any money in the stores. It was a very small reward. Reward? Shame turned in her again.

"I can just wait here and take a bus," Maria said, and she sat down, clutching the bench for resolve.

"Please yourself," Elsie said.

Their bus was a block away at the stop light. Just before the light changed, a taxi turned into the street.

"Taxi!" Maria called out, an arm thrown up to stop the traffic, to halt the indifferent flow of events, to take charge of her life again. "Taxi!"

# THE INVESTMENT YEARS

If Roger had wanted to explain his mood, there were plenty of ordinary, unflattering reasons for it: his thirtieth birthday last month, the measles that Peter had brought home from school and given the younger two, the argument Nancy had started about his taking business trips just to get out of the house. But Roger didn't want to explain his mood, being a man who found it easier to take than to lay blame, in his marriage anyway. After all, Nancy had good reason to be exhausted and to dread five days alone, and, though he could not postpone the trip, he was certainly glad of it.

"My wife," said Bert as they sat in the car eating hamburgers after a long, uncertain sales meeting, "thinks these business trips are just a piece of cake: five hundred miles on the road, hambrugers so you can get a mickey out of your expenses in order to put yourself to sleep in a second rate motel while some other guy is still watching tv or making it with somebody he won't have to listen to the next morning."

"Some other guy?" Roger asked, to be flattering. He only saw Bert on these trips and worked at being good humored without being really friendly.

"Well, if there wasn't one for the road occasionally, who'd ever take a job like this?" And cheered, Bert contemplated the possibilities of two or three of the carhops.

There was nothing to make the swallowing of Roger's hamburger any better, neither mickey nor girl. He couldn't even use the few dollars he was saving to buy a present for Nancy or more than candy bars or a few pencils for the kids. The hot water heater had gone last week, two months before they'd finished paying for a new roof.

"How about that one?" Bert suggested, gesturing with the last bite of hamburger. "Maybe we could go halves."

"Thanks anyway," Roger said.

"Trouble with you, boy, is that there's never any cake at all."

True. Unless you could call a night when he didn't have to get up with a sick child cake. And that's all Nancy would mean, for just those few hours to die into her own sleep. Thinking of Nancy like that depressed him. He tried to think, instead, about the vacation they were planning, the same one they had planned and not gone on last year and the year before because of their endless calendar of chicken pox, broken arms, and unexpected bills.

"I'll walk back to the motel," Roger suggested. "I need the exercise."

"There's a tv at home . . ."

"Well . . ." Roger said, leaving his dollar and maneuvering carefully out from under the long, thin tray.

Ordinarily, Roger would not have felt martyred by his own good sense. Ordinarily, if he controlled a mood on a walk like this, it was smugness at the thought of his good, intelligent wife, his three, lively, loving children, his well kept house, his roses. If they were tired sometimes, if they didn't get away on a vacation, it wouldn't be long; these were the investment years. He and Nancy looked on the bright side. Tonight the blazing car headlights he walked toward blinded him, and he was at first sullen and then angry because it was true: for him there was never any cake at all.

Instead of going directly to his room, Roger stopped in the office and asked for a local paper.

"Anything going on in town tonight?"

"Bingo at church and beer at the hotel," the proprietor answered. "And a lousy movie."

In the city there would be a concert or a foreign film or a play, not that Roger and Nancy went to any of those things. Like their vacation, they talked about going and stayed home. It was only seven-thirty. If he had taken his own car, he could start home now, but what would be the point of driving all night? He couldn't sleep once he got there, the kids up, Nancy doing the morning vacuuming. Well, at least she didn't have to spend her evenings in the forty-watt glow of a motel room. Her television set didn't take quarters. Roger found a quarter for his and sat down in the cracked leatherette chair, designed for someone with three foot long thighs and an eight inch backbone and sold to every motel of this sort in the country. In the middle of the third commercial, there was a knock on the door.

"No luck," Bert said without sign of great disappointment.

"Come watch the commercials," Roger suggested politely.

"Let's at least go out for a beer. Come on."

"And waste my quarter?"

"No, I wouldn't ask anyone to do that," Bert said, flipping a quarter at Roger. "My treat."

"You've finally found my price," Roger said, and he got up out of the damaging chair, turned off the set and put his wallet back in his pocket.

Having agreed to go, Roger tried to look cheerful, but he could find nothing less depressing about the beer parlor than he had about the motel. It was too early for a crowd, yet the tables were already patterned with spilt beer and dirty ashtrays. At one end of the room a juke box worked at trying to obliterate the human silence. At the other, a television set offered the same commercials Roger had recently deserted.

"What I like about this town . . ." Bert began, but Roger couldn't hear whatever rudeness followed.

They were on their third beer before the place began to fill up, a small crowd coming in from the movie, perhaps even a guilty few from gambling at the church. That would explain why the fat woman was carrying a pop-up toaster under her arm.

"You think she won it?" Bert asked. "No kidding? I'm going to ask her."

Roger was mildly embarrassed by the idea, but he didn't try to stop Bert who, after a few exchanges, was leading the fat woman and her husband back to the table.

"You were right," Bert said.

"I'm just lucky," the fat woman said. "Even won me a trip east once, and I got me the old man here in a poker game."

Roger didn't really try to follow the conversation after that, though he contributed to it occasionally. The fat woman was cheerful, and her husband was pleased with her. By the time the beer parlor closed, it seemed right that Roger and Bert go home with them to find out whether or not the toaster really worked.

Roger felt like a kid again as Bert blundered along dark roads following shouted and conflicting directions. Only when Bert brought the car to an ordered halt and they got out did Roger suddenly want to draw back, but he resisted the impulse guiltily, knowing himself to be a snob. The shack they went into was more orderly than the bottle-littered yard they had picked their way through, not clean of course, but there was a cheerful slovenliness about it. The bingo winner cleared dirty dishes from a table and set the new toaster down in the proud center. Then while her husband plugged the toaster into a swinging light bulb socket overhead, she looked for bread. Bert was setting out beer from a carton, and there was also a bottle of whisky which Roger had bought, not wanting to be less generous than the others.

They were all very serious about the toaster, and, when it performed, toast leaping into the air, bouncing onto the table and onto the floor, they were delighted. They drank to the church, to the lucky winner, to the toaster and to themselves.

"Got to get these young fellas girls," the fat woman said. "Can't have a party without girls."

"Too late," Roger protested. "Just get me some jam, that's all."

"Girls," Bert said. "Why not?"

It was three in the morning when the next guest arrived, not two girls as had been hoped, but one, remarkably ugly, her hair still up in curlers, one child asleep in her arms, another trailing behind her in pajamas.

"You're a sport, Sally," the lucky fat woman shouted.

"Had to bring the kids," Sally said.

"Never mind. Put them to bed in the other room."

Roger was very drunk, but just as the deepest sleep couldn't distract him from the need of one of his own children, he could not be indifferent now to what he saw. He stood up unsteadily about to make an indignant protest. At the sight of him, the independent child burst into tears.

"Oh, pack it up, Charlie," Sally said. "Come on, get in here and get to bed."

"I've had enough," Roger said. "Would somebody please phone me a cab?"

"Now don't worry," the prize husband said, "Sal will do for the both of you."

"He doesn't go halves," Bert said. "Call him a cab."

"You don't deserve a toaster," Roger said with great dignity before he walked out of the shack and waited in Bert's car until the cab arrived.

Five hundred miles is a long way to drive with a bad hangover, conscience and temper. Roger might have got some ease by feeling as angry and disgusted with Bert as he was with himself. In fact, before they met for a late attempt at breakfast, Roger was planning to take that ease, but Bert was in one of his wry, cheerful moods which made Roger's righteous indignation look more like childish sulking. They had driven more than a hundred miles before Roger risked any moral unpleasantness.

"I keep thinking about those kids," he said.

"Charlie went right off to sleep," Bert said. "You didn't really scare him."

That was not the response Roger had expected. He looked around for what he had been about to say next and couldn't find it.

"So you get a little stupid and you get a little ugly . . . so what? Everybody cuts out one time or another. I don't mind. I just told her you had too much to drink. Nobody's feelings were hurt. Forget it."

Roger was too busy recovering from his indignation to follow this explanation at all well. He said, "You call that cake?"

"Are you kidding?" Bert asked. "Look, I've just said I don't mind saving you from a dog, but let's not pretend I like it, okay?"

"Why didn't you leave when I did?"

"We couldn't both leave, not after she'd got the kids up and come all the way over."

Roger sat with that for several bitterly confusing moments. Bert was telling him he'd been rude. The idea, inconceivable to him, was shocking and simple. From Bert's point of view, Roger had been unkind not only to his host and hostess and that incredibly ugly and irresponsible woman but to Bert.

"How much did it cost you?" Roger asked.

"Keep the quarter," Bert said with a grin. "You had to pay for the cab."

"I'm out about thirty bucks," Roger said.

"Just get me some jam, you said," Bert laughed.

Roger laughed, too, but his head hurt, and so did his stomach as if he had suddenly been swung up-side-down. It was thirty dollars he had to account for, and he had not made a habit of lying to Nancy. An experience increasingly inexplicable to him would be a marriage-threatening disaster to Nancy. She had not agreed to share her life with the sort of man who got drunk with a fat woman, went home with her to try out her toaster, got a whore and two children out of bed at three in the morning and then left Bert to a gallantry Roger could still hardly conceive of. Nancy thought even Archie Bunker was sordid. No explanation, short of being robbed, would be creditable, given this months's bills.

"We should have gone to the bingo game," Roger said glumly.

"Would have cost ten more for the same evening eventually. All roads lead to Rome."

All roads, for Roger, led to home. Even his apprehension did not get in the way of his relief to be out of Bert's car and walking up his own well kept path into the quiet of his sleeping children and the welcome of his wife. He even looked forward to the litany of new domestic catastrophes to restore him to the sane, unlucky man he used to be.

"Oh, honey, you'll never guess what I'm going to do," Nancy said, her arms tight around him.

"What?" he asked.

"I felt so mean after you left. I thought it will be a minor miracle if he ever comes home again . . ."

"Oh, Nancy . . ." He began to protest on her behalf.

"I was talking to Alice, telling her about the hot water heater, the measles, me, and what it must feel like to be you. Anyway, we decided to do something. We're going to have a garage sale."

"What will you sell?" Roger asked, willing to forgive her anything, even his favorite fishing rod.

"Just junk around our houses. And in the process the basement will get cleared out and the shed and the store room, and even the hall closet. The kids can help," she said, as she led him into the kitchen. "We baked you a cake. I'm so glad you're home."

Roger looked at the cake, a misshapen masterpiece of

chocolate energy, and laughed.

"A piece of cake! A piece of cake!"

It was the first thing he'd been able to eat all day, and Nancy poured them both glasses of cold, sweet milk.

"How was your trip?"

The question gave him a twinge, and he did not say, you'll never guess what I did.

"Awful, he answered. "I blew an extra thirty dollars."

"Never mind," Nancy said. "We'll get breathing room."

She wasn't even interested to know what had happened to that thirty dollars. He didn't have to tell her. One day, when he was thirty-five or perhaps forty, he might tell her the story of the pop-up toaster and his asking for jam, and they would both laugh at the boy he'd been, even at thirty. Now he was a man, eating a second piece of cake under his nearly paid for roof, knowing he didn't deserve his luck any more than that woman deserved her toaster.

# A GOOD KID IN A TROUBLED WORLD

"I'd rather have a do-it-yourself nervous breakdown any-way," Cornelia said. "A kit for manic-depressives . . ."

"I think it's too bad your mother doesn't believe in psy-chiatrists," Nigel said in his light, ominous voice.

"I think it's too bad she doesn't believe in liquor. If she did, I could afford all kinds of other things . . ."

"You don't drink all that much," Nigel said, helping himself to more gin. "It's all the money Rick wants. Cornie, that boy . . ."

Nigel was an expert on boys, poor thing. Very different from being an expert with them. Cornelia often wondered why she put up with his long, dyspeptic lectures on the younger generation or his drinking bottles and bottles of her gin or his waspishness about the state of her wardrobe and her psyche. She was sorry for Nigel, and, in fact, he wasn't bad company when he was in a gossipy or reminiscing mood. He occasionally took her out to dinner, which was all right in the winter time when he confronted the public with nothing more than crested blazers and polka dot cravats. In the summer time, the Bermuda shorts that girdled his gour-met belly were enough to keep her cooking for him even when he was in a generous mood.

"Not the sort of man to have around the house," her mother said, just for something to be unpleasant about in

171

the winter, but in the summer, when Rick was home from college, she would say, "He's just another of those bad influences on the boy. It's no wonder Rick locks himself up with a guitar and a room full of spiders."

Cornelia had never been clever at finding good influences, either for herself or for Rick. Truthfully, his own father, if he had lived through the war, would not have been a psychologist's choice, undomesticated genius of bizarre accidents, hilarious, baffled, more lovable than loving. He'd got himself killed for lack of a better solution, of that Correlia was sure. She had been urgently unhappy about it, but unsurprised. And her life was not much changed by it, for marriage hadn't been even a brief interruption of her mother's domination. Middle class soldiers didn't support their wives. His pay became her pension, that little margin between her real liquor bill and the one her mother was willing to pay, as a social necessity in a wicked world. Cornelia should have gone to work or married again or both. She was liberally educated, and she had skills, but not of the lucrative or socially acceptable sort. Plans to play the virginal professionally or open a blacksmith shop were treated not only by her mother but by her friends as whimsical.

"A woman's place is with her child," her mother said.

"Barf," Cornelia answered, out of her mother's hearing.

The trouble was Cornelia loved her child and enjoyed being with him. Because declaring independence from her mother was tangled with declaring independence from him, she did not get around to it. Nor did she get around to finding another husband.

"Lucky fluke I got married at all," she'd say, sprawled in a large chair.

Her friends were the sort to laugh at her rather than give her advice about hair style, make-up, clothes. So many of them were, in any case, suffering from marriage that they were glad of a place to come where it didn't exist, where there was just dear, old Cornie, grumbling and raging about her mother or worrying with great energy and lack of direction about Rick.

"Aside from being nearly blind, knock-kneed and crazy, he's not a bad little kid," she'd say. "But I've got to teach him values, lasting values."

That principle her mother and Cornelia agreed on, but they couldn't agree on any value in particular, and that was a source of nearly as much nerve damaging conversation as the number and kinds of Cornelia's bills. It always came back to the problem of good influences.

Cornelia had known a great many interesting people, even some talented and responsible ones, but those who did not become martyrs to conscience or of politics, tended to alcohol, jail, or suicide.

"It's a troubled world," Cornelia would try to explain, but even she had to admit that her corner of it sometimes seemed more troubled than others, dangerously troubled for a bright child with her short-circuiting nervous system. "Not a system at all, as far as I can figure out. We're proof of the law of the random."

She and Rick shared asthma and Scarlatti and an absorbed slovenliness, which included all their various projects and a number of unlikely pets, spiders being the most persistent variety. She tried to give him those other, more conscious things: a sense of compassion and duty toward minorities, some comprehension of the miraculous.

"Is this faith-in-man or faith-in-God day?" Rick would ask with tiresome irony, which discouraged her.

"Just because things don't always work out . . ."

Like the time she sent him to Friendship Camp and he came home with a skull fracture. Or that week-end with the fake swami who sold her an overpriced Buddha and gave Rick a distinctly unsavory lecture about things of the spirit. And last Christmas vacation, she'd made a really bad mistake, just through scatty-mindedness, talking Rick into going on that civil rights march.

"Isn't there an easier way to go to jail?" he'd wanted to know.

Then he gave in and went in the middle of a late afternoon snow storm. She was awakened at four in the morning by a bitter and bitterly cold son.

"It wasn't a civil rights march," he said. "It was an historical reenactment of Washington's march on the something-or-other. A bunch of history buffs."

"Well, I'm sorry," she said. "I must have read it wrong in the paper."

"Yeah, you must have."

He was in bed with pneumonia on Christmas day. That's why she'd gone ahead and bought the electric guitar to go along with the new microscope and the jeep. What else could she do after he'd said, "I'd burn my draft card for you if I could see well enough and breathe well enough to get one worth burning."

"His father *died* in the last war," Nigel said haughtily, making it sound like an accomplishment. "Patriotism . . ."

Cornelia didn't count the number of times Nigel practiced that speech before he delivered it to Rick in June. Rick pointed out that he had no choice about serving his country, but it was too mild a comment to stem Nigel's rhetoric. Rick's greatest handicap was not his poor eyesight or his uncertain lungs but a weary good humor, which made him victim not only to all Cornelia's friends, but to his grandmother and Cornelia as well. His only retaliation, if so strong a word could be used, came in occasional songs he wrote for his own and sometimes Cornelia's entertainment. Things like, "Nobody ever called my granny Cornie," which forced him into some disrespectful rhymes but never into malice.

"Spiders, my dear boy, are basic," Nigel said, on another of his favorite topics. "Your obsession with them is an insult to your mother."

"She doesn't mind them."

"Of course she does. She hates her own mother."

"Poor, rich old Granny? Oh, no. It would be like trying to hate the bank or the stock exchange."

"What's so difficult about that?" Nigel demanded.

"Well, you have a point, but I don't think Mother's a socialist."

"We were discussing your spiders," Nigel said.

"Would you like to see my new ones?"

"I would not! I can't stand them."

Rick did not go on to make any unpleasant assumptions about Nigel's relationship with his own mother. Instead, he made Nigel an ice cream cone and then asked him about his famous friends. Nigel had known everyone, briefly. Perhaps his basis for being rudely impatient with both Cornelia and Rick was that they could go on putting up with him two or three times a week, year in and year out, when people of character and achievement crossed the street to avoid him.

"I gave a little luncheon the other day," he said, "and simply nobody came."

In that mood, Nigel was nearly intolerable to Rick, who expressed desperation by raising topics calculated to make someone much more tolerant than Nigel threaten to bury the whole generation. But Rick had so little invested in drugs and long hair that he couldn't sustain Nigel's anger for long. Then back Nigel would go to his social sorrows until Rick retreated to his spiders, which required wonder but not sympathy. Or he'd invent another song for himself, "I'm a Drop-out with the Drop-ins."

Cornelia's mother had learned not to drop in. She had her heart to consider. She inspected once a month and otherwise expected to be called upon. Rick minded that requirement less than Cornelia did. He was fond of his grandmother, who provided an abrasive moral sanctuary. There was really very little difference between her pronouncements and Nigel's, except that they were laced with neither gin nor self-pity. "Straight-laced talk and straight-laced tea from my straight-laced granny is enough for me." Along with the generous checks, larger if she had been particularly critical.

"We are being bought," Cornelia protested. "Have you thought of joining the Peace Corps?"

Rick gave her a speechless look before his eyes went back down to his strumming hand.

"Well, anyway, let's go down to the Red Cross and give some blood."

"Whose?" Rick asked, but he went, knowing in advance that his wouldn't do, being hardly adequate for himself.

"I do such bad things to you," Cornelia said. "I'm a lousy mother."

Just for example, she never seemed to be able to get a meal for him at a time when it was reasonable for him to eat it. Breakfast wasn't a problem because he slept through it, but Cornelia could never remember lunch; and dinner, even when she concentrated, hardly ever got to the table before ten in the evening, by which time Rick had either eaten himself past hunger or gone to a movie. He didn't seem to mind, but she did, measuring her boy against all her friends' enormous sons and knowing that she had failed.

After the episode at the Red Cross, Cornelia was full of reforming remorse. She would feed Rick red meat on time. In her zeal she bought too much and decided to ask Nigel as well. It would be good for him to be fed at seven before he was so sleepy with drink that she had to wake him not just between courses but between bites.

Nigel, not used to being invited until he'd already been at the house for several hours, was in an uncommonly good mood, which meant his barbs were less frequent but more accurate. He had dressed specially in a long African shirt, which didn't require trousers, and Rick, to help him with the spirit of the thing, found a record of African chants. Cornelia was actually out in the kitchen at six-forty-five, trying to locate the olive oil, when the door bell rang.

It was her friend, Lucile, who had just, by an act of maternal will, succeeded in dropping her youngest child at the movies. Rick helped her from the front door to a chair as far away from Nigel as possible. None of Cornelia's friends liked each other.

"Lucile would like some rum," he said to his mother, his voice perfectly normal, his eyes crossed to indicate Lucile's present condition.

"How about something to eat, Lucile?" Cornelia suggested.

"I've eaten," Lucile decided. "But don't let me . . . you know . . . innerupt. Ricky, you're a nice boy. What are you doing out of jail? You know my Tom's in jail? In jail. I'm so proud. Did I tell you that, Cornie? About my Tom? Wouldn't take bail, no sir. He wrote me a postcard: 'Dear Mom, The food isn't so good, but I am o.k.' Have you got any rum, Cornie? Just a drop. I won't innerupt. You just go ahead."

"What did Tom do, steal a car?" Nigel asked.

"Certainly not! He hit a policeman. He just went right up and gave him a good sock inna nose."

"Commendable," Nigel said.

"What the hell have you got on, Nigel?"

"This is an African robe," Nigel said.

"Looks like drag to me."

Rick and Cornelia drew in simultaneous asthmatic gasps and wheezed into a duet of suggestions. But Nigel and Lucile had located the two games they wanted to play. Nigel was going to be the big white supremacist, and Lucile was going to be the defender of young manhood against *that* kind of decadence. They obviously couldn't be left alone. Cornelia sat down while Rick went for rum and asthma pills and his guitar. Dinner would have to wait.

Cornelia wasn't drinking, but in her attempt to keep jovial peace between her two guests her speech became as slurred as theirs, her remarks as random, until after an hour had passed she seemed, if anything, drunker than either of her guests. Rick leaned against the wall accompanying the conversation with his guitar, usually softly, shifting from protest to Uncle Tom songs as was appropriate. Sometimes he played into something from the First World War or hummed an Irish ballad. When he couldn't soothe or mute in this way, he would for a moment censor comments with violent strumming. One of these finally irritated Lucile.

"What are you doing, Ricky? What are you trying to prove?"

"We shall overcome . . ." Rick began to sing.

"It's not funny. Tom's in jail. My sister's son is out killing the Viet Cong, and all you do is stay home and sponge off your grandmother and play that silly guitar . . ."

"I've got problems," Rick said, amiably. "It's bad blood, for one thing, but I'm not being funny . . . really. All I've got is a voice . . ." and he began to sing again. "How many roads must a man walk down before they call him a man?"

"Why don't I get us all something to eat?" Cornelia offered.

"I've eaten," Lucile said.

"So have we all," Nigel said, "at one time or another."

"I'm going to cook the dinner."

"Before Lucile resorts to cannibalism after the fashion of her favorite natives," Nigel said, unsteadily pouring himself another drink, "I think it's a good idea."

"Do you want me to do anything?" Rick asked following Cornelia out into the kitchen.

"If we leave them alone, they'll kill each other. But maybe that's the most humane solution. Why should you be a decoy anyway?"

Blank-eyed, Rick gave a professional immitation of a duck.

"Why don't I just tell Lucile to go home?"

"She can't drive," Rick said. "She's got to have something to eat."

"Drunks don't eat."

The door bell rang again. This time it was George, an organist gone wrong in the electronic music center, where he now did nothing but record and tamper with supersonic sounds.

"Listen to this, Rick—where's Cornie?—I want you to hear this," George was saying, already putting a tape on. "You won't believe it. It's originally only two sounds. The natural drift is fantastic."

"Must we?" Nigel asked.

"You'll like it, Nigel," George encouraged, and there was something so ingeniously certain about him that even Nigel could not reply to the wry contrary.

Out in the kitchen, above the boiling and broiling, Cornelia could distinguish the by now familiar sounds of outer space. George would certainly not have eaten. She cut another of the blood building steaks in half. It was nearly nine o'clock. So much for her resolutions. Now along with the sustained and drifting tones, Cornelia heard Rick's voice, singing.

It wasn't just that she was his mother. She was the first to admit that he was half blind, anemic, and crazy. And she hadn't done a good job of what health he had. He would probably never be either in the army or in jail. But whether he could march or not, he could sing. She carried the food into the dining room and then stood to listen, which was what Rick was doing really. He listened, then joined, a voice in communication with the sounds of stars, of engines, of the under sea.

Nigel sat, not asleep as Cornelia would have expected but staring out above the hand that covered the rest of his face into a lunar space of his own. Lucile looked at Rick with the tear-bleared, drowning eyes that kept her conscious in spite of herself. George smiled.

What need did Rick have for blood, eyes, breath for the roads? He was at home with the miraculous. He was generous with this hardest minority of all: Nigel, Lucile, George and herself. Cornelia had had just this sense before and then lost it. Tomorrow there would be another blood drive or march or swami, but just now Rick was still singing.

# SLOGANS

Jessica did not say, "I am dying." She said, "I live from day to day," that cliché of terminal therapy. Some people never did learn to say the word, *cancer*, but nearly everyone could master a slogan.

Already divorced before her first bout, the children all away at school or college, Jessica bought a wig, took a lover, and in the first remission went with him to Europe.

"Serious about him? Of course not," she explained to a friend they visited. "I'm not serious about anything."

After the second bout, she put a pool in at her summer place and then nearly regretted it.

"The children come home not only with lovers but with pets. I am being overrun with dogs and budgies and a bob-tailed cat."

"It's given her permission to be selfish," her critical sister observed.

"She's finally doing what she pleases," explained an admiring friend.

"I live from day to day," was Jessica's only answer.

For some that obviously meant doing what they'd always done, going to work every day or not dropping out of the bridge club or still having everyone for Christmas. For Jessica it meant something quite different, lovers, trips and swimming pools. Finally, at the end of her second remission, when

181

she discovered it was not arthritis in her back but cancer of the spine, she took a trip across the continent to see her birthplace, to attend her twenty-fifth reunion at college, to resurrect old friends who had not been much more than signatures on Christmas cards for years.

"If I'd known you were planning to go to the reunion," Nancy wrote, "I would have planned to go myself," a lie, for not having married, given birth or divorced, Nancy was uncertain what she might say to friends of twenty-five years ago, even if it was also to be Jessica's premature wake. "Come and see me on your way home," she added.

When Jessica accepted her invitation, Nancy tried to remember what kind of a friendship theirs had been. They lived in the same dorm, and they both had clownish reputations, teeth too strong, brows too high to be pretty. So they were funny instead, co-operatively so, setting each other up in song or gag or prank, protecting each other, too, from being thought to be just fools. Jessica had been clever as well, good at winning elections, and Nancy was smart. They were never roommates, never a team, but Jessica was in the crowd Nancy took home for a week of spring skiing, and Nancy was among the few friends Jessica took home singly to keep her holiday company in the house of a much younger sister, reclusive father and put-up-with-it mother, both long since dead of wasting diseases. Nancy's parents were still skiing the slopes, and, if she needed a slogan, it was learning how to live forever.

Jessica and Nancy hadn't much confided in each other, but they came to depend on each other in a casual way, more like sisters than like friends but without sisterly intolerance. Nancy knew first hand about what Jessica called, "the gloom of the ancestral mansion," and Jessica knew that Nancy didn't care a fig about the slopes. "Oh God . . ." they were apt to say to each other just before Christmas holidays.

But one evening, toward the end of their senior year, Nancy went to Jessica's room to borrow a book or check an

assignment and stayed for a cigarette, then another. Jessica
was obviously in a mood she was trying to joke herself out
of.

"Mother says I must simply resign myself to a tailored
exterior. I don't tell her about my underwear. I give half a
dozen pairs of white cotton pants to the Good Will every
year and spend my pocket money on black lace and apricot
ruffles. Do you believe me?"

Jessica opened a bureau drawer to reveal stacks of what
Nancy's mother would have called "whorish" underwear.

"Some people are too rich to worry about being old
maids," Jessica said.

"I won't even be able to afford to marry a poor man."

Had Jessica actually asked Nancy what she was going
to do, or had she, out of embarrassment at Jessica's vul
nerability or some moody need of her own, simply offered
her confession?

"I'm a lesbian. I don't suppose I will marry."

"Oh, God," Jessica said. "What is it about me that people
are always telling me such awful things? Why do I have to
bear it?"

It was years before Nancy again risked a friendship with
that information. It did seem to her that she had taken unfair advantage of Jessica, presumed far too much on her good
will. Jessica hadn't dropped her, but they were both careful,
in the months before graduation, to avoid being alone together.

They had met only once in the years since by accident
on the street in Edinburgh, both there for the same festival,
Nancy with Ann, her lover, and Jessica with her stiff young
husband, George. They were glad to see each other and
raucous about it, like the college girls they had recently been.

"Come help me buy a set of bagpipes," Nancy suggested.
"I've decided I can't have them unless I can manage to play
them."

While an embarrassed Ann and George stood by, Nancy
blew mightily into the instrument they found without being

able to make a sound over Jessica's laughter. Only when Nancy had left the bagpipes on the counter and crossed the shop to consider the kilts, did there come a soft groan of air like a creature expiring.

"That doesn't count," Jessica said firmly.

When they were back in the street, taking their leave of each other, Jessica explained, "We're having to cut our trip short. My father's dying."

Faithfully over the years, they wrote their Christmas notes to each other, Jessica reporting the progress of her children, the success of her husband's business, the move to a city apartment when the last child went to boarding school, Nancy describing her work, the house she and Ann had bought together, the progress of neices and nephews, the health of parents.

They had nothing in common really. What held them to their ritual was the shadow of guilt that one evening had cast over their otherwise easy friendship, Nancy's for her burdensome indiscretion, Jessica's probably for her lack of sympathy. That they had both aged into a more permissive climate made that guilt nothing more than a seasoning for their yearly good will. Yet without it, there would have been no reason for putting a good face on year after year.

Then Jessica divorced, apparently with great relief. She asked Nancy some practical questions about getting a job, and Nancy gave what advice she could, but across a continent and the years, Nancy could not easily imagine with Jessica what she might do. It became obvious that Jessica entertained the idea of a job only to be entertained. When the children weren't at home, she found cruises, courses in art history, and shopping for new clothes enough to occupy her. Probably the post-cancer lover had not been the first. Remembering the underwear, Nancy speculated that he might have been one of many over the years.

Now with a spine of fast multiplying cells which would this time surely kill her, Jessica was crossing the continent and coming for dinner and the night.

Ann was fixing the guest room, twin-bedded now that Nancy's parents preferred it when they were away from their own king-sized. It was an arrangement that suited an increasing number of their friends, a less melodramatic symbol of decline than a visit from a dying friend, but it saddened Nancy simply. She had decided, she wasn't sure why, to bake cookies. Motherly gestures, whatever the occasion, occurred to her more and more often these days. She wondered if she'd ever said, in one of her Christmas notes, that she was white-haired now.

"Are you going to smoke in front of her?" Ann asked.

"I hadn't thought about it," Nancy said, handing Ann a cookie to sample.

Nancy got out the large cookie tin, brought to them once by a would-be lover neither of them had liked, partly for that reason. They had kept the tin because they did like it, a wreath of old fashioned flowers stenciled on the lid, in the center of which was the motto:

> To the House
> of a Friend
> The Road is
> Never long.

It reminded Nancy of the petit-pointed mottos of her great-grandmother and her great-aunts which used to hang in the stairwell of an old summer house. In childhood, Nancy had been surrounded by protective, promising slogans and superstitions, making wishes on everything from a load of hay to the first raspberries of the season, crossing fingers against her own white lies, wearing a small cache of herbs around her neck to ward off germs.

The tin was too large to put on the table unless they had a crowd. Then always someone began to read the verses stenciled on its four sides.

> Monday's child is
> Fair of Face
> Tuesday's child is
> Full of Grace

Nancy could never remember the day she was born. She knew it was one of the hard ones, either "Thursday's child has far to go," or "Saturday's child works hard for a living." It was easy to remember that Ann was Friday's child.

Friends usually didn't know their own days either. Nancy didn't always tell them to look in the back of the phone book where the years were blocked out, in silly dread that someone would discover a Wednesday birthday and be "full of woe."

"I'd better put the cookies on a plate," Nancy decided.

"Doesn't Jessica know?" Ann asked surprised.

"Oh, that, sure, I told her years ago when we were still in college."

The tin was also, of course, an 'in' joke, which was why it had been given them:

> The child that is born
> on the Sabbath Day
> Is bonny, blythe, good
> and gay.

It was Wednesday, not Sunday, from which Nancy wished she could protect Jessica.

Coming toward Nancy through the clutter of people at the baggage claim area, Jessica didn't look as if she needed protection. Though her hair was short and the flesh had begun to fall away from her jaw line, she looked very much like herself. Only when they embraced, a gesture that startled Nancy, could she feel Jessica's thinness under her disguising clothes. Then Jessica was standing her off to look at her.

"I've decided there are two categories of classmates: totally unrecognizable or made up to play the part of a forty-six-year-old woman. You're in category two. That hair's fantastic. Is it a wig?"

"No, my very own."

"So's mine," Jessica said proudly, taking a handful to demonstrate. "But not as distinguished as yours. And mine's a suspicious length. I look like a man recently out of the army or prison."

"You look elegant," Nancy said and meant it.

Jessica hadn't rejected her mother's advice. But the suit she wore, a combination of suede and cashmere, was expensively soft and becoming.

"Do you like it?" Jessica asked, looking down at herself. "It's even more important to divorce a rich man once you've married him. I bought it at Carmel last week."

Claiming her bag, walking to the car, driving home, they talked in their old casual easiness. There were, after all, all those people and those four years they had in common, a larger store than Nancy had imagined, not coming directly from a reunion.

"Vera, do you remember Vera?" Jessica asked. "Sure you do. She was that little blonde who was funny *and* pretty. Well, she's still the belle of the ball. She divorced her husband, got a huge settlement, the house, alimony, and now he's moved back in and wants to marry her again. Nothing doing! She likes him better as a star boarder. She says it's much more romantic and practical, because now she's the only woman he can afford."

"Was Larsen there?" Nancy asked.

"Oh, no. The really colorful ones, the really interesting ones, like Larsen, like you, don't go to reunions."

"Like me?" Nancy asked surprised.

"Being a lesbian by now, even in those conservative circles is, well, admirably scandalous. And then you have a career . . ."

"I call it a job," Nancy answered.

"Well, we weren't trained to have jobs, were we? Not like girls today. Even mine. The college is a different place, you know. No curfew, men in the rooms. Some of our classmates were shocked about that. But I said the only thing that shocked me was how stupid we were to put up with all those rules."

"Do you remember," Nancy said, "when we got campused for a week-end for opening a side door after six o'clock?"

"We'd probably be expelled now. There are locks everywhere, even on the rooms. If you want to go out, even to the library, after dark, you have to call the campus escort," Jessica said.

"What about Dr. Ryan?" Nancy asked.

"She gave the dinner speech. She retires next year. She's *old*, Nancy, dottery."

Once they arrived at the house and Nancy could look directly at Jessica, she saw the sudden death's head strain in Jessica's face.

"Rest?" she asked.

"Yes," Jessica agreed simply.

Jessica was still in the guest room when Ann got home from work.

"How is she?"

"Just the same ... and dying," Nancy answered. "I don't know."

"How are you?"

"Very glad she's come," Nancy said, "and frightened for her."

"Can she talk about it?"

"She hasn't."

They began to prepare dinner together without exchanging the ordinary bits of their separate days.

By the time Jessica joined them she had refreshed herself. She embraced Ann as warmly as she had Nancy, as if to include her in that old friendship though they had met only once.

"No drink, thanks. Do go ahead," she encouraged. "And if you smoke, please smoke. I can't stand the role of Hamlet's ghost."

" 'Swear,' " Nancy intoned dramatically, remembering that they used to say that, not remembering why.

"I also hate to waste time resting," Jessica said. "They'll have to put me in again and do something about me when I get home."

"It must be awful," Nancy said.

"It is," Jessica answered. "Do you know what I hate most? All those articles about the 'cancer personality,' trying to make you feel guilty as well as sick."

"It's the medical profession, passing the buck," Ann said.

"And the friends and relatives. My daughter thinks it's God's wrath for my wicked ways. I said to her, 'Ducky, the only reason I have to die is that we all do. You find me a survivor, and I'll repent.' "

"Why is everyone so stuck on cause and effect, I wonder?" Ann asked.

"A combination of Newtonian physics and Christianity," Nancy suggested, "when we need Einstein and possibly Zen."

"Nobody said anything remotely like that at the reunion," Jessica said, laughing. "Nancy, you don't disappoint me."

Nancy remembered how little anyone at college had ever talked about what interested her, how Jessica had always covered for her accidents of seriousness and turned them into a joke.

"Well, as one of our gallant classmates put it, if divorce makes you a high risk for cancer, at least it lowers the risk of being found chopped in pieces."

"What a ghoulish way of putting it" Nancy said.

"But Josie Enright (she was in one of the hill halls, do you remember?) had that distinction, haven't you heard, and her 'widower' got off scot free," Jessica said.

"It's not the sort of thing that gets into the class newsletter," Nancy said.

"She was in the obits. In the *Quarterly*, not with the gory details. 'Suddenly,' I think it said," Jessica said.

"Is the general consensus against marriage by now?" Ann asked.

"Oh, I don't suppose so: Sore heads tend to congregate. Ninety percent of us were really majoring in marriage after all. The awards go to those getting ready for their silver anniversaries with one pregnant child or child-in-law. On some, smugness is even becoming. Do you remember Judy Framton?"

Nancy nodded as she got up to clear the table.

"Well, she's proto-grandmother of the first category, totally unrecognizable."

"I wouldn't have the courage to go back," Ann said.

"It was fun," Jessica said. "I haven't laughed that much in a long time."

Nancy brought the plate of cookies to the table.

"Home made?" Jessica asked.

"It's what lesbians do when they're alone together," Nancy said.

"Now I wish I'd known *that* before the reunion," Jessica said. "There are still sheltered lives among us. Gosh, I haven't baked cookies in years. Do you remember the enormous chocolate chip cookies they used to make at college? They still do."

Nancy remembered the short-and-thicks, milkshakes you had to eat with a spoon, and fresh orange juice at the college shop.

"I had to buy the whole pitcher of it once," Jessica remembered, "because Donna (she was my roommate) was so hungover she couldn't write her exam without it."

The remembering went on over coffee, which Jessica didn't drink. She and Nancy apologized to Ann, who said she knew some of the stories as well as they did and could even join in on a punch line or two. But Jessica was tiring.

"You have a long trip tomorrow," Nancy said.

"Oh, I know," Jessica said.

Ann and Nancy went into the kitchen to finish loading the dishwasher.

"What about Einstein and Zen?" Ann asked.

"We have to accept the random. We know all the leaves are going to fall, but we have no way of knowing when any particular one . . ."

They heard Jessica coming down the hall to the bathroom. She stopped at the kitchen door.

"I forgot to say about the flowers in my room. They're lovely. Goodnight."

For a few moments they moved around the kitchen without speaking.

Then Nancy said, "Zen masters write death poems. Odd things like:

> Seventy-seven long years
> I've reviled the Scriptures,
> Zen itself. A failure through
> And through, I piss on Brahma."

Ann gave a startled laugh and then said, "Maybe you should have . . ."

Nancy shook her head, "It's just another slogan."

# THE END OF SUMMER

Canchek arrived promptly at eight in the morning in what looked like a new work shirt and trousers, boots that had been carefully cleaned. Even his beard looked freshly laundered. So well covered by hair and cloth, his age was readable only in his eyes, young enough still for consternation and hope.

"Your holiday's done you good," Judith Thornburn said.

"Got her pumped out?" he asked, ignoring her civility in a way she didn't mind. He was a man who didn't like wasting other people's money.

"Yes, they've just left. They couldn't see any cracks in it. Neither could I."

"You looked in it yourself?" he asked, surprised.

"I wanted to know," she answered.

Judith had been waiting for nearly a month to get this last of the summer problems solved before she closed the house for another year. There had been too many of them, a leaky skylight, a failed pump, and finally this seeping septic tank whose pungent odors had driven her guests off the new back terrace with its lovely view. One man had dug down to it.

"It's cracked," he told her. "You'll probably have to get it replaced."

193

When she called Canchek in urgent concern, he said, "I'm going sailing for three weeks. She probably just needs patching. I'll do her when I get back."

There was only one other man who could be called about such things, Thompson, but, once you'd had one work for you, the other wouldn't come back unless you made it clear that you were switching sides. Thompson was an older man, garrulous, who told the widows and grass widows he worked for, "Don't go looking for trouble. Just don't put no paper down her, and don't clean your sinks with nothing to interfere with the natural process. These old places, they don't like to be disturbed, any more than you do. Old plumbing is old plumbing."

"He's a harmless old coot, and at least he's friendly," those who sided with Thompson would say, and they'd add, "And he'll take a neighborly drink and he doesn't still live with his mother.

Canchek wouldn't, and Canchek did. Judith wasn't old enough yet, in her mid-thirties as Canchek was, to appreciate Thompson's vulgarity. And she was a person who liked to look for trouble, get to the bottom of it and solve it. Canchek was her man even if she had to wait.

They walked around the house together, she carrying the trowel she had been using when he arrived.

"I thought I might lift some of the plants if you show me where you have to dig."

"Don't know yet," he said, flashing a light into the tank.

"It's odd," she said. "I even saw the cracks when we uncovered the outside, right about there, and I would have sworn they went right through. Fiberglass isn't that thick."

Canchek blew out his breath harshly before he spoke. "Not cracked," he said, and then he walked down the sodden earth below the tank, "but she's been leaking all right, for quite a while."

"Is that why that plum tree looks so sick?"

"Lost two of my own apples just to run off. Probably." He put a sympathetic hand on the trunk as he looked up to the blackened rather than turning leaves. "They're only drawn to so much water. Not like a man."

Even Canchek people said he was a dour, silent man, but good at what he did, hardworking and reliable. Perhaps that's why she valued these small attempts at conversation. They made her know that Canchek liked her, or at least didn't disapprove of her as she suspected he did a lot of people, even those who chose to be his particular customers. She didn't know why he did. She drank and smoked, both of which would probably be against his beliefs. Nobody seemed quite sure what sect it was he and his mother were the lonely representatives of. He was willing to drive a truck; he even did emergency work on Sunday, but his beard looked more like a religious than a personal choice. Judith knew so little about religious choices, she wasn't sure what anybody believed or was supposed to believe. She was not yet divorced, but the prospect seemed more and more likely. Surely Canchek wouldn't approve of that. He could easily have heard the gossip, if he listened to such things, about the Thornburn woman, out here most of the summer by herself. Husband bought her the place to get her out of the way, as so many of them did. A fancy car, a boat, whatever else she wanted or he wanted for her to show that she was well provided for. He didn't give her the one thing a man ought to give a woman: a child. Maybe, in a world increasingly both careless and frantic about money, Canchek liked her simply because the Thornburns were willing to pay the cost promptly of having things fixed.

"You can save the daisies," he said, pointing. "I'll save only some of the bulbs." Did he notice her regret when he added, "but bulbs just turn up, don't they?"

She wanted to save what flowers she could, but she also felt less guilty about asking him, or anyone, to do such an unpleasant job if she didn't flinch from it herself, and worked along with him.

"Funny thing," Canchek said as he began to dig in the area she'd indicated. "Man's the only animal that doesn't like his own smell."

Judith heard the lines, "And all is seared with trade; bleared, smeared with toil;/And wears man's smudge and shares man's smell." Certainly Hopkins didn't like it.

It was warm enough, now that the early morning fog was burning off, for another workman to take off his shirt. Canchek would not. Judith had to imagine his shoulders, the muscles of his back. She was not so much attracted to him as curious. The skin on her husband's back already began to feel like the skin of a puppy which would grow into a large dog.

Judith supposed he still made love to her the way he still paid the bills, as a responsibility. He hadn't said anything about a divorce yet. When he first became involved with another woman and Judith confronted him, he said he expected her to be civilized about it. In front of him, she was. Alone her hysterical crying fits and destructive rages so humiliated her that he was the last person she'd subject to them. Judith hadn't even spoken to her close friends because her grief and her shame were both so boring and so predictable, as was her fantasy of being his mistress instead of his wife, the one he ran away to. This last summer, in fact, he was occasionally running away from his mistress to Judith or the quiet life she provided at what they called "the cottage." It was a good-sized house, set in some acres of woods, just across the road from the sea. His mistress was not being civilized, or she owned a vicious cat.

"At this point, my dear," said a friend Judith hadn't confided in, "they go back to their wives."

Judith couldn't see why. There were no children for whose sake things should be done. For herself, he didn't any longer seem much of a prize for her good behavior: "Home is the sailor, home from the sea, and the hunter home from the hill." She would never expel him from the world he had paid for, but she would not move out once he'd left either.

"Look," Canchek said. "This must be the crack you saw."

She walked over and looked at the exposed curve of a badly damaged septic tank.

"That's it," she agreed.

"Well, she's not yours. She's another one."

"Really?"

"They must of broken this one putting her in, just smashed her up a bit more and put in this other one."

"Why didn't they take the broken one out?"

"Couldn't be bothered maybe. These guys with machines won't get off them. Some of them don't even own a shovel."

Canchek pulled great pieces of fiberglass out of the soil until he and she could have played at a giant jigsaw puzzle, but he was not interested in the wreckage. He wanted to find out what was leaking. As he dug, he occasionally grunted in discovery and disgust.

"There's no septic field here at all, nothing but some tile and mud. I'll have to get pipe."

He had done enough work around the place for her to know he begrudged any purchase of new material if what was around could be used. Whether it belonged to the rich or the pensioned, money was money.

"We'll need some rocks," he said, kicking about in the tall grass where cultivation ended.

"There's a pile over here," she offered. "They came out of the garden."

He did not look up or acknowledge her offer, intent on his own search which seemed to her odd. Judith would not have looked for rocks like Easter eggs in the field grass.

Canchek grunted and sank down on his haunches, like a hunter checking prints and droppings, only the crest of his dark hair visible among the tassle tops. Then he stood up, shaking his head.

"You know, there's as sure a wrong way to do it as there is a right way. Look at this."

Judith followed his path to where he stood, and there spreading out beside him was a sprawling pile of stones nearly uniform in size, hidden in the tall grass. She remembered having seen it in spring, matted over with last year's rot before new grass began to grow again.

"Why do they even dump it on the site if they don't intend to use it?" he asked himself and then gave his answer. "They call in the inspector just before they're going to lay the pipe. He sees the trenches. He sees the pile of rock, says, 'Okay, boys, that's good.' And the minute he turns his back, they bulldoze the trenches and go home. What did I tell you? Not a shovel to their name!"

It was a long speech for Canchek. He walked over to the collapsed septic tank and dragged it over to his van.

"I'll take this to the dump on my way to get the pipe," he said.

"You can fix it then?" she asked.

"Sure, today," he answered and smiled at her slumping relief.

Judith had had her frugal lunch before Canchek returned, knowing he would have stopped for a man's lunch with his mother, a woman Judith had never met. Mrs. Canchek spoke only enough English to call her son to the phone or say when he would be back. As far as Judith knew, she never left the place, a well-made log cabin in a clearing as neat and bare as a table top between meals. Canchek did their shopping. Occasionally Mrs. Canchek could be seen behind the high deer fence around the vegetable garden, hoeing, drab kerchief around her head, skirts to the ground, a peasant in a painting. There were neither chickens nor dog to keep her company. The only sign of companionability was a bird feeder outside what was probably a kitchen window. No one was ever invited in.

Judith did not go out at once to greet him. She stayed at her own kitchen table and watched him work, shoveling new trenches away from the uncovered septic tank, like fingers stretching away from a palm, down hill. It was hot now, and, though the tank had been emptied, the soil he dug in must be putrid with clogging waste. Yet he was taking time, like a man not reckoning the hours, to sift what good

bulbs he found and pile them for her to replant in the restored bed. As son to woman, obedient to her love of
flowers, though there were none in his own beaten and swept
yard. Was he, in fact, good to his mother? Or did he go home
and sit sullen with the burden she was to him and let her
bring him servile offerings?

The phone rang. Judith let it ring six times before she
answered it.

"Outdoors, were you?" her husband asked, his dictating
cheerfulness always freshly insulting her.

Judith wanted to answer truthfully, but instead said,
"I'm digging out the septic tank with Canchek."

"My God, Judy, martyrdom doesn't have to go that
far. Surely, the man is paid enough—If I recall the last bill
correctly—to do it himself."

"I wanted to save the bulbs," she answered defensively.

"Buy more; buy a carload."

Is there any point? Is there going to be a next year, she
wanted to ask him, but she didn't.

"One of the reasons Canchek's so expensive is that he's
too cheap to buy himself machinery. Is he out there with a
shovel? I bet he is."

"He says it's the only way to do it properly," Judith
answered.

"Once a shit shoveler, always a shit shoveler. Is he going
to get it done by the week-end?"

"He said he'd be finished today."

"Good. I'll be down then, tomorrow."

"Driving?"

"No, I'm beat. I'll take the early train."

He didn't ask her to meet him any more than he would
ask to come down. At first, she had canceled whatever other
plans she had made either to go out, which he wouldn't want
to do, or have friends in, because she didn't trust herself to
keep up the facade with an attentive audience. Lately, she
had not made week-end plans, a time she spent either in relieved loneliness or in nervous dread that this would be the

last time. By now, she was equally afraid that he would decide to re-establish himself in their life or end it.

Canchek was now kneeling, replacing the terracotta tiles he had dug up. It would have been no use or terrible use to have had a son, if not materially bound to her as Canchek was to his mother, still guilty to leave her as his father had done before him. People said it was harder for a man to leave when there were children. Was it? Sometimes Judith imagined her husband regretting his refusal to be a father, easier to leave her in children's distracting company than alone. But that allowed him some concern for her feelings. He didn't want to know she had any.

Canchek was now laying the long black perforated pipe along a trench, his feet planted on either side, walking backwards. She envied him a task to be absorbed in, then remembered the stench of it for a man whose only known pleasure was sailing, the freshening breeze taking him far out from shore until salt purified the odors of earth and the far horizon promised nothing, nothing at all.

He was standing at the back door.

"Have you got a bucket?" he asked.

His eyes were darker than they had been in the morning, as if they had absorbed the color of earth. He had put on a sweat band. It pressed at his hairline, forcing his hair to stand up like a dark crop.

She found two buckets and went out with him to gather stones from the pile he had found. A wheelbarrow would have been more efficient, and there was one in the garden shed, but she did not want to think her husband's thoughts. A breeze had come up from shore with the faintest bite of autumn in it, cooling the afternoon, making their harvesting of rock easier. Sometimes he stopped to shovel dirt over the rock they had strewn, leaving her to haul by herself, and alone with her own job she felt more companionable with him, as if he accepted a simple partnership.

It was nearly six o'clock when they finished, the light nearly gone. She washed out the buckets while he collected scraps and tools.

"May I get you something?" Judith asked. "Coffee? A cold drink?"

"Fill her up as soon as you can," he said. "I'll cover her up tomorrow, some time before dark."

She nodded but waited, keeping the question between them.

"Her," he said finally, nodding his head in a homeward direction.

An apology, an excuse. Was that how her husband left his woman with that grunted female pronoun and a nod in the direction of the sea? Perhaps Canchek preferred a mother to a woman with more ambiguous needs and motives. Nothing bound him really but his acceptance of the bond.

"Thank you," she said. "I'm so glad it could be done."

"There's always a way to do it right," he said.

Canchek had not returned by the time Judith left to meet her husband's train. There was still an hour of daylight. To defend Canchek, she wanted him to have come and gone before she returned. For herself, she wanted him to be there when she got back, she couldn't say why. Canchek could not prevent anything from happening or make it happen, a dark figure in the dusk, shoveling.

"He doesn't look quite human," her husband observed out the kitchen window, pouring himself a drink.

"He said yesterday, 'Man's the only animal that doesn't like his own smell.' "

"What's that supposed to mean?" her husband asked.

"Just that, to him," Judith answered.

"To you?" her husband asked, and she heard in his tone what she had been waiting for, hopefully, then dreadfully, for months.

"A reason for being civilized?" she suggested mildly.

He took a long drink and set the glass down. There wasn't a trace of summer in his face, of sea or earth. He was bleached with tiredness. She couldn't offer him anything either. He had, in his own house, helped himself.

"I've appreciated it," he said flatly.

The months' long fuse of her fury sputtered up toward an explosion right behind her eyes. The second before it ignited, Canchek's fist on the back door banged it out.

"She's done," he said.

"Come have a drink," Judith's husband suggested, humanly enough, "after a stinking job like that."

But Canchek had turned away quickly after his announcement and was gone. Judith stood in the doorway, looking out at the buried tank, its now secret fingers also properly rock-and-earth-covered, the surface carefully raked to prepare for bulbs, the old ones Canchek had saved and the carload her husband wanted her to buy. They would camouflage and be nourished by man's "smudge and smell," which Canchek, and perhaps all men, called by the name of "she," as they did ships which would bear them away. Judith turned back to her husband.

"Thank you," he said.

"You're welcome," Judith answered, seeing him for the first time in months as clearly as she saw Canchek, but this man was her husband, at home.

# THE PRUNING OF THE APPLE TREES

"He wants to move back in," Edna said to her friend Dorothy over a diet Pepsi.

They sat in Edna's backyard, a patch of flat ground scarred by an abandoned sandbox and a half collapsed dog run. By the garage there was a cracking, grass-threatened square of concrete, poured by enthusiastic amateurs as a basket shooting court only a few years ago. Half of the now derelict vegetable garden had been sacrificed to it. Two aging and neglected apple trees had survived, and here and there minor attempts had been made at clean-up and restoration. Some rather hard-done-by snapdragons bloomed dustily by the fence, and there was a young azalea bush by the back steps, but much remained to be done to make the yard the grandmotherly retreat it could have been.

"Did he say why?" Dorothy asked.

"She's too young for him, too demanding. She doesn't do his laundry."

"He didn't actually say that!"

"No," Edna admitted. "He said he missed the children. I said, 'I do, too.' He doesn't even remember they've all gone."

"Did he say he missed you?"

"His courage failed him," Edna said, laughing. "What do

you suppose is the matter with me? I can't even be angry with him."

"You don't want him back after all this time, do you?" Dorothy asked.

"Oh, he'd be like something to wear to a party, on the positive side."

"At my college reunion last year, the woman who was the star of the occasion had divorced her husband, got a whopping settlement as well as alimony, and now her ex has moved back in with her, but she won't marry him again. She likes it just as it is being the lady of the house with a star border."

"Are they happy?"

"Obviously, she is," Dorothy said.

"Charlie has never asked for a divorce," Edna said.

"You're protection, after all," Dorothy said. "Men don't want to remarry any more than they want to marry in the first place, do they?"

"I guess not," Edna said.

She had not been bold enough to trap Charlie into marriage. She'd begun to talk about traveling, maybe even innocently until she discovered how angry the idea made that normally mild mannered young man.

"You girls!" he had said, in real fury. "You don't worry about careers or saving money. You just work a while until you've got enough to take off, and then you say men have all the freedom."

"Would you like to travel?" she asked him.

"That's like asking would I like a million dollars. Who wouldn't?"

It wasn't for Charlie a desire but a taunting impossibility, like being a famous athlete or the prime minister.

"What would somebody like you get out of it, anyway?" he asked later. "You haven't even mastered another language."

Charlie was mastering French as well as studying to pass examinations to become a chartered accountant. Edna was

more touched by his seriousness than offended by his scorn.
He was quite right really. She hadn't the ambition to master
anything.

"I could go to England," she suggested.

"You'd never figure out how to cross the street, never
mind the money."

"There's this tour of Scotland, Ireland, and England," she
persisted.

"It costs two thousand dollars!" he said, outraged.

"Well. I've got two thousand dollars."

"That's nearly enough for a down payment on a house."

"So?"

"If you think you can go off on a trip like that, blow
all your savings, and then come home and . . . and dump
yourself on me . . ."

Edna focused again on her friend Dorothy and said,
"He married me for my money," and laughed. "Two thousand dollars! Mind you, in those days it was nearly enough
for a down payment on a house . . . this house."

They both turned to look at it, a comfortably aging large
stucco box.

"You could get a couple of hundred thousand dollars for
it now, do you know that?" Dorothy asked.

"I suppose so," Edna said.

Charlie hadn't left until the mortgage was paid, just after
his fiftieth birthday.

"A hundred and sixty dollars a month, the payments
were," Edna said. "You couldn't rent a room with that
now."

"You don't have to have him back, you know," Dorothy
said. "You're not obligated. Five years is a bit long for these
casual affairs modern marriages are supposed to accom-
modate so easily. It's even legally desertion by now."

"The war separated some people nearly that long," Edna
mused.

"The war!"

"Charlie's older brother was in the war. He said to me

once, not long after Charlie left, he thought that was maybe what was wrong with Charlie, that he'd just never been anywhere or done anything."

"Who has?" Dorothy asked. "Gus and I went to Palm Springs once, and he didn't like it."

"Oh, Gus!"

"Well, he's no more of a stick-in-the-mud than Charlie used to be. I tell you, I watched him pretty closely for a while there," Dorothy confessed.

Edna didn't say that she'd watched Charlie, too. To this day she didn't know whether Joan had caused his diet or the diet Joan. Edna had, of course, been pleased that he was losing weight though finally he looked haggard rather than healthy. She had even suggested a holiday, somewhere in the sun where he could show off his new trimness and at the same time get some color back into his face.

"Accountants don't take winter holidays," he'd snapped. "You should have married a lawyer if you wanted a winter tan."

She didn't say it was his vanity rather than her own she was trying to cater to. Charlie wasn't ordinarily a bad tempered man. Only great strain or risk made him rude as he was when he had proposed. Edna did not realize he was working himself up to another kind of proposal, and not to her.

"What's so unfair," Dorothy said, "is that they do all the things they claim to hate once they find someone else, liking going out to dinner or mowing the lawn. Gus has a friend who baby-sits his woman's kids while she goes out to a movie. They aren't even his. His own he wouldn't even *take* to a movie."

"Charlie was a pertty good father. He doesn't see any of them now."

"Well, he's not shameless, but that's not much good to the kids, is it?"

"They're at an age where parents are chiefly an embarrassment anyway. I wouldn't be surprised if the boys don't secretly a bit admire him, 'Look what the old duffer had the gumption to do.' "

"Oh, no!" Dorothy said. "Maybe they don't write or phone as often as they should, but those are loyal boys, Edna."

Loyal. That's a word she would have used to describe Charlie for all those years. What on earth did it mean? That she could count on him not to make rude remarks about her cooking in front of the children or guests? Well, she could, but what she meant was something more like standing by her or the kids, no matter what, really *no matter what.*

"They get it from their father," Edna said.

"Don't be sarcastic about your own kids."

"I'm not," Edna said. "I could just as easily call Charlie as either of the boys if I ever needed anything."

"But you don't."

"No," Edna said. "I haven't asked Charlie for anything, but he saw the kids through college even if he didn't see them, and he sent me the same housekeeping money even after they left until I sent some of it back. I couldn't eat like four horses."

"So now he can afford to take her out to dinner. Doesn't that make you mad?"

"Not any more. If you want to know the truth, I didn't exactly feel sorry for him. I felt guilty."

"Now that's the living end!" Dorothy said. "It's all your fault, right? You bought the wrong underwear. You gave him ring-around-the-collar. You didn't flatter him more than ten times a day. How many times do you have to tell a man that bald is sexy?"

"I never flattered Charlie. It's the one thing we fought about. He was so easily flattered by anybody. His head was just like a balloon. One little puff of hot air, and you could see it begin to swell. We argued about it so often we couldn't be bothered finally to go over it all again. I'd say, 'Don't be so easily flattered by the world,' and he'd say, 'Don't be so easily offended by it.' And then we'd laugh."

"Gus is one great arguer. All he ever says is 'Period.' "

"So maybe I should have." Edna said.

"Should have what?"

"Told him what a great guy he was."

"Now's kind of a hard time to begin," Dorothy suggested.

"We'd both die of embarrassment," Edna said.

"What did you say to him?"

Edna stared out into the apple trees. "I didn't."

He hadn't, of course, said anything at all about Joan except that he wasn't any longer living with her, and it was petty of Edna to want to know why, who left whom, for all the day-dreaming reasons she had spent the first two years of their separation concocting. Anyway, she knew perfectly well Charlie hadn't left Joan. Charlie hadn't left Edna. She'd thrown him out. She hadn't even given him that impossible option, "Choose!" Nor bothered with the rhetorical question, "How could you?"

There was nothing for him to explain to her then or now. It was his stupid vanity. And had that changed? Not likely. Faults like that got worse, not better. Unless, of course, Joan had taught him a real lesson, been the selfish bitch Edna had prayed she was, really *hadn't* done his laundry.

"Do you know what I can't stand about any of this?" Edna demanded of Dorothy. "Everything I've thought and felt for the last five years is so ordinary, and that's awful."

"There's ordinary good and there's ordinary awful," Dorothy said. "Ordinary good says Gus wants his dinner on time."

And ordinary awful, Edna thought, as she went into her own kitchen, is that I don't care when I eat or what. She suspected Charlie, methodical and disciplined as he was, was probably better at living alone than she was. She had a sudden and ridiculous image of him cooking a solitary hamburger on a small hibachi on his studio apartment balcony in an apron that said, "Boss." Their large family barbecue sat rusting in the garage, moved there by one of the boys because she couldn't stand the sight of it. She'd had his chair in the living room moved to the basement as well.

Right now Dorothy and Gus were sitting down together to dinner, and Dorothy was saying to Gus, "You're not going to believe this: Charlie's come crawling home, and I think she's going to let that bastard back in, after *five years.*"

Why, after all, did he want to come home? He missed being something more than a cheque book to the children, but he could change that without her. He said the house needed painting. She said what it probably needed was to be put up for sale.

"What are your plans, Edna?" he asked.

"I don't know. Maybe it's time I took that trip to Europe."

"Maybe we could go together," he said, "now that the kids are through college."

He wasn't looking at her. He was figuring out that it had been five years since the apple trees had been pruned.

"Why don't I come over next Sunday and do a bit of work around here?"

Edna scrambled herself some eggs, ate a whole tomato and a carrot, finished off with a digestive biscuit, distracting herself with planning Sunday's menu.

Maybe he was as tired of being a villain as she was of being a wronged woman. But that's what they were, and how did they ever get past that? Wouldn't they just begin saying all over again, "How could you be so vain?" and "Why do you have to be so offended?" She used to think that a marriage with only one basic argument was a pretty remarkable thing, as long as there was loyalty, as long as *no matter what . . .*

"I kicked the bugger out," she said into her coffee cup, "and alienated his kids and bad mouthed him to our friends."

What was so boring, ordinary, and impossible was not the argument but being left with only one side of it endlessly repeating in her head.

"Charlie," she said into the phone, "why do you want to

come home?"

"Because I flatter myself with the hope that you want me to," he said.

"You can do that for yourself now?"

"Maybe it's just a gimmick," he admitted.

Edna was tempted to say, maybe it wasn't, because she'd certainly learned to offend herself in the last five years, no help from anyone. But she had a more important confession to make.

"I do, Charlie," Edna said. "I do want you home."

# INLAND PASSAGE

"The other lady . . ." the ship's steward began.

"We're not together," a quiet but determined female voice explained from the corridor, one hand thrust through the doorway insisting that he take her independent tip for the bag he had just deposited on the lower bunk.

There was not room for Troy McFadden to step into the cabin until the steward had left.

"It's awfully small," Fidelity Munroe, the first occupant of the cabin, confirmed, shrinking down into her oversized duffle coat.

"It will do if we take turns," Troy McFadden decided. "I'll let you settle first, shall I?"

"I just need a place to put my bag."

The upper bunk was bolted against the cabin ceiling to leave headroom for anyone wanting to sit on the narrow upholstered bench below.

"Under my bunk," Troy McFadden suggested.

There was no other place. The single chair in the cabin was shoved in under the small, square table, and the floor of the minute closet was taken up with life jackets. The bathroom whose door Troy McFadden opened to inspect, had a coverless toilet, sink and triangle of a shower. The one hook on the back of the door might make dressing there possible. When she stepped back into the cabin, she bumped into

211

Fidelity Munroe, crouching down to stow her bag.

"I'm sorry," Fidelity said, standing up, "But I can get out now."

"Let's both get out."

They sidled along the narrow corridor, giving room to other passengers in search of their staterooms.

Glancing into one open door, Troy McFadden said, "At least we have a window."

"Deck?" Fidelity suggested.

"Oh, yes."

Neither had taken off her coat. They had to shoulder the heavy door together before they could step out into the moist sea air. Their way was blocked to the raised prow of the ship where they might otherwise have watched the cars, campers, and trucks being loaded. They turned instead and walked to the stern of the ferry to find rows of wet, white empty benches facing blankly out to sea.

"You can't even see the Gulf Islands this morning," Troy McFadden observed.

"Are you from around here?"

"Yes, from North Vancouver. We should introduce ourselves, shouldn't we?"

"I'm Fidelity Munroe. Everyone calls me Fido."

"I'm Troy McFadden, and nearly everyone calls me Mrs. McFadden."

They looked at each other uncertainly, and then both women laughed.

"Are you going all the way to Prince Rupert?" Fidelity asked.

"And back, just for the ride."

"So am I. Are we going to see a thing?"

"It doesn't look like it," Troy McFadden admitted. "I'm told you rarely do on this trip. You sail into mist and maybe get an occasional glimpse of forest or the near shore of an island. Mostly you seem to be going nowhere."

"Then why . . . ?"

"For that reason, I suppose," Troy McFadden answered,

gathering her fur collar more closely around her ears.

"I was told it rarely gets rough," Fidelity Munroe offered.

"We're in open sea only two hours each way. All the rest is inland passage."

"You've been before then."

"No," Troy McFadden said. "I've heard about it for years."

"So have I, but I live in Toronto. There you hear it's beautiful."

"*Mrs.* Munroe?"

"Only technically," Fidelity answered.

"I don't think I can call you Fido."

"It's no more ridiculous than Fidelity once you get used to it."

"Does your mother call you Fido?"

"My mother hasn't spoken to me for years," Fidelity Munroe answered.

Two other passengers, a couple in their agile seventies, joined them on the deck.

"Well . . ." Troy McFadden said, in no one's direction, "I think I'll get my bearings."

She turned away, a woman who did not look as if she ever lost her bearings.

*You're not really old enough to be my mother,* Fidelity wanted to call after her, *Why take offense?* But it wasn't just that remark. Troy McFadden would be as daunted as Fidelity by such sudden intimacy, the risk of its smells as much as its other disclosures. She would be saying to herself, *I'm too old for this. Why on earth didn't I spend the extra thirty dollars?* Or she was on her way to the purser to see if she might be moved, if not into a single cabin then into one with someone less . . . more . . .

Fidelity looked down at Gail's much too large duffle coat, her own jeans and hiking boots. Well, there wasn't room for the boots in her suitcase, and, ridiculous as they might look for walking the few yards of deck, they might be very useful for exploring the places the ship docked.

*Up yours, Mrs. McFadden, with your fur collar and your
expensive, sensible shoes and matching bag. Take up the
whole damned cabin!*

All Fidelity needed for this mist-bound mistake of a
cruise was a book out of her suitcase. She could sleep in
the lounge along with the kids and the Indians, leave the
staterooms (what a term!) to the geriatrics and Mrs.
McFadden.

Fidelity wrenched the door open with her own strength,
stomped back along the corridor like one of the invading
troops, and unlocked and opened the cabin door in one
gesture. There sat Troy McFadden, in surprised tears.

"I'm sorry . . ." Fidelity began, but she could not make
her body retreat.

Instead she wedged herself around the door and closed
it behind her. Then she sat down beside Troy McFadden,
took her hand, and stared quietly at their unlikely pairs of
feet. A shadow passed across the window. Fidelity looked
up to meet the eyes of another passenger glancing in. She
reached up with her free hand and pulled the small curtain
across the window.

"I simply can't impose . . ." Troy finally brought herself
to say.

"Look," Fidelity said, turning to her companion, "I
may cry most of the way myself . . . it doesn't matter."

"I just can't make myself . . . walk into those public
rooms . . . alone."

"How long have you been alone?" Fidelity asked.

"My husband died nearly two years ago . . . there's no
excuse."

"Somebody said to me the other day, 'Shame's the last
stage of grief.' 'What a rotten arrangement then,' I said. 'To
be ashamed for the rest of my life.' "

"You've lost your husband?"

Fidelity shook her head, "Years ago. I divorced him."

"You hardly look old enough . . ."

"I know, but I am. I'm forty-one. I've got two grown daughters."

"I have two sons," Troy said. "One offered to pay for this trip just to get me out of town for a few days. The other thought I should lend him the money instead."

"And you'd rather have?"

"It's so humiliating," Troy said.

"To be alone?"

"To be afraid."

The ship's horn sounded.

"We're about to sail," Troy said. "I didn't even have the courage to get off the ship, and here I am, making you sit in the dark . . ."

"Shall we go out and get our bearings together?"

"Let me put my face back on," Troy said.

Only then did Fidelity let go of her hand so that she could take her matching handbag into the tiny bathroom and smoothe courage back into her quite handsome and appealing face.

Fidelity pulled her bag out from under the bunk, opened it and got out her own sensible shoes. If she was going to offer this woman any sort of reassurance, she must make what gestures she could to be a bird of her feather.

The prow of the ship had been lowered and secured, and the reverse engines had ceased their vibrating by the time the two women joined the bundled passengers on deck to see, to everyone's amazement, the sun breaking through, an ache to the eyes on the shining water.

Troy McFadden reached for her sunglasses. Fidelity Munroe had forgotten hers.

"This is your captain," said an intimate male voice from a not very loud speaker just above their heads. "We are sailing into a fair day."

The shoreline they had left remained hidden in clouds crowded up against the Vancouver mountains, but the long wooded line of Galiano Island and beyond it to the west the mountains of Vancouver Island lay in a clarity of light.

"I'm hungry," Fidelity announced. "I didn't get up in time to have breakfast."

"I couldn't eat," Troy confessed.

When she hesitated at the entrance to the cafeteria, Fidelity took her arm firmly and directed her into the short line that had formed.

"Look at that!" Fidelity said with pleasure. "Sausages, ham, bacon, pancakes. How much can we have?"

"As much as you want," answered the young woman behind the counter.

"Oh, am I ever going to pig out on this trip!"

Troy took a bran muffin, apple juice and a cup of tea.

"It isn't fair," she said as they unloaded their contrasting trays at a window table. "My husband could eat like that, too, and never gain a pound."

Fidelity, having taken off her coat, revealed just how light bodied she was.

"My kids call me bird bones. They have their father to thank for being human size. People think I'm their little brother."

"Once children tower over you, being their mother is an odd business," Troy mused.

"That beautiful white hair must help," Fidelity said.

"I've had it since I was twenty-five. When the boys were little, people thought I was their grandmother."

"I suppose only famous people are mistaken for themselves in public," Fidelity said, around a mouthful of sausage; so she checked herself and chewed instead of elaborating on that observation.

"Which is horrible in its way, too, I suppose," Troy said.

Fidelity swallowed. "I don't know. I've sometimes thought I'd like it: Mighty Mouse fantasies."

She saw Troy try to smile and for a second lose the trembling control of her face. She hadn't touched her food.

"Drink your juice," Fidelity said, in the no-nonsense, cheerful voice of motherhood.

Troy's dutiful hand shook as she raised the glass to her

lips, but she took a sip. She returned the glass to the table without accident and took up the much less dangerous bran muffin.

"I would like to be invisible," Troy said, a rueful apology in her voice.

"Well, we really are, aren't we?" Fidelity asked. "Except to a few people."

"Have you traveled alone a lot?"

"No," Fidelity said, "just about never. I had the girls, and they're still only semi-independent. And I had a friend, Gail. She and I took trips together. She died last year."

"I'm so sorry."

"Me, too. It's a bit like being a widow, I guess, except, nobody expects it to be. Maybe that helps."

"Did you live with Gail?"

"No, but we thought maybe we might . . . someday." Troy sighed.

"So here we both are at someday," Fidelity said. "Day one of someday and not a bad day at that."

They both looked out at the coast, ridge after ridge of tall trees, behind which were sudden glimpses of high peaks of snow-capped mountains.

Back on the deck other people had also ventured, dressed and hatted against the wind, armed with binoculars for sighting of eagles and killer whales, for inspecting the crews of fishing boats, tugs, and pleasure craft.

"I never could use those things," Fidelity confessed. "It's not just my eyes. I feel like that woman in the Colville painting."

"Do you like his work?" Troy asked.

"I admire it," Fidelity said. "There's something a bit sinister about it: all those figures seem prisoners of normality. That woman at the shore, about to get into the car . . ."

"With the children, yes," Troy said. "They seem so vulnerable."

"Here's Jonathan Seagull!" a woman called to her

binocular-blinded husband, "Right here on the rail."

"I loathed that book," Troy murmured to Fidelity.

Fidelity chuckled. "In the first place, I'm no friend to seagulls."

Finally chilled, the two women went back inside. At the door to the largest lounge, again Troy hesitated.

"Take my arm," Fidelity said, wishing it and she were more substantial.

They walked the full length of that lounge and on into the smaller space of the gift shop where Troy was distracted from her nerves by postcards, travel books, toys and souvenirs.

Fidelity quickly picked up half a dozen postcards.

"I'd get home before they would," Troy said.

"I probably will, too, but everybody likes mail."

From the gift shop, they found their way to the forward lounge where tv sets would later offer a movie, on into the children's playroom, a glassed-in area heavily padded where several toddlers tumbled and stumbled about.

"It's like an aquarium," Fidelity said.

"There aren't many children aboard."

"One of the blessings of traveling in October," Fidelity said. "Oh, I don't feel about kids the way I do about seagulls, but they aren't a holiday."

"No," Troy agreed. "I suppose I really just think I miss mine."

Beyond the playroom they found the bar with only three tables of prelunch drinkers. Troy looked in, shook her head firmly and retreated.

"Not a drinker?" Fidelity asked.

"I have a bottle of scotch in my case," Troy said. "I don't think I could ever . . . alone . . ."

"Mrs. McFadden," Fidelity said, taking her arm, "I'm going to make a hard point. You're not alone. You're with me, and we're both old enough to be grandmothers, and we're approching the turn of the 21st not the 20th century, and I think we both could use a drink."

Troy McFadden allowed herself to be steered into the bar and settled at a table, but, when the waiter came, she only looked at her hands.

"Sherry," Fidelity decided. "Two sherries," and burst out laughing.

Troy looked over at her, puzzled.

"Sherry is my idea of what you would order. I've never tasted it in my life."

"You're quite right," Troy said. "Am I such a cliché?"

"Not a cliché, an ideal. I don't know, maybe they're the same thing when it comes down to it. You have style. I really admire that. If I ever got it together enough to have shoes and maatching handbag, I'd lose one of the shoes."

"Is that really your coat?" Troy asked.

Fidelity looked down at herself. "No, it belonged to Gail. It's my Linus blanket."

"I've been sleeping in my husband's old pajamas. I had to buy a nightgown to come on this trip," Troy confided. "I think it's marvelous the way you do what you want."

Fidelity bit her lip and screwed her face tight for a moment. Then she said, "But I don't want to cry any more than you do."

The waiter put their sherries before them, and Fidelity put a crumpled ten dollar bill on the table.

"Oh, you should let me," Troy said, reaching for her purse.

"Next round," Fidelity said.

Troy handled her glass more confidently than she had at breakfast, and, after her first sip, she said with relief, "Dry."

"This is your captain," the intimate male voice asserted again. "A pod of killer whales is approaching to starboard."

Fidelity and Troy looked out the window and waited. No more than a hundred yards away, a killer whale broke the water, then another, then another, their black backs arching, their bellies unbelievably white.

"They don't look real," Fidelity exclaimed.

Then one surfaced right alongside the ferry, and both women caught their breath.

"This trip is beginning to feel less like somebody else's day dream," Fidelity said. "Just look at that!"

For some moments after the whales had passed, the women continued to watch the water, newly interested in its possibilities for surprise. As if as a special reward for their attention, an enormous bird dropped out of the sky straight into the sea, then lifted off the water with a strain of great wings, a flash of fish in its talons.

"What on earth was that?" Fidelity cried.

"A bald eagle catching a salmon," Troy replied.

The ship had slowed to navigate a quite narrow passage between the mainland and a small island, its northern crescent shore fingered with docks, reached by flights of steps going back up into the trees where the glint of windows and an occasional line of roof could be seen.

"Do people live there all year long?" Fidelity asked.

"Not many. They're summer places mostly."

"How do people get there?"

"Private boats or small planes."

"Ain't the rich wealthy?" Fidelity sighed.

Troy frowned.

"Did I make a personal remark by mistake?"

"Geoff and I had a place when the boys were growing up. We didn't *have* money, but he earned a good deal . . . law. He hadn't got around to thinking about . . . retiring. I'm just awfully grateful the boys had finished their education. It scares me to think what it might have been like if it had happened earlier. You just don't think . . . we didn't any- way. Oh, now that I've sold the house, I'm perfectly com- fortable. When you're just one person . . ."

"Well, on this trip with the food all paid for, I'm going to eat like an army," Fidelity said. "Let's have lunch."

Though the ship wasn't crowded, there were more people in the cafeteria than there had been for breakfast.

"Let's not sit near the Jonathan Seagulls," Fidelity said,

leading the way through the tables to a quiet corner where they could do more watching than being watched. Troy had chosen a seafood salad that Fidelity considered a first course to which she added a plate of lamb chops, rice and green beans.

"I really don't believe you could eat like that all the time," Troy said.

"Would if I could."

Fidelity tried not to let greed entirely overtake her, yet she needed to eat quickly not to leave Troy with nothing to do.

"See those two over there?" Fidelity said, nodding to a nondescript pair of middle-aged women. "One's a lady cop. The other's her prisoner."

"How did you figure that out?"

"Saw the handcuffs, That's why they're sitting side by side."

"They're both right handed," Troy observed critically.

"On their ankles."

"What's she done?"

"Blown up a mortgage company," Fidelity said.

"She ought to get a medal."

"A fellow anarchist, are you?"

"Only armchair," Troy admitted modestly.

"Mrs. McFadden, you're a fun lady. I'm glad we got assigned to the same shoe box."

"Do call me Troy."

"Only if you'll call me Fido."

"Will you promise not to bark?"

"No," Fidelity said and growled convincingly at a lamb chop but quietly enough not to attract attention.

"Fido, would it both antisocial and selfish of me to take a rest after lunch?"

"Of course not," Fidelity said. "I'll just come up and snag a book."

"Then later you could have a rest."

"I'm not good at them," Fidelity said. "I twitch and have

horrible dreams if I sleep during the day. But, look, I do have to know a few intimate things about you, like do you play bridge or Scrabble or poker because I don't, but I could probably scout out some people who do . . . ."

"I loathe games," Troy said. "In any case, please don't feel responsible for me. I do feel much better, thanks to you."

A tall, aging fat man nodded to Troy as they left the cafeteria and said, "Lovely day."

"Don't panic," Fidelity said out of the side of her mouth. "I bite too, that is, unless you're in the market for a ship-board romance."

"How about you?" Troy asked wryly.

"I'm not his type."

"Well, he certainly isn't mine!"

Fidelity went into the cabin first, struggled to get her case out from under the bunk and found her book, Alice Walker's collection of essays.

"Is she good?" Troy asked, looking at the cover.

"I think she's terrific, but I have odd tastes."

"Odd?"

"I'm a closet feminist."

"But isn't that perfectly respectable by now?" Troy asked.

"Nothing about me is perfectly respectable."

"You're perfectly dear," Troy said and gave Fidelity a quick, hard hug before she went into the cabin.

Fidelity paused for a moment outside the closed door to enjoy that affectionate praise before she headed off to find a window seat in the lounge where she could alternately read and watch the passing scene. An occasional deserted Indian village was now the only sign of habitation on the shores of this northern wilderness.

The book lay instead neglected in her lap, and the scenery became a transparency through which Fidelity looked at her inner landscape, a place of ruins.

A man whose wife had died of the same cancer that had

killed Gail said to Fidelity, "I don't even want to take someone out to dinner without requiring her to have a thorough
physical examination first."

The brutality of that remark shocked Fidelity because
it located in her her own denied bitterness, that someone
as lovely and funny and strong as Gail could be not only
physically altered out of recognition but so horribly trans-
formed humanly until she seemed to have nothing left but
anger, guilt, and fear, burdens she tried to shift, as she
couldn't her pain, onto Fidelity's shoulders, until Fidelity
found herself praying for Gail's death instead of her life.
Surely she had loved before she grew to dread the sight of
Gail, the daily confrontations with her appalled and appalling
fear. It was a face looking into hell Fidelity knew did not
exist, and yet her love had failed before it. Even now it was
her love she mourned rather than Gail, for without it she
could not go back to the goodness between them, believe in
it and go on.

She felt herself withdraw from her daughters as if her
love for them might also corrupt and then fail them. In the
way of adolescents they both noticed and didn't, excused
her grief and then became impatient with it. They were
anyway perched at the edge of their own lives, ready to be
free of her.

"Go," she encouraged them, and they did.

"I guess I only think I miss them," Troy said. Otherwise
this convention of parent abandonment would be intolerable,
a cruel and unusual punishment for all those years of intimate attention and care.

And here she was, temporarily paired with another
woman as fragile and shamed by self-pity as she was. At
least they wouldn't be bleeding all over the other passengers.
If they indulged in pitying each other, well, what was the
harm in it?'

Fidelity shifted uncomfortably. The possibility of harm
was all around her.

"Why did you marry me then?" she had demanded of

her hostile husband.

"I felt *sorry* for you," he said.

"That's a lie!"

"It's the honest truth."

So pity, even from someone else, is the seed of contempt.

Review resolutions for this trip: be cheerful, eat, indulge in Mighty Mouse fantasies, and enjoy the scenery.

An island came into focus, a large bird perched in a tree, another eagle no doubt, and she would not think of the fish except in its surprised moment of flight.

"This is your captain speaking . . ."

Fidelity plugged her ears and also shut her eyes, for even if she missed something more amazing than whales, she wanted to see or not see for herself.

"Here you are," Troy said. "What on earth are you doing?"

"Do you think he's going to do that all through the trip?" Fidelity demanded.

"Probably not after dark."

"Pray for an early sunset."

It came, as they stood watching it on deck, brilliantly red with promise, leaving the sky christened with stars.

"Tell me about these boys of yours," Fidelity said as they sat over a pre-dinner drink in the crowded bar. "We've spent a whole day together without even taking out our pictures. That's almost unnatural."

"In this den of iniquity," Troy said, glancing around, "I'm afraid people will think we're exchanging dirty post-cards."

"Why oh why did I leave mine at home?"

Fidelity was surprised that Troy's sons were not better looking than they were, and she suspected Troy was surprised at how much better looking her daughters were than she had any right to expect. It's curious how really rare a handsome couple is. Beauty is either too vain for competition or indifferent to itself. Troy would have chosen a husband for his character. Fidelity had fallen for narcissistic good looks, for which her daughters were her only and lovely reward.

"Ralph's like his father," Troy said, taking back the picture of her older son, "conservative with some attractive independence of mind. So many of our friends had trouble wth first children and blame it on their own inexperience. Geoff used to say, 'I guess the more we knew, the worse we did.' "

"What's the matter with Colin?" Fidelity asked.

"I've never thought there was anything the matter with him," Troy said, "except perhaps the world. Geoff didn't like his friends or his work (Colin's an actor). It was the only hard thing between Geoff and me, but it was very hard."

The face Fidelity studied was less substantial and livelier than Ralph's, though it was easy enough to tell that they were brothers.

"We ought to pair at least two of them off, don't you think?" Fidelity suggested flippantly. "Let's see. Is it better to put the conservative, responsible ones together, and let the scallywags go off and have fun, or should each kite have a tail?"

"Colin won't marry," Troy said. "He's homosexual."

Fidelity looked up from the pictures to read Troy's face. Her dark blue eyes held a question rather than a challenge.

"How lucky for him that you're his mother," Fidelity said. "Did you realize that I am, too?"

"I wondered when you spoke about your friend Gail," Troy said.

"Sometimes I envy people his age," Fidelity said. "There's so much less guilt, so much more acceptance."

"In some quarters," Troy said. "Geoff let it kill him "

"How awful!"

"That isn't true," Troy said. "It's the first time I've ever said it out loud, and it simply isn't true. But I've been so afraid Colin thought so, so angry, yes, *angry*. I always thought Geoff would finally come round. He was basically a fair-minded man. Then he had a heart attack and died. If he'd had any warning, if he'd had time . . ."

Fidelity shook her head. She did not want to say how easily that might have been worse. Why did people persist in the fantasy that facing death brought out the best in people when so often it did just the opposite?

"How does Colin feel about his father?"

"He always speaks of him very lovingly, remembering all the things he did with the boys when they were growing up. He never mentions those last, awful months when Geoff was remembering the same things but only so that he didn't have to blame himself."

"Maybe Colin's learning to let them go," Fidelity suggested.

"So why can't I?" Troy asked.

There was Fidelity's own question in Troy's mouth. *It's because they're dead,* she thought. *How do you go about forgiving the dead for dying?* Then, because she had no answer, she simply took Troy's hand.

"Is that why your mother doesn't speak to you?" Troy asked.

"That and a thousand other things," Fidelity said. "It used to get to me, but, as my girls have grown up, I think we're all better off for not trying to please someone who won't be pleased. Probably it hasn't anything to do with me, just luck, that I like my kids, and they like me pretty well most of the time."

"Did they know about you and Gail?"

"Did and didn't. We've never actually talked about it. I would have, but Gail was dead set against it. I didn't realize just how much that had to do with her own hang-ups. Once she was gone, there didn't seem to be much point, for them."

"But for you?"

"Would you like another drink?" Fidelity asked as she signaled the waiter and, at Troy's nod, ordered two. "For myself, I'd like to tell the whole damned world, but I'm still enough of my mother's child to hear her say, 'Another one of your awful self-indulgences' and to think maybe she has a point."

"It doesn't seem to me self-indulgent to be yourself," Troy said.

Fidelity laughed suddenly. "Why that's exactly what it is! Why does everything to do with the *self* have such a bad press: self-pity, self-consciousness, self-indulgence, self-satisfaction, practices of selfish people, people being themselves?"

"The way we are," Troy said.

"Yes, and I haven't felt as good about myself in months."

"Nor I," Troy said, smiling.

"Are we going to watch the movie tonight, or are we going to go on telling each other the story of our lives?"

"We have only three days," Troy said. "And this one is nearly over."

"I suppose we'd better eat before the cafeteria closes."

They lingered long over coffee after dinner until they were alone in the room, and they were still there when the movie goers came back for a late night snack. Troy yawned and looked at her watch.

"Have we put off the evil hour as long as we can?" Fidelity asked.

"You're going to try to talk me out of the lower bunk."

"I may be little, but I'm very agile," Fidelity claimed.

The top bunk had been made up, leaving only a narrow corridor in which to stand or kneel, as they had to to get at their cases. Troy took her nightgown and robe and went into the bathroom. Fidelity changed into her flannel tent and climbed from the chair to the upper bunk, too close to the ceiling for sitting. She lay on her side, her head propped up on her elbow.

It occurred to her that this cabin was the perfect setting for the horrible first night of a honeymoon and she was about to tell Troy so as she came out of the bathroom but she looked both so modest and so lovely than an easy joke seemed instead tactless.

"I didn't have the courage for a shower," Troy confessed. "Really, you know, we're too old for this."

"I think that's beginning to be part of the fun."

When they had both settled and turned out their lights, Fidelity said, "Good night, Troy."

"Good night, dear Fido."

Fidelity did not expect to sleep at once, her head full of images and revelations, but the gentle motion of the ship lulled her, and she felt herself letting go and dropping away. When she woke, it was morning, and she could hear the shower running.

"You did it!" Fidelity shouted as Troy emerged fully dressed in a plum and navy pant suit, her night things over her arm.

"I don't wholeheartedly recommend it as an experience, but I do feel better for it."

Fidelity followed Troy's example. It seemed to her the moment she turned on the water, the ship's movement became more pronounced, and she had to hang onto a bar which might have been meant for a towel rack to keep her balance, leaving only one hand for the soaping. By the time she was through, the floor was awash, and she had to sit on the coverless toilet to pull on her grey and patchily soggy trousers and fresh wool shirt.

"We're into open water," Troy said, looking out their window.

"Two hours, you said?"

"Yes."

"I think I'm going to be better off on deck," Fidelity admitted, her normally pleasurable hunger pangs suddenly unresponsive to the suggestion of sausages and eggs. "Don't let me keep you from breakfast."

"What makes you think I'm such an old sea dog myself?"

Once they were out in the sun and air of a lovely morning, the motion of the open sea was exciting. They braced themselves against the railing and plunged with the ship, crossing from the northern tip of Vancouver Island to the mainland.

A crewman informed them that the ship would be putting in at Bella Bella to drop off supplies and pick up passengers.

"Will there be time to go ashore?" Fidelity asked.

"You can see everything there is to see from here," the crewman answered.

"No stores?"

"Just the Indian store . . . for the Indians," he said, as he turned to climb to the upper deck.

"A real, lived-in Indian village!" Fidelity said. "Do you want to go ashore?"

"It doesn't sound to me as if we'd be very welcome," Troy said.

"Why not?"

"You're not aware that we're not very popular with the Indians?"

Fidelity sighed. She resented, as she always did, having to take on the sins and clichés of her race, nation, sex, and yet she was less willing to defy welcome at an Indian village than she was at the ship's bar.

They were able to see the whole of the place from the deck, irregular rows of raw wood houses climbing up a hill stripped of trees. There were more dogs than people on the dock. Several family groups, cheaply but more formally dressed than most of the other passengers, boarded.

"It's depressing," Fidelity said.

"I wish we knew how to expect something else and make it happen."

"I'm glad nobody else was living on the moon," Fidelity said, turning sadly away.

The Indian families were in the cafeteria where Troy and Fidelity went for their belated breakfast. The older members of the group were talking softly among themselves in their own language. The younger ones were chatting with the crew in a friendly enough fashion. They were all on their way to a great wedding in Prince Rupert that night and would be back on board ship when it sailed south again at midnight.

"Do you work?" Troy suddenly asked Fidelity as she put a large piece of ham in her mouth.

Fidelity nodded as she chewed.

"What do you do?"

"I'm a film editor," Fidelity said.

"Something as amazing as that, and you haven't even bothered to tell me?"

"It's nothing amazing," Fidelity said. "You sit in a dark room all by yourself, day after day, trying to make a creditable half hour or hour and a half out of hundreds of hours of film."

"You don't like it at all?"

"Oh, well enough," Fidelity said. "Sometimes it's interesting. Once I did a film on Haida carving that was shot up here in the Queen Charlottes, one of the reasons I've wanted to see this part of the country."

"How did you decide to be a film editor?"

"I didn't really. I went to art school. I was going to be a great painter. Mighty Mouse fantasy number ten. I got married instead. He didn't work; so I had to. It was a job, and after a while I got pretty good at it."

"Did he take care of the children?"

"My mother did," Fidelity said, "until they were in school. They've had to be pretty independent."

"Oh, Fido, you've done so much more with your life than I have."

"Got divorced and earned a living because I had to. Not exactly things to brag about."

"But it's ongoing, something of your own to do."

"I suppose so," Fidelity admitted," but you know, after Gail died, I looked around me and realized that, aside from my kids, I didn't really have any friends. I worked alone. I lived alone. I sometimes think now I should quit, do something entirely different. I can't risk that until the girls are really independent, not just playing house with Mother's off-stage help. Who knows? One of them might turn up on my doorstep as I did on my mother's."

"I'd love a job," Troy said, "but I'd never have the courage . . ."

"Of course you would," Fidelity said.

"Are you volunteering to take me by the hand as you did yesterday and say to the interviewer, 'This is my friend, Mrs. McFadden. She can't go into strange places by herself?' "

"Sure," Fidelity said. "I'll tell you what, let's go into business together."

"What kind of business?"

"Well, we could run a selling gallery and lose our shirts."

"Or a bookstore and lose our shirts . . . I don't really have a shirt to lose."

"Let's be more practical. How about a gay bar?"

"Oh, Fido," Troy said, laughing and shaking her head.

The ship now had entered a narrow inland passage, moving slowly and carefully past small islands. The Captain, though he still occasionally pointed out a deserted cannery, village or mine site, obviously had to pay more attention to the task of bringing his ship out of this narrow reach in a nearly silent wilderness into the noise and clutter of the town of Prince Rupert.

A bus waited to take those passengers who had signed up for a tour of the place, and Troy and Fidelity were among them. Their driver and guide was a young man fresh from Liverpool, and he looked on his duty as bizarre, for what was there really to see in Prince Rupert but one ridge of rather expensive houses overlooking the harbor and a small neighborhood of variously tasteless houses sold to fishermen in seasons when they made too much money so that they could live behind pretentious front doors on unemployment all the grey winter long. The only real stop was a small museum of Indian artifacts and old tools. The present Indian population was large and poor and hostile.

"It's like being in Greece," Fidelity said, studying a small collection of beautifully patterned baskets. "Only here it's been over for less than a hundred years."

They ate delicious seafood at an otherwise unremarkable hotel and then skipped an opportunity to shop at a mall left open in the evening for the tour's benefit, business being what it was in winter. Instead they took a taxi back to the ship.

"I think it's time to open my bottle of scotch," Troy suggested.

They got ice from a vending machine and went back to their cabin, where Fidelity turned the chair so that she could put her feet up on the bunk and Troy could sit at the far end with her feet tucked under her.

"Cozy," Troy decided.

"I wish I liked scotch," Fidelity said, making a face.

By the time the steward came to make up the bunks, returning and new passengers were boarding the ship. Troy and Fidelity out on deck watched the Indians being seen off by a large group of friends and relatives who must also have been to the wedding. Fidelity imagined them in an earlier time getting into great canoes to paddle south instead of settling down to a few hours' sleep on the lounge floor. She might as well imagine herself and Troy on a sailing ship bringing drink and disease.

A noisy group of Australians came on deck.

"You call this a ship?" they said to each other. "You call those cabins?"

They had traveled across the States and had come back across Canada, and they were not happily prepared to spend two nights in cabins even less comfortable than Fidelity's and Troy's.

"Maybe the scenery will cheer them up," Fidelity suggested as they went back to their cabin.

"They sound to me as if they've already had more scenery than they can take."

True enough. The Australians paced the decks like prisoners looking at the shore only to evaluate their means of escape, no leaping whale or plummeting eagle compensation

for this coastal ferry which had been described in their bro-
chures as a "cruise ship." How different they were from the
stoically settled Indians who had quietly left the ship at
Bella Bella shortly after dawn.

Fidelity and Troy stayed on deck for the open water
crossing to Port Hardy on Vancouver Island, went in only
long enough to get warm, then back out into the brilliant
sun and sea wind to take delight in every shape of island,
contour of hill, the play of light on the water, the least event
of sea life until even their cloud of complaining gulls seemed
part of the festival of their last day.

"Imagine preferring something like The Love Boat,"
Troy said.

"Gail and I were always the ferry, barge, and freighter
types," Fidelity said.

Film clips moved through her mind, Gail sipping ouso in
a café in Athens, Gail hailing a cab in London, Gail . . . a
face she had begun to believe stricken from her memory
was there in its many moods at her bidding.

"What is it?" Troy asked.

"Some much better reruns in my head," Fidelity said,
smiling. "I guess it takes having fun to remember how often
I have."

"What time is your plane tomorrow?" Troy asked.

The question hit Fidelity like a blow.

"Noon," she managed to say before she excused herself
and left Troy for the first time since she had pledged herself
to Troy's need.

Back in their cabin, sitting on the bunk that was also
Troy's bed, Fidelity was saying to herself, "You're such an
idiot, such an idiot, such an idiot!"

Two and a half days playing Mighty Mouse better than
she ever had in her life, and suddenly she was dissolving into
a maudlin fool, into tears of a sort she hadn't shed since her
delayed adolescence.

"I can't want her. I just can't," Fidelity chanted.

It was worse than coming down with a toothache,

breaking out in boils, this stupid, sweet desire which she simply had to hide from a woman getting better and better at reading her face unless she wanted to wreck the last hours of this lovely trip.

Troy shoved open the cabin door.

"Did I say something . . . ?"

Fidelity shook her head, "No, just my turn, I guess."

"You don't want to miss your last dinner, do you?"

"Of course not," Fidelity said, trying to summon up an appetite she could indulge in.

They were shy of each other over dinner, made conversation in a way they hadn't needed to from the first few minutes of their meeting. The strain of it made Fidelity both long for sleep and dread the intimacy of their cabin where their new polite reserve would be unbearable.

"Shall we have an early night?" Troy suggested. "We have to be up awfully early to disembark."

As they knelt together, getting out their night things, Troy said, mocking their awkward position, "I'd say a prayer of thanks if I thought there was anybody up there to pray to."

Fidelity *was* praying for whatever help there was against her every instinct.

"I'm going to find it awfully hard to say good-bye to you, Fido."

Fidelity had to turn then to Troy's lovely, vulnerable face.

"I just can't . . ." Fidelity began.

Then, unable to understand that it could happen, Fidelity was embracing Troy, and they moved into love-making as trustingly as they had talked.

At six in the morning, when Troy's travel alarm went off, she said, "I don't think I can move."

Fidelity, unable to feel the arm that lay under Troy, whispered, "We're much too old for this."

"I was afraid you thought I was," Troy said as she slowly and painfully untangled herself, "and now I'm going to prove it."

"Do you know what I almost said to you the first night?" Fidelity asked, loving the sight of Troy's naked body in the light of the desk lamp she'd just turned on. "I almost said, 'what a great setting for the first horrible night of a honeymoon.'"

"Why didn't you?"

"You were so lovely, coming out of the bathroom," Fidelity explained, knowing it wasn't an explanation.

"You were wrong," Troy said, defying her painful stiffness to lean down to kiss Fidelity.

"Young lovers would skip breakfast," Fidelity said.

"But you're starved."

Fidelity nodded, having no easy time getting out of bed herself.

It occurred to her to disturb the virgin neatness of her own upper bunk only because it would have been the first thing to occur to Gail, a bed ravager of obsessive proportions. If it didn't trouble Troy, it would not trouble Fidelity.

As they sat eating, the sun rose over the Vancouver mountains, catching the windows of the apartment blocks on the north shore.

"I live over there," Troy said.

"Troy?"

"Will you invite me to visit you in Toronto?"

"Come with me."

"I have to see Colin . . . and Ralph. I could be there in a week."

"I was wrong about those two over there," Fidelity said. "They sit side by side because they're lovers."

"And you thought so in the first place," Troy said.

Fidelity nodded.

"This is your captain speaking . . ."

Because he was giving them instructions about how to disembark, Fidelity did listen but only with one ear, for she had to keep her own set of instructions clearly in her head. She, of course, had to see her children, too.

# BLESSED ARE THE DEAD

"Such a satisfying death!" Martin said, shaking out the *Vancouver Sun* and settling more comfortably in his chair. "Even in the eulogies, all his sins are being remembered."

"Are we going to the funeral?" Lily asked, handing him a very much thinned scotch.

"I wouldn't miss it, would you? There will be all the children and mistresses of the first marriage, the second Mrs. Kurr with all her children and all the—what does one call them?—companions of the second 'open marriage,' various bartenders and lawyers: a bloody circus!"

"You haven't spoken to him for five years," Lily said.

"The very best reason not to miss the opportunity to cut him dead one last time."

"Doesn't it scare you to be that callous?"

"Lily, my skin is as thin as my old mother's. I quiver with feeling. How often in a life do we experience for ourselves a sense that—what's that wonderful line in Christopher Fry?—that the brick has been 'richly deserved and divinely delivered.' Most drunken, whoring old buggers are rewarded with appointments to the bench and life into the nineties. I feel on the edge of conversion."

"As a died-again Christian?" Lily asked.

"That's going too far, of course. It's more a Sunday school nostalgia," Martin admitted, "when I really did

237

believe bastards like Wally Kurr would be struck dead. I've lived so many years with irony, with knowing it's more likely that boy scouts like me would drop dead at fifty, snow shovel in hand, after a life of one watered down scotch before dinner, a workout three times a week, and a cigar on my birthday. Now, even if I die on Friday of smug pleasure at his funeral, I'll still have the satisfaction of having outlived him."

"He's the first one, isn't he?" Lily mused, "if you don't count Clara Kurr's suicide or Jim Wilson's plane crash."

"The first what?"

"One of us to . . . just die."

"Well, there're your parents and my father . . ."

"I mean, our age, more or less. Wally was a year ahead of me at UBC."

"And two years behind me. He was only forty-eight," Martin said, checking the paper. "You know, I think we ought to go out for dinner and celebrate the fact that there's some justice left in the world."

"The way to get a man to go out to dinner is to put him on a diet. Then he's willing to make anything a cause for celebration: an old friend's death, a daughter's abortion."

"Wally Kurr was never really a friend of mine, and we don't have a daughter and I didn't know I was on a diet."

"Daughter-in-law."

"It's not the same thing," Martin said. "I'm perfectly willing to celebrate not having a daughter. Imagine living in incestuous terror for nearly twenty years of your life!"

"Oh, Martin."

"Now, none of that fashionable feminist revulsion. Husbands don't like it at all."

"I'll go out to dinner as long as it's not the Club," Lily said.

"But don't you like to see your friends?"

"They're your friends."

"Friends are friends, Lily, and they are the best insurance

there is for you against finding the company of your husband a bore."

"You've never bored me," Lily said.

"Where would you like to go?"

"The Club," she answered. "I'll have to change."

Martin preferred to be recognized in public, and he could count on that only at the Faculty Club. Elsewhere Lily attracted admiring attention because of her Sunday talk show on Channel 2. Neither of them would be much noticed a hundred miles or more from Vancouver unless they went where Vancouverites go or to an academic symposium. Martin had an international reputation among a limited number of scholars for his work on the nature of tragi-comedy, its important Christian underpinnings.

"It's still perfectly acceptable to write about Christianity as long as you aren't one" was Martin's social explanation, particularly at Lily's studio parties which were short on professors and long on people who did things (as opposed to teaching them or writing about them).

Lily did allow a certain number of writers on her talk show, mostly in deference to Martin's taste. As a breed, they didn't interview well, either monosyllabic or uninterruptable, vain about everything but their looks, probably because they spent most of their time with their backs to the world.

"I really think people who care about posterity should wait for it," she said.

As a lecturer as well as a scholar, Martin felt he had the best of both worlds, the here and the heareafter, of which he had a clear picture in his mind. It was a library in which his book, *The Nature o Grace, A Study of Tragi-Comedy*, was prominently displayed. It was such a concrete reassurance against the unimaginable faces of his great-great-grandchildren about whom he knew only the one thing: they would remember him.

Martin finished his scotch and stood to greet his

expensively dressed wife who wore, on a silk suit her public had not yet seen, the Tony Calveti pin he had given her on their last anniversary.

"Why on earth did we ever have children?" he asked her.

"How else would you know how to enjoy being free of them?" she asked him.

"If either of my sons had ruined your figure, I would have murdered them in their cribs. As it is, I don't harbor an ounce of ill will toward them."

Martin held the door of the Mercedes Lily had given him for an anniversary present several years ago and felt the satisfaction of knowing that he could sell it now for more than she had paid for it. With the house mortgage paid off, holidays already scheduled (Mexico fro Christmas, England in May), Martin and Lily were on the good side of these bad times.

As they drove along the shore, the late sun shone on picnicing families at the beach, on freighters at anchor waiting for berths in the inner harbor, on sailboats, on the water itself, golden and slate grey. The bushes were still in wonderfully vulgar bloom in the rose garden, but the flag by the Faculty Club was at half mast.

"Not for Wally!" Martin exclaimed.

"He was a graduate," Lily reminded him.

"We don't lower the flag for every graduate! We'd have to leave it there permanently. Maybe someone's shot the Prime Minister."

"We aren't in Texas," Lily said.

A notice at the front desk informed them that the lowered flag was, indeed, for Wallace Kurr.

"You weren't all that glum at the space he took up on the front page," Lily reminded him, "and, after all, we're eating out in his honor."

"But the flag is for prominent, not notorious citizens."

"They're more or less indistinguishable."

Here their conversation was interrupted by greetings from Martin's colleagues and their wives, rather more of them than

Martin had expected on a week night until he remembered that there was a cocktail party scheduled in the lower lounge for a retiring dean whom Martin despised.

"Oh God, now that we're here, I suppose we should just . . . nod in."

But, of course, there was no nodding in on such occasions. The speeches had just begun.

Why ever had he let Lily give in to him about coming here where such pomposities as this could so often override conviviality? Looking at the numbers in the room, Martin worried that he would not get a table, certainly not a good table, in the dining room. Nearly everyone here was old enough not to be leashed to a babysitter and could easily stay on. Perhaps the thing to do was to persuade Chester and Margerie over there to go downtown with them for dinner.

Oh, these deadly phrases, "inspiring mentor," "distinguished contribution," for a man who had been elevated to dean in order to spare him and his department the embarrassment of dwindling enrollment in his ill-prepared and haltingly presented lectures, to get rid of his reactionary presence on committees. It was as ridiculous as lowering the flag for Wally.

Yet Martin's basic satisfaction reasserted itself at the thought of Wally, at this very moment a cold corpse waiting for flames and worms. Retirement after all was a little death, this ceremony a dress rehearsal, at which the corpse, unlike the bride, was present.

It was too much to hope that the parting gift would be something witty and original like, say, a goldfish bowl or a spittoon. Occasionally a man with a confessed hobby got a fishing rod or some golf clubs, but this fellow was handed his retirement on the expected silver platter, unsuitable for either carving turkey or handing round martinis, its only function to be cleaned.

Because they were at the back of the room, Martin and Lily did get a table, a window table, in the dining room, and

Chester and Margerie, whom they'd known since their undergraduate days, came to join them.

"What a surprise!" Chester said. "I thought such politicing was beneath you."

"An honest mistake," Martin explained. "We came over to celebrate the just demise of Wally Kurr."

"Ah, Wally," Margerie said. "He was my first rabbit test."

"I guess, when you live in the fast lane, you get there quicker," Chester observed mildly.

"He was not in the fast lane," Martin said. "He's been right off the rails for years."

"You've never forgiven him Clara's suicide, have you?" Margerie asked.

"If I had to list the number of things that I haven't forgiven Wally, that nobody should forgive Wally, we'd be here all night. Shall we start with snails?"

"Lovely," Lily agreed.

"It says here 'escargot.' "

"Have we been speaking French?" Martin asked.

"Martin is only purely bilingual," Lily reminded them.

"Otherwise we'll get the English equivalent to *joual.*"

"Snails it is," Chester agreed. "I'm sure that's what Peter Trudeau eats in Toronto."

"When we saw the flag, Martin wondered if he'd been shot."

"Who decides about that flag, Chester?" Martin demanded.

"A committee," Chester answered from behind the wine list.

"Everybody knew Wally," Margerie said, "After all."

"Without Wally the local papers would have had to shut down for lack of news," Chester said.

"For lack of scandal."

"The difference?" Lily asked. "Martin's faith in destiny has been restored tonight."

"Surely not?" Chester looked at Martin.

"No, but still it is wonderful to see justice with her sweet, impartial face visit this planet. She is not after all in permanent eclipse."

"Death's boatman takes no bribe, nor brings E'vn skilled Prometheus back from Hades' shore," Chester intoned in his unfortunate tenor.

"Is it really necessary to gloat?" Margerie asked. "What about his present wife and all those children? Where's the justice for them?"

"He settled all his property on her before the last time he declared bankruptcy, and that's over two years ago, plenty of time for him to have dealt himself back into the game."

"Were you a tiny bit jealous of him, Martin?"

"If I was, I am no longer. May he rest in peace," Martin said, raising his glass.

"Were you really ever jealous of Wally?" Lily asked on their way home.

"Why is it that women have always excused Wally?" he asked in return. "I suppose it's understandable that a nice girl like Margerie would go to bed with him when she was nineteen. She didn't know any better. But why defend him now?"

"He died good looking and, you think, rich."

"Good looking? He was as thin as a stork."

Lily was tactfully silent.

The phone was ringing as they walked in the door. Lily answered it, listened for a moment, raised her eyebrows, and then said, "Just a minute. He's right here." She put her hand over the receiver and said, "It's Joan Kurr."

"I don't even know her," Martin mouthed frantically.

Lily shrugged and held the phone out to him.

"Yes?" he said, he hoped with some sympathy in his tone.

Then, after a long pause, he said, "Yes," again, and it came out more like a reluctant admission of guilt.

244

When he hung up the phone, Martin said in disbelief, "Do you know what I've just agreed to do? I've just agreed to be one of the pall bearers!"

"You were an usher in his first wedding," Lily reminded him.

"For Clara's sake," he protested.

"And now for Joan's?"

"It isn't her idea. It was Wally's, one of his mortal broodings after Clara died, no doubt."

"Well, you did want to go to the funeral anyway."

"But not as his . . . accomplice!"

"He's dead, after all."

"O death, where is thy sting. O grave where is thy victory?"

"Oh, Martin, where is your sense of humor?"

Martin flung himself into a chair, stared at the empty fireplace and said, "How could he do this to me?" silently adding *again*.

Martin, dressed in his only three-piece suit, which was dark grey, expected to be the only respectable man at the coffin. He did not worry about the safety of his wallet or his watch, for Wally's friends would be in the upper echelon of crooks and gamblers who managed real estate in the city, sporting gold nuggets from their own mines on their watch chains. He did worry about his own good name among them in the report of this religious farce in the evening paper.

Having looked up the burial service in the prayer book, Martin discovered that the church, probably in times when the dead were buried in the churchyard, was suggested only in inclement weather for a ritual intended for the graveside. It was a cloudy day.

What choices among the ironies would the minister fall upon? "He heapeth up riches, and cannot tell who shall gather them" or "Raise us from the death of sin unto the life of righteousness" or—and he read this one out to Lily as she was putting on her hat—"make me not a rebuke unto the foolish."

"Which would be intended for us, no doubt," Lily observed.

Even though they arrived early, finding a parking place was difficult. Martin cursed the limousines which dwarfed his beloved Mercedes, but he was able to squeeze into a place that a Lincoln had just failed to negotiate. His moral superiority was intact.

"Do try not to look smug," Lily said. "I'll save you a seat on the aisle."

Martin turned to see that the other men loitering on the steps waiting for direction as pall bearers were all known to him not from the gossip columns but from the university, a classmate who had become a doctor, the president of Wally's own class, a quite respectable corporation lawyer, the owner of a fish-packing company who had also been an usher at Wally's first wedding.

He said to Martin, "To tell the truth, I wouldn't be here if Mrs. Kurr hadn't specifically asked me . . ."

One by one each confessed to a similar uncertainty, not having seen Wally in years, but each also felt an uneasy loyalty to those old ties of friendship when they had been young together, poaching on each other's female territory, wrecking each other's cars, predicting ill-favored futures for each other, and standing up at each other's weddings.

Nobody wanted to say what they all probably assumed, that Wally had no other friends. Martin tried to remember if he'd felt any less cynical and out of place at Wally's wedding. Martin had agreed to that only because he'd been in love with Clara himself and didn't want anyone else to know it. But what humiliation had he to cover up here that made him agree to be in this bewildered company?

Between the funeral director and the minister, they were soon instructed on their simple duties and could join the crowd moving into the church.

"Who are all these people?" Martin muttered to Lily, for the church was full.

As he himself had facetiously predicted, they were all Wally's old loves and his children. Also there were both prominent crooks and their bankers with their second and third wives. Across the church Martin spotted Chester and Margerie who would witness his embarrassment with some amusement.

Then he eyed the coffin, resting below the altar banked with pretentious flowers, which he and the comrades of his youth were to bear away.

"Behold, I shew you a mystery; we shall not all sleep, but we shall be changed in a moment, in a twinkling of an eye, at the last trump. for the trumpet shall sound, and the dead shall be raised incorruptible . . ."

Martin snorted loudly. What they should have planned to do was drop the coffin in the aisle and let the body roll out for all to see the essentially corrupted remains of Wally Kurr, the womanizer, the crook, the killer, for he had killed Clara as surely as if he'd shot her himself.

Yet Martin found himself chanting, along with hundreds of other unbelievers, "Christ, have mercy on us." And, sharing a hymnal with Lily, he raised his voice to sing, "Rock of Ages, cleft for me . . ." and pondered the lines, "All for sin could not atone/ Thou must save and thou alone . . ."

Where was the justice in all this? Though Martin believed no more in hell than in heaven, if he had to be burdened with Christian imagery, surely there should be a little more crackling of flames for this particular sinner.

At the end of the final prayer, Martin rose with the other men and walked up the aisle to the coffin. Unrehearsed and unaccustomed to manual tasks, they were clumsy with the flowers, clumsier still lifting the coffin and getting it down the steps, though it wasn't really very heavy. By this time Martin was too anxious not to make a fool of himself to think of making a fool of Wally Kurr's corpse. When the men had the coffin on the straight away of the aisle, they figured out the necessity of walking in step, and Martin had a sudden sense of the theatrical dignity of their task. So strong was the form that, though he believed not at all in redemption, he knew he and the others had become agents of grace, only needing to bear and forbear to the grave to defeat completely the justice he had come to witness.

As mechanical, as arbitrary as any device in the tragi-comedies he had studied so long, Martin, the righteous man, shouldered his part of the burden of body and box out to the waiting hearse, then out of the hearse over the uncertain turf of the cemetery to the grave site on which a gentle rain began appropriately to fall.

Among the weeping women, including Margerie and Lily, Martin stood without solace.

"From henceforth blessed are the dead . . ."

# POWER FAILURE

Laura Thornstrom was watching the late news, a habit which often gave her nightmares but consoled her that she hadn't much longer to live, when the power failed. The color fled from the screen like water going down the drain, and she heard the silencing of all the small hummings in the house, fridg, freezer, pump. In the dark she heard only her heart beating and wondered at its independence from all those other gadgets she needed to stay alive. Every time this winter the power had failed, she tested the notion that she was too old to stay on alone on this little island so vulnerable to the weather and isolated enough to wait sometimes several days for help. In a power failure she had to haul not only wood for heat and cooking but water from the rain barrels, if they weren't frozen, for washing and flushing the toilet. Even the thought wore her out.

She reached for the matches on the table beside her and lighted a candle. With its light she located one of the battered fluorescent lights, safer than any of the old fashioned lanterns now that she was both inclined to stumble and to be absentminded. She would do nothing tonight but go to bed, getting her extra quilt out to make up for the failure of her electric blanket. There was no wind; so perhaps there would be power in the morning.

The weight of the quilt on her arthritic feet made her

moan, a bad habit born of living alone, for the sound of it didn't comfort her, only made her feel sorrier for herself. But what did it matter when there was no one else around to be troubled by her moods? In the two years since Thorny had died, Laura had retreated not into a second childhood but into a second adolescence. Often sulky, melodramatic, and clumsy, she wondered if the only incentive to be an adult was an intimate audience before whom one was ashamed to brood and complain. Certainly, it was only since Thorny had died that she'd been angry with him in that hopeless way of adolescents, so often angry about what couldn't be helped, shouting, "It isn't fair!"

Well, it wasn't fair that the power was out and her feet hurt and her husband was dead. She didn't complain ever to her children because they would only say she was mad to stay here and should move back to the mainland where among them they could look after her.

She and Thorny hadn't had enough money to retire in the city. They didn't care. They sold their city house and fixed up their summer place, insulating it, getting a good wood stove, and putting in electric heaters for when they were too old to chop and haul wood. It had more bedrooms than they needed, but that had assured them visits from children and grandchildren, occasions Laura now anticipated with a mixture of pleasure and dread. She hadn't really the energy any more to cook for them all and cope with the boisterous energy of the little ones. But, if she admitted that to anyone, the pressure was on again for her to leave the island.

They always came in the spring, summer, and fall when Laura loved the island and knew she would never leave it. She wore herself out before they even arrived, making sure no daughter or daughter-in-law would find the oven neglected, the kitchen floor sticky, the spare rooms fit only for spiders which were Laura's undisturbed companions when she was alone. Her sons and sons-in-law were less insistent with her, helped instead by seeing to it she had plenty of wood to last the winter, stacked conveniently near the house, checking gutters, floor boards, light switches. Nobody expected her to take over Thorny's jobs to prove she could stay on alone. Sometimes she wanted to snap at the girls, tell them she didn't have to keep an AA motel rating for half a dozen guests to be permitted an independent old age. But she knew temper, too, was one of the signs.

Turning painfully in her bed, she tried to stop listening to all those voices, to the absolute silence of the house. Had she remembered to turn off everything, lights, heaters, the electric stove, the television so that the house wouldn't blaze her into waking if the power came on before morning? It wouldn't. And she didn't care if it did. It was simply stupid to worry about being wakened when she couldn't go to sleep.

It snowed in the night. Laura could tell by the white light in her bedroom when she opened her eyes. She could tell by the coldness of her nose that the power was still off. She felt entombed in her bed, the heavy quilt weighing down on her stiff, painful joints. Then she thought of the birds. In the snow they must be fed, particularly her pair of variegated thrushes who stayed with her through the winter, not like those rascal aristocrats who, like her closest human neighbors, went south for the winter. She and Thorny had, too, for a month or so, but they were always glad to get home.

Laura groaned as she hoisted herself out of bed, this morning so slowly that she knew one of these mornings she just wouldn't make it. She had just finished her slow and layered dressing when there was a knocking at her door.

"Come in!" she shouted, knowing it would take her painful minutes to get to a door she never locked.

"It's me, Jimmy," called the voice in uncertain, deep register, "come to start your wood stove."

"Why aren't you in school?" she asked, having made it to her bedroom door which opened onto the living room.

"It's Saturday, Mrs. Thornstrom," Jimmy said to her, balancing an armload of kindling and logs. "I already swept your path, but I'll bring in enough wood for the day."

"That's very kind of you, Jimmy."

"My dad says there's no use in having ten kids if they're all good for nothing," Jimmy answered with a grin. "If the power's still off tonight, Peter's going to stop by. He's not worth much unless you tell him."

"He's only seven, Jimmy," Laura reminded him.

"Yeah, but his memory's as bad as old Mr. Apple's. Senile at seven!"

Laura knew there was no point in offering to pay Jimmy. The O'Hea children were raised to do favors for people just like their father who managed to put enough food on the table because they all dressed out of the thrift shop.

"Can I make you a cup of cocoa?" Laura offered. "Think maybe there's a doughnut around somewhere, too."

"Don't mind if I do," Jimmy said. "I'll just get you some water."

"I'm afraid the barrels will be frozen."

"Nope. I checked. I'll bring enough in to put some in the tub."

As the kitchen warmed, Laura moved around more easily. She found the doughnuts, some stale bread and seeds for the birds, and, when she and Jimmy sat down together, she wondered why she had fretted in the night. A power failure, snow, anything of that sort turned an ordinary day into a holiday. What boy in the city would come pounding at her door ready to do all her chores for nothing but a snack which he stayed for more to keep her company than because he wanted it?

Laura knew not to ask about school. Jimmy was at an age when he fretted to be out of the classroom and into the woods or onto a fishing boat. His father would have let him, but his mother was determined that all the kids were going to finish high school. They spoke instead about the logging truck that had gone off the road last week, three fires in as many days so that the volunteer firemen all finally went home to bed and said either the island would burn down or the kids and women would have to cope with the next one.

Once Jimmy had gone and the birds were fed, Laura was briefly at loose ends without the chores she had expected to do for herself. Then she realized that on such a day she could simply settle to read while she had the light to. There was not even any point in cleaning up Jimmy's muddy boot prints since Peter's would be there this evening. A power failure was even a sort of luxury, if it didn't go on too long.

By evening, however, when her eyes were too tired to read by poor light, when there was no television, and Peter had so overloaded the stove that she would have to wait for hours to bank it, she decided to take her battery radio to bed, feeling the same kind of discouragement she had the night before. "If I should die before I wake" had seemed to her a morbid prayer when she was a child. Now she understood it as a prayer for the old, not morbid at all but simply mortal.

Static on the radio woke her, but, when she reached to turn it off, it was not on. Fire. Something was on fire! For no more than a second, those reluctant old bones held her prisoner of a prayer. Then she moved, no longer aware of pain. It was the kitchen, somehow the stove . . . The kitchen door, like a great hearth cast huge heat and light into the living room which had begun to fill with smoke. Laura backed away from it toward her front door, stepped into her boots, grabbed a coat and flashlight and stepped out into the shocking cold.

It woke her but left her inside the nightmare of fire, where she now must think what to do. It had already been too late to grab the fire extinguisher, too late to phone the fire department, too late to think what to save. She moved slowly, stupidly down the path and then turned back to believe what was happening. The fire had eaten into the second floor and flowered onto the roof. Even if the firemen arrived—and how could they when they didn't know?—it was already too late to save the house.

Laura watched the upstairs corner bedroom fold in on

itself. She thought of the closet full of Thorny's clothes which she'd never got round to giving away and found herself weeping for them, the things of his life like his life itself gone. How perfectly silly she was, in tears over his clothes when she had nothing but the nightgown, coat and boots she stood in, *nothing.*

"Not so much as my handbag," she said aloud.

Then she saw flames dance into the cedar next to the house and realized the danger as well as the loss. She did not know if she'd been standing there a minute or half an hour. She must get help at once. Her nightgown fluttering in the snow around her boots, she lighted her way to the empty house of her neighbors. Fortunately she had left their key under a flower pot on their deck, fearing that otherwise, in her absent-mindedness, she would misplace it.

The fire number was stickered to their phone as it was in every island house. Once Laura had made the call, she sat in the dark house waiting to hear the fire station siren and then realizing it could not sound without power. Everyone would have to be phoned. What would they do if the woods were ablaze by the time they got there? Should she go back and try to attach the hose? The well pump was useless. In any case, Laura was too cold and weak to move. Should she call her son?

Laura didn't want any of her children to know, but they would have to know. She hadn't even a handkerchief to blow her nose. It made her feel guilty, sitting there sniffing, and then resentful, bitterly resentful to be cold and alone in the middle of the night. How she hated the night which had become like a personal enemy to her!

It must have been the overloaded stove . . . or a fire in the chimney. Well, what difference did any of that make now? She thought of her books from the Open Shelf Library. She would have to pay to replace those. She'd have to phone the bank for another cheque book. Things, after all, could be replaced. They were insured. Even the house was insured. But surrounding these reasonable thoughts, threatening to engulf them was the darkness.

Laura heard the wailing siren of the fire truck. Then its lights swung into view on the lane that passed this house on its way to hers. Behind the yellow fire engine came the tanker truck, and behind that a line of cars. Only when they had all gone by did Laura think she should let them know where she was.

She got as far as the deck and could go no further. Her stiff old bones simply refused to carry her back to that roaring, collapsing house. Then a late, lone car came along, and she signaled it with her flashlight.

It was Jim O'Hea with his three oldest boys.

"Run for it!" he ordered them.

Then he got out of the car, bounded up onto the deck and surrounded her with a strong arm.

"Come on," he said gently, "I'll take you home to Mum," as he always referred to his wife.

Laura did not protest. The little will she had had left her. In most of the houses they passed she could see the demented darting of fire, and it frightened her newly each time, as if the whole neighborhood were kindling for disaster. In several she also saw random arcs of flashlights.

"The damned power!" Jim muttered. "We ought none of us to pay our bills this month. They should have had a crew here today."

"Well, at least I won't have to worry about the food in my freezer," Laura commented cheerfully, her social self functioning out there beyond the shuddering anxiety.

"You don't have to worry about a thing now," Jim said gently.

Even the younger O'Hea children were up, their mother urging them to finish glasses of milk so that she could herd them back to bed again.

The large room in which they cooked, ate, and entertained themselves was amply warmed by the wood stove, and it was cheerfully lighted by kerosene lamps. Laura gratefully accepted an old chair by the stove and the offer of a cup of tea.

"I sent over to Lyvia's for some clothes for you," Kathleen O'Hara said. "She's about your size. She ought to be here any minute."

"It's the middle of the night," Laura protested.

"About five in the morning by now, not much more than an hour before she'd be up anyway, and the engine's woke everybody anyway. Phone's been ringing off its ear."

"Oh dear," Laura said. "Oh dear."

"Burned right down, is it?" Kathleen asked.

"I suppose so. I waited at my neighbors."

"Sensible."

"I hope they can save the woods at the back."

"They'll do the best they can. How did it start, do you know?"

"In the chimney probably," Laura said, realizing that she didn't want little Peter implicated, though she was sure Jimmy would think to suspect him.

"Have you phoned your kids?"

"Not yet," Laura said. "I'll wait until they're up."

"One of them will want to be on the morning ferry."

"Oh, I don't want to go over there!" Laura said.

"Have to go some place," Kathleen commented reasonably.

Lyvia Tey was at the door with a large, cardboard box full of clothes.

"My poor dear!" she exclaimed. "Are you all right?"

Then followed the same questions Kathleen had asked before Lyvia got around to the box.

"I didn't know about shoes," Lyvia said. "Whether they'd fit you, but I brought some."

"Oh, my boots should do until I can get something else."

"It's a good thing I remembered underwear! Nothing but your nightgown?"

"Why don't you go into our bedroom and try them on?" Kathleen suggested.

Once alone in the bedroom with its large, unmade bed,

Laura wanted simply to crawl into it, turn out the lamp and fall asleep, leaving all the horror and confusion and kindness behind her. She didn't want to put on Lyvia's clothes. She didn't like Lyvia's clothes. Her snobbish ingratitude shocked and oddly reassured her. At least her own taste hadn't burned up in the fire. Of course, she had to get dressed. She couldn't go on through the day in her nightgown, coat and boots, and day was coming.

Laura looked through the contents of the box, holding up a dress, then a pair of slacks, a blouse, a sweater, examining them in the shadowy light. It touched and shamed her that Lyvia hadn't brought over anything but her very best. Laura found a vest and underpants, discarded a bra, found a pair of socks. Then she didn't try on the shoes. There was only a small cracked mirror on a table, in which Laura could dimly see only her uncombed hair and unmade face. She hadn't a comb or lipstick to her name, and she looked simply awful. Thank heaven she had most of her own teeth, for no one could see that her bridge, soaking in the bathroom, had also been lost.

"How are you coming along in there?" Kathleen called. "May I come in?"

She brought with her a pitcher of warm water and a bowl, covered with a towel on which there was a comb and lipstick.

"I wish I could offer you a nice, hot bath," Kathleen said.

"Oh, that's just wonderful. I look such a fright!"

"You're all right. That's the main thing."

Other women had arrived by the time Laura reappeared. On the family's dining table were casseroles, bowls of salad, plates of cookies, pies, dozens of eggs, a ham, and in boxes piling up by the door were more clothes, bedding, towels, even a little battery radio.

"Oh, I can't accept all this!" Laura protested in dismay. "I don't even have anywhere to put it."

"You will," they reassured her.

She shouldn't have been surprised. In her years on the island she, too, had hurried to whatever place sheltered a burned out family, fire so terrifyingly common a disaster, taking food and clothing, household goods, and, if there was no insurance, money. It simply had never occurred to her that it would ever happen to her. Whatever was given she was bound to accept; yet it felt a kind of madness to her, things piling up around her when she had no place to go.

The children were getting up again as dawn light began to take over the shadows. Kathleen, helped by the other women, was getting breakfast ready. She sent one of the older girls on her bicycle to tell the firemen there would be breakfast ready for them when they were done.

Laura couldn't eat. She accepted another cup of tea and said, "I suppose I must call my son."

"My fishing tackle, too?" he asked, incredulous, and then took himself in hand.

It was only Thorny's clothes she had thought to mourn, not the closets full of belongings of her children and grandchildren, about which she hadn't concerned herself since her own were grown. She had no idea how many pairs of riding boots, tennis rackets, fishing rods, skin diving suits, to say nothing of ordinary clothing had been lost in the fire. She could only assure her son that it was everything. "Even my bridge," she added wryly.

"Your what?"

"My bridge: my teeth."

It was so ridiculous a conversation that Laura began to laugh, which, far from reassuring her son, convinced him she was hysterical. He promised to be on the morning boat.

"What day of the week is it?" Laura asked as she turned away from the phone.

"Sunday," Peter said, and then he leaned up against her, offering the burden of his small weight to comfort her. It did.

Kathleen's daughter came breathlessly back into the house, her presence commanding everyone's attention. It occurred to Laura that anyone from so large a family would have no self-consciousness in public speaking since even asking for the butter had to be done before a large audience.

"They said to say they were sorry, Mrs. Thornstrom, but it was pretty well gone before they got there."

Laura nodded. It was no news to her.

"But they've got the woods pretty well out, and they're just coming in for breakfast, except for Jimmy and one other who have to stay behind to watch."

The children were urged to finish breakfast quickly to give up their places to a dozen soot blackened and tired men who came discouragedly into the house, shaking their heads, cursing the power company which had so delayed their response, telling Laura how damned sorry they were, but there was nothing much left but the chimney and the bathtub. She had seen enough island fires to know what it would look like. She would not, as some did, try to sift through the ashes in hope of finding, oh, anything.

"Shut up a minute, all of you," Jim O'Hea commanded. "Can you hear that?"

It was the hum of the refrigerator. The power was back on.

"Thank God!" Kathleen said. "You can all wash."

One of the kids went immediately to the televison and turned it on. Another tried all the by now unnecessary light switches. The women urged the men off to the bathroom to leave the kitchen sink free for washing dishes for the next round of breakfast.

All through the morning, more people arrived, bringing food and gifts. Only much later Laura also found in a handbag several hundred dollars in cash. She was offered places to stay, advice about rebuilding, "Hell of a way to get a new house, but it makes nice work for some of us."

By the time Thorny junior arrived, his stricken face looked out of place in the cheerful crowd. But Laura was very glad to see him. Maybe he could figure out what to do with the carloads of goods turning the O'Hea's into a warehouse.

"Now that you're here, darling, I think I'll just lie down for a while."

Kathleen led her back into the bedroom which she had somehow managed to straighten. Laura lay down and slept for a few minutes or an hour, waking to escape the fire that burned all around her, hoping, until she realized where she was, that it was only her dream that had frightened her.

Her room at Thorny junior's house was no more reassuring as she woke again and again from dreams of fire. She wept for ridiculous things like her own needle and thimble, her little travel clock, and was unconsoled by the swiftness with which her children replaced them She was furious with herself that such irrationalities only made them more convinced that the fire was a blessing in disguise to bring her back to what senses she had left.

"Think of this as your house now, Mother," Thorny junior said.

"But it isn't," she protested. "It's yours."

If only she could get one good night's sleep, she could begin to pull herself together.

"You mustn't keep waiting on me like this," she said to her daughter-in-law as she came in with the now accustomed breakfast tray.

"It's no trouble, Mother. At your age, you've got a right to start the day slowly."

"Most days never get started at all," Laura observed.

"You just rest."

Resting gave Laura time to grieve for her house, yet what had it been but a place too big for her with too much of her own and other people's clutter? The memories, well, they hadn't burned after all. She didn't need the house to go on being mad at Thorny for being dead.

It was the insurance release papers that got her out of bed.

"No, I'm not signing them, son."

"But why not?"

"Because I'm going to rebuild."

"What?"

"I only just realized it," Laura said. "But a small house, one my own size."

"Where?"

"Why, right where the other one was. And don't tell me there's no one to look in on me over there."

"But, Mother, you're too old to live alone."

"No, I'm not. I'm too old to live any other way."

"But we don't want to be worrying about you. We want to look after you. Why, Mother, some days you can't even get out of bed."

"Because I don't have to," Laura replied. "Oh, there will be mornings when breakfast in bed will sound like heaven, but, until I'm actually there, it's better for me to get up. Who's feeding my birds, I'd like to know?"

Her other children were invited to dinner that night in order to persuade her to change her mind, to live in the city at least, if not with one of them.

"I can't afford to live in the city," Laura answered them. "And I don't want to."

They were irritated with her, even angry, but finally she could begin to see them giving way, giving up, washing their hands of her. They were dim-witted city people, every last one of them. Nobody on the island would be surprised to see her back. With the insurance money, she could be a paying guest in Lyvia's spare room until the new house was built, a project which would provide much needed work for Jim O'Hea and several others. It was not just Laura's way of saying thank you. It was getting back into the rhythm of give and take, the rhythm of living.

"I'll be going back," Laura told her children, "next week."

# PUZZLE


Even in her late seventies Ella Carr was still trying to put her life together like a puzzle which, when she'd finally managed it, she could live in terms of, a character out of Mary Poppins walking into the completed picture. Some of the pieces of it were not difficult. The largest part had always been her work, and it was central—husband, children, lovers all at the hard edges. Oh, there were dark areas, moments when she wished she had made other choices, to write well instead of successfully, not to write at all so that she could have been the wife her husband expected, the mother she hired for her children instead. But Ella Carr was too accomplished an entertainer far too handsomely re-warded to sustain serious regret, even about the several for-tunes less generous people might have said she'd squandered on the children, on friends, and on herself.

At the height of her career, magazine sales tripled while one of her novels was being serialized. Airlines paid her to fly for the use of her name. She had never kept track of foreign translations or even movie rights. To the well over a hundred books credited to her name had to be added as many again which she had written under a pen name or ghosted. Writing was her compulsion. Her first novel had been published when she was seventeen, and, though her work was now suffering the shift of popular taste, her

263

publishers tended to complain about her ability to change with the times rather than about her outdated plots.

"You can't have homosexual characters in a book of yours," they protested. "What will your readers think?"

"All my readers are dead," Ella Carr replied.

In her prime, she had turned out three books in a summer and was paid a hundred thousand dollars apiece for them.

"In the thirties," she'd remind you, "that was a lot of money."

Now she managed, against failing energy and eyesight, only one book a year and worried about doctor's bills and taxes, because advances were small, sales a meager ten thousand. People still knew who she was, though more and more often it was expressed in surprise not only that she was still writing but still alive. One young reviewer dealt ungenerously with her latest book as if it were a posthumous work. She sent a postcard which read, "Don't speak ill of the dead," and signed it Ella Carr.

She had had her own television program. The great movie stars had been her friends. Her fan mail hadn't stopped.

She could still fall in love, her chief diversion since she could remember. When she was hardly more than a child, Ella had herself written fan letters, love letters not only to actors and actresses, dancers, singers, concert pianists, but to any attractive friend of her parents, to her school teachers. She was rarely ignored, for those who present themselves to the world, even so unlikely a part of it as the classroom, do so to be admired and loved whatever other motive their modesty requires. To be out of love now and then, sometimes for weeks at a time, was for her like a serious illness. Ella had to be in love to get anything done. All the paraphernalia of that, the signed programs and photographs, the notes and letters, had long since gone to university archives waiting for a biographer she hoped would be less impressed than amused at the times beyond number she had offered her heart and other parts to a tasteless range of the accomplished. Though Ella enjoyed her celebrity and treated her own fans with attentive kindness, what inspired her still was other people's gifts. At the moment she was corresponding with the most promising tenor at the Met, her son's new law partner, and a young starlet whose fortune was probably in her legs.

"I've never tried to resist a good looking woman," she was the first to admit now that she was old and the world had begun to catch up with her.

Those infatuations, though occasionally alarming and inevitably disappointing whether requited or not, went on being as necessary to her as they had been when she was thirteen. Now in her old age they had the quality of those first loves, involving far more ardor than appetite. Recently without the least envy or regret, Ella had seen her thrice-divorced daughter marry a man she was in love with herself. Ella suspected it was a gesture of gallantry toward herself since he knew how she fretted over that child, who, no matter which way she was turned, had never fitted into her mother's life.

Children don't, even the ones who do as you tell them and grow up to correct all your own mistakes. Ella had a daughter like that, too, who loved being a mother and didn't believe in hiring other people to do your dirty work for you. She was quite a good painter, but it was a hobby, nothing more. Her real name was Rebuke. In fact, she was proud of her mother's accomplishments and ready to be daily dutiful even through a long dying.

When her own mother was dying, Ella was taking up nearly a floor at the Savoy in London. She was in China when her father died. She wasn't at home even when her first born son was killed in an automobile accident. The only one she had been there for was her husband, but, holding him in her arms, they both knew it was years too late.

"How did we miss it?" he asked.

He had walked out, for obvious reasons: he couldn't stand the demands of four children under five years old; he was jealous of her work; he was sexually deprived. She could not stand to have him come into the same room. She began to shake.

Years later, a doctor said, "There's nothing abnormal about that. You were exhausted. You had to protect yourself. Four children in five years is too many, particularly now that they all live."

If Ella had had the pill, there might never have been children. She might have had her marriage instead. But could he have shared her with her work before he'd established his own place in the world? She doubted it. She wouldn't have found it easy to give up children, but for him she could have done it. Writing, no. What she gave up as involuntarily as she shook was her husband. Free of his support, writing and motherhood could not be in conflict. She had to support the children.

"Every writer needs a wife. Sex hasn't anything to do with it," Ella Carr had repeated in too many interviews, as if confessing would protect her from judgment.

No one paid the slightest attention. She was a woman "alone" with four children.

"I might as well not exist!" Tudy cried.

In public, yes, but holding Tudy up to private scrutiny revealed her as the essential fact of life. How many successful men felt the same resentful humiliation when they recognized their success depended on the sacrifice of their wives? At least Ella hadn't sacrificed her husband. Perhaps somewhere he had pensioned off his own guilty discard as she had hers. And bought her silence.

Ella had supervised the burning of the letters because they would have brought at least ten thousand dollars to the archives since they covered the twenty years of Ella's life when she had been the most sought after, probably the most highly paid writer in the world. After the first three years, they were love letters only out of duty, but no one could have mistaken the nature of the relationship. Ella, who had never in her life written an explicit love scene, had been graphic in letters home to a woman she no longer desired but could not live without.

The children never knew. Tudy was for them their caretaker and tyrant, who could also, but incidentally, reduce their mother to tears. They called her Tudy, one of those inexplicable, nearly interchangeable children's names for people whose power they would like to soften. If she appeared in Ella's biography, she would be the excellently paid, intermittently resented children's nurse and sometimes housekeeper who, aside from nervous breakdowns, served faithfully until she was retired with a generous pension to Arizona.

Once, after her husband died, Ella almost called Tudy back, thinking she would go mad alone with all her losses, but she kept remembering how bitterly difficult it had been to get rid of Tudy, something neither of them could go through again.

"Oh Mother," her motherly daughter agreed, "Tudy's too old now to be any help. If you're lonely, borrow one of your grandchildren for a while."

Instead Ella wrote a novel about an old woman, saintly in her love for her possessive and ill-tempered nurse/jailor. One of the secrets of Ella's success was to write lives she could not have lived. In the month it took to write, she confirmed that she could work again and be alone. Work had always been her rationalization.

The guilt, however, was never more than dormant, woke as she increasingly did in the dark hours of the morning and stank like something dead but undisposed of in the house. It was so unlike what she felt for her husband and her son, whom she missed and regretted and tried to call back from the dead. Ella was secretive about the seances except among a small group of like-minded people as unresigned as she was to losing those they loved.

Her husband and she had been the great loves of each other's lives. They had not divorced, neither of them having any reason to. Once the shock of separation settled to being the catastrophe they had not been able to avoid, each reached out to the other across the necessary distance. He never remembered the children's birthdays; he never forgot hers. She sent him congratulatory notes as his own successes became a matter of public record. When he read she was giving a speech in Chicago, he suggested they have dinner. They met like that a couple of times a year. When she was forty, two months after a hysterectomy, they became lovers again. Tudy had her second nervous breakdown, part of her cure a promise that she would never be betrayed again. That promise was not kept. Meetings between husband and wife became elaborately secret, a week-end stolen from a lecture tour, a fictitious business meeting in New York with agents and publishers. They were far better lovers than they had been, and they were still in love. When the last child left, he said to her, "I want to come home."

Ella never explained about Tudy. He was intuitive and tactful. He had to wait two years for Ella to bully and buy Tudy out of the house to make room for him to return. A month after he finally came home, he had a stroke. In a year he was dead.

Ella could not lay him to rest. She had too recenlty got him back. Though she believed they would finally be re-united in the eternal marriage only imperfectly managed in this life, she could not wait.

The child named Rebuke, when she found out about the seances, said, "Well, if it's any comfort to you, why not?"

It was, though Ella was never certain she had any direct contact. Trying gave her something to wait for other than death.

Ella's first born had been her favorite, perhaps only because she'd been able to pay absolute attention to him for the first year of his life. She knew him as she never knew the others. He was the only one Tudy hadn't taken over. He was the only one who didn't fiercely resent Tudy once he was grown. He had married a girl Ella was hardly less in love with herself. Visits to them had to be nearly as clandestine as those with her husband.

"It's not unnatural for me to want to see my grandchildren," Ella argued.

"It's not them. It's her you want to see . . . and him," Tudy answered sullenly, accurately.

"Of course, I do. Why not?"

"I've shared you with four children. I've shared you with the world. I put up with your fans. I've put up with your infatuations, your lies, your dirty weekends. I've given up my own family, my own life . . ."

"I didn't ask you to."

"You didn't have to ask. I *gave*."

"What do you expect? What do you want?"

"You."

"Don't you have me? Do you have to lock me in a cage as well?"

"Sometimes I'd like to."

Tudy had been a pretty woman, but like so many who spent their days with peanut butter sandwiches, donuts, and chocolate milk, their nights awake with one sick child or another, she was thirty pounds overweight, and her hair was permanently frizzy and limp from all the steaming for croup and asthma. What made her and so many like her unattractive was a face deprived of gratitude.

Ella was grateful. She could not have lived her life without Tudy. A present for Tudy was more important than presents for the children when Ella came home from a trip. Tudy treated any gift as insufficient and suspect.

"You haven't known my size for fifteen years," about a sweater that didn't fit. "When would I have time to read?" about a book. The closest she came to being pleased would be when she said something like, "Well, you must have had quite a time!"

Ella was guilty. She tried to make life easier for Tudy, hired maids Tudy nearly always fired, bought household gadgets Tudy refused to use, sent the children to camp so that she and Tudy could take holidays together, catastrophes because Tudy could be jealous of a palm tree if Ella admired it, and Ella's fans were everywhere, discovered her even when she traveled under another name.

"I can't help having a recognizable face!" she protested. "You can't live without attention."

Since Ella couldn't avoid it, was it such a crime to enjoy it? The cost, Tudy's hour-long crying jags, from which she recovered enough to continue accusations, was too high. Their only peace was at home when Ella was working twelve hours a day and needed to be guarded against all interruptions, even a child's broken arm.

"Don't whine for your mother. She's got to pay for it," Tudy would say, stern and matter-of-fact.

It was Tudy who left their bed to tend the nightmares and earaches.

"You need your rest."

Ella did spend time with the children, special time, like any loving and normally busy and preoccupied father. She could make that loss up to them but Tudy had to be their mother.

"She did the best she could," Rebuke admitted. "It was just that we wanted you, and you always seemed to be away or working."

Ella never gave way to the temptation to justify herself to the children. Tudy did that for her as well, of course. She reminded them that their mother paid for the food on the table, the roof over their heads, the clothes on their backs. If they weren't appreciative then, they grew up to be pleased by cars and trips to Europe. Ella bought them houses when they married, paid their psychiatrist's bills, paid for their children's dental hardware, paid and paid and paid.

It was Tudy they finally learned to understand and forgive. All three of her surviving children still wrote to Tudy, sent her Christmas presents, even sometimes went to visit her.

"She was there," Ella's younger son explained. "We

took her too much for granted."

Her thrice-divorced and recently married daughter said, "If she'd adored us, we might have forgiven her sooner. She didn't. Like all the world, she adored you."

Alert even now for betrayals, Ella knew Tudy would never discuss her own feelings with the children. She had not even been able to confide in the very sympathetic psychiatrist called in to help her through her second crack-up. It was Ella who told him. He had comforted Ella, but whether he had ever importantly reached Tudy Ella doubted.

It wasn't the sex that was wrong but the claims made as a result. Ella, who had decided she was not only frigid but hysterical about any adult body within twenty feet of her, was wonderfully surprised and comforted by Tudy's love-making, which gave her surer pleasure than she had found in her marriage bed and a new arrogance in the pleasure she could return.

Ella concluded that she should have been a man. Should she have seen instead that no one should be a woman? It was a question she had made sure her biography would never include the information to pose. For herself, she still hoped she would not be required to answer it.

Ella wanted to remove Tudy from her life in such a way that there was no hole, or, if Ella had to look at that jagged emptiness, she'd rather have others to blame, the children who had played with the puzzle of her life and lost some of the pieces, Tudy herself who had changed in those years out of all recognition until there simply was no place for her in Ella's life, which had also changed.

"People outgrow each other," Ella said to herself and then revised, as she rarely did in her work, to "one person outgrows another." Still, the betrayal is basically inadvertent. Ella had not meant to grow away from Tudy any more than she had meant to shrink from her husband. If only she and he had had more than his dying year, their love might have closed over those intervening years, healed the interlude with Tudy until it ached only before occasional thunderstorms.

As it was, her marriage could bracket but not bridge either Tudy or the children, who acknowledged their father as he lay dying only out of obedience to Ella. He handed out his blessings in the same spirit.

"There were always so many of them," he said, tired and weakened by the thought.

For Ella there were only three. She had buried their first-born son two years before his father died, who had not been at her side. Tudy was.

When Ella saw her at the airport, she understood the Greek custom of murdering the bearer of bad news. Fate and feeling are outside the laws of justice.

"I don't want you at the funeral!" Ella shouted. "Gloating!"

Of course, Tudy went, and if her tears were more for Ella than for the boy, there was no malice in her even for the young widow. She opened her arms to the next generation of fatherless children, grandchildren who had long since abandoned Ella as had their mother for a new husband, but they still saw Tudy without knowing she had ever been a threat to them.

"Nobody's abandoned you, darling," Rebuke reassured her. "Look at all these birthday cards and presents."

From fans, from old lovers, from children and grand-children, but there was none from Tudy.

"Once I leave this house, don't expect me to be like him, sending you stupid roses. Once I leave this house it's over; it's dead. When you find out you can't live without me, *tough*!"

Tudy also assured Ella there would be no meeting in the next world.

"It's bunk!"

"Maybe it is," Ella had agreed bitterly. "We've had hell enough in this one."

Now she badly wanted husband or son to send some message that they were there waiting, would be, when the time came, on her right hand and on her left, to hold and protect her at last from the fiery call if it came. There was, however, no more message from them than from Tudy.

One day there was no mail. For the next week Ella could not work, waiting for it to happen again. Then her daughter was ill and did not come to see her for ten days. Even the television, which she saw inadequately anyway, flickered and blurred.

"The world is going out," she confided in herself. "Surely that isn't dying."

Dying is gathering up the pieces, the bright and the dark, fitting them together, puzzling out the true picture, seeing it at last. Ella couldn't any longer see. There was no one there to help her.

"Isn't anyone going to show me how? Isn't anyone going to teach me?"

The last sentence Ella Carr wrote might have been the title for her next book, "Death is not that Kind of Lover," for it modified the truth, that death is no lover at all, as she had always been able to in fiction, as she had not managed to in life.

**Inland Passage and Other Stories** by Jane Rule. 288 pp.
ISBN 0-930044-56-8     $7.95
ISBN 0-930044-58-4     $13.95

**A Hot-Eyed Moderate** by Jane Rule. Essays. 252 pp.
ISBN 0-930044-57-6     $7.95
ISBN 0-930044-59-2     $13.95

**We Too Are Drifting** by Gale Wilhelm. A novel. 128 pp.
ISBN 0-930044-61-4     $6.95

**Amateur City** by Katherine V. Forrest. A mystery novel. 224 pp.
ISBN 0-930044-55-X     $7.95

**The Sophie Horowitz Story** by Sarah Schulman. A novel. 176 pp.
ISBN 0-930044-54-1     $7.95

**The Young in One Another's Arms** by Jane Rule. A novel. 224 pp.
ISBN 0-930044-53-3     $7.95

**The Burnton Widows** by Vicki P. McConnell. A mystery novel.
272 pp. ISBN 0-930044-52-5     $7.95

**Old Dyke Tales** by Lee Lynch. Short Stories. 224 pp.
ISBN 0-930044-51-7     $7.95

**Daughters of a Coral Dawn** by Katherine V. Forrest. Science
fiction. 240 pp. ISBN 0-930044-50-9     $7.95

**The Price of Salt** by Claire Morgan. A novel. 288 pp.
ISBN 0-930044-49-5     $7.95

**Against the Season** by Jane Rule. A novel. 224 pp.
ISBN 0-930044-48-7     $7.95

**Lovers in the Present Afternoon** by Kathleen Fleming. A novel.
288 pp. ISBN 0-930044-46-0     $8.50

**Toothpick House** by Lee Lynch. A novel. 264 pp.
ISBN 0-930044-45-2     $7.95

**Madame Aurora** by Sarah Aldridge. A novel. 256 pp.
ISBN 0-930044-44-4     $7.95

**Curious Wine** by Katherine V. Forrest. A novel. 176 pp.
ISBN 0-930044-43-6     $7.50

**Black Lesbian in White America.** Short stories, essays,
autobiography. 144 pp. ISBN 0-930044-41-X     $7.50

**Contract with the World** by Jane Rule. A novel. 340 pp.
ISBN 0-930044-28-2     $7.95

**Yantras of Womanlove** by Tee A. Corinne. Photographs.
64 pp. ISBN 0-930044-30-4     $6.95

**Mrs. Porter's Letter** by Vicki P. McConnell. A mystery novel.
224 pp. ISBN 0-930044-29-0      $6.95

**To the Cleveland Station** by Carol Anne Douglas. A novel.
192 pp. ISBN 0-930044-27-4      $6.95

**The Nesting Place** by Sarah Aldridge. A novel. 224 pp.
ISBN 0-930044-26-6      $6.95

**This Is Not for You** by Jane Rule. A novel. 284 pp.
ISBN 0-930044-25-8      $7.95

**Faultline** by Sheila Ortiz Taylor. A novel. 140 pp.
ISBN 0-930044-24-X      $6.95

**The Lesbian in Literature** by Barbara Grier. 3d ed.
Foreword by Maida Tilchen. A comprehensive bibliography.
240 pp. ISBN 0-930044-23-1      $7.95

**Anna's Country** by Elizabeth Lang. A novel. 208 pp.
ISBN 0-930044-19-3      $6.95

**Prism** by Valerie Taylor. A novel. 158 pp.
ISBN 0-930044-18-5      $6.95

**Black Lesbians: An Annotated Bibliography** compiled by
JR Roberts. Foreword by Barbara Smith. 112 pp.
ISBN 0-930044-21-5      $5.95

**The Marquise and the Novice** by Victoria Ramstetter.
A novel. 108 pp. ISBN 0-930044-16-9      $4.95

**Labiaflowers** by Tee A. Corinne. 40 pp.
ISBN 0-930044-20-7      $3.95

**Outlander** by Jane Rule. Short stories, essays. 207 pp.
ISBN 0-930044-17-7      $6.95

**Sapphistry: The Book of Lesbian Sexuality** by Pat Califia.
2nd edition, revised. 195 pp. ISBN 0-930044-47-9      $7.95

**The Black and White of It** by Ann Allen Shockley.
Short stories. 112 pp. ISBN 0-930044-15-0      $5.95

**All True Lovers** by Sarah Aldridge. A novel. 292 pp.
ISBN 0-930044-10-X      $6.95

**A Woman Appeared to Me** by Renee Vivien. Translated by
Jeannette H. Foster. A novel. xxxi, 65 pp.
ISBN 0-930044-06-1      $5.00

**Cytherea's Breath** by Sarah Aldridge. A novel. 240 pp.
ISBN 0-930044-02-9      $6.95

**Tottie** by Sarah Aldridge. A novel. 181 pp.
ISBN 0-930044-01-0      $6.95

**The Latecomer** by Sarah Aldridge. A novel. 107 pp.
ISBN 0-930044-00-2      $5.00

## VOLUTE BOOKS